QUEEN ABIGAIL THE WISE

and "Abigail's Christmas Cookies"

by Grace Brooks

www.QueenAbigail.com
Facebook.com/QueenAbigailtheWise/

For Mackenzie and Harvest
and all the other
nearly perfect
children I know

Queen
Abigail
the Wise

Introduction

THIS IS THE STORY of how Abigail Alverson from Benton Bend, Missouri gave away something very precious on Holy Saturday and how she got everything back on Pascha Sunday. But we're not going to start there.

It's also the story of how the Every Tuesday Girls Club began to fix people's problems. But we're not going to start the story there, either.

We won't start with how Abigail got her icon or how Xenia beat her brothers' score at ZooBlastex or even why Maggie's baby brother briefly had a dotted line on his face.

We're going to start before any of that happened. We'll go all the way back to the first Sunday in Lent, when the late winter sun was shining, the icicles were dripping ... and Abigail was trying very hard to think up a rhyme for the word "flyswatter."

Chapter one

ABIGAIL SAW THE FLY IN CHURCH before anyone else did. If you've seen the inside of an Orthodox church, you know that they come in all sizes. Some are just rooms or stores that are rented for Sundays, but others are great cathedrals with white pillars and lots of carved wood. Abigail's church, St. Michael the Archangel, was rather large and had a great dome in the ceiling, as many Orthodox churches do. So, it was natural that Abigail saw the fly first, because, as usual, during the morning service, her mind was wandering and her eyes had drifted all the way up to the ceiling.

The church was filled with solemn icons in glittering frames and the music of the Divine Liturgy — the priest chanting to the people and the choir singing in reply. And the scent of incense wafted throughout — the very perfume of holiness. But what is a ten-year-old to do? Although Abigail knew very well that she was supposed to be looking at the church altar or following along in the service book or praying silently — her mother had told her these things often enough — she became fascinated by the little insect flying in and out of the dome's sunbeams like an airplane doing tricks at a show.

Maybe she wouldn't have started composing a song to the fly if the service hadn't been quite so long. Just that morning, she had asked her mother, very politely, if there were going to be any extra prayers or anything that would make the service take longer than usual. Abigail had noticed, in a very scientific way, that her ability to stay out of trouble had a lot to do with the service being as short as possible. And so, very politely, she had asked about it as they were driving to church.

Mrs. Alverson answered, "Abigail." Just that.

Abigail was surprised. "What?" she asked innocently.

Abigail's brother Mark answered her from the front seat. "You ask that *every* Sunday, Abby."

Did she? *Every* Sunday? "No, I don't," she protested. She knew for a fact that the previous Sunday her little sister had interrupted just as she was going to ask. Still, she had eventually received assurance from her mother that that day's service would be no longer than usual.

So she thought she'd be all right. But right in the middle of the service, her mother left the choir and came to where Abigail was sitting. "Abigail, I forgot!" she whispered. "This is the Sunday of Orthodoxy — the Sunday with the icons."

Abigail looked blank, so her mother said, "You know, the icons? The pictures in church?"

Abigail knew what icons were. When the Alversons started coming to the Orthodox church, Fr. Andrew told them all about icons. "The icons should have their own Sunday," Abigail said with affection. She liked looking at the pictures of saints and thought they liked looking at her. There was something about them that made her happy.

"There's a procession at the end," her mother continued. "We all walk around the church holding icons." Abigail still looked blank. "It means the service today will be longer," said her mother simply. Abigail stopped thinking about icons. She stopped being happy.

"You said there was nothing extra today," she said. Some things were just unfair.

"I know," Mrs. Alverson said, glancing around as other choir members looked at her. "I just forgot. I'm sorry, Abigail. I didn't — " But the next song started and her mother had to begin singing again, so Abigail never found out what she was going to say.

Well!

That had made things more difficult. It was hard to look at the glowing icons with their serious but joyful faces. She knew she was being a little childish, but she couldn't help feeling like they were to blame somehow, and she couldn't face them without feeling a little annoyed.

If only she could be like her brother Mark in church, or like Hillary or Vanessa, or any of the older kids who could be so completely quiet and attentive. Or else like her little sister Elizabeth — Bet, they called her — who was allowed to move around in church and look at picture books because she was too little to do any better.

But, as her mother and father had told her many times, she was older now; she was almost 11, and they expected more from her. They expected her not to make up such strange things and talk so loud and start dancing when there was no music. Especially in church, they expected her to be like the other children who could sit quietly and pay attention.

Abigail wished she could. She wanted to be like her friend, Maggie-May Peasle, who never seemed to get into trouble. Maggie was so good that her parents probably just smiled at her all the way home from church.

Abigail wanted to be that good, but she found it very difficult. If only she had a job to do, something important to be involved in. She couldn't sing with the choir or serve on committees or make money to repair the roof. But Abigail was secretly longing to do something important. There were people all around her — not just her own friends, but teenagers and old people and mothers and fathers — and sometimes they would look grumpy or sad in a way that made her want to help them. She didn't know why she felt like that — she knew she should just finish her math homework or play and do crafts. But she couldn't help it. She wanted to do real things and help people with their problems.

But instead...

Abigail frowned deeply and crossed her arms. Instead she was in church and the service was going to go extra long today and she didn't know what to do.

She wanted to be good.

But then, there was that fly.

WHEN ABIGAIL saw the fly, she stopped thinking about anything else. It was much more interesting to follow its lazy loops in the sunbeams. Up in the dome, with the apostles in their gold and blue and purple robes, the fly danced and offered all that it had to give.

Oh, little fly,
Won't you please rest?

Abigail was surprised to find that she had started a poem about the fly. But once she did, she knew just what music would go with it. There was a TV commercial for Glabbo Gum that had people in orange jumpsuits dancing in a factory, and the music had been going around in her head for a week. But what would come after the first line?

We know you've done
Your very best.

That sounded all right. She said the first two lines to herself a time or two and decided they were pretty good. But what should come next? The fly had started buzzing around people in the choir, and Abigail thought she should mention the problems it was causing.

"Don't make us get … a big flyswatter."

That was a good third line. But she didn't just think it this time — she said it out loud. A few people in the choir turned to look at her. Mr. Broadmere, who had been wishing very much for a flyswatter, said, "Amen to that."

But what rhymed with flyswatter?

Tap-water? Sea otter?

The good thing about having a poem to work on was that it helped pass the time. Before she knew it, the service had ended and Fr. Andrew came out to give announcements before the procession. "Sign-up sheet for our retreat… Thanks for prayers after Fr. Tamil's surgery… And I see that Jeff Rayner is here with his granddaughter."

Granddaughter! What a great word to use!

People in church began to move about and get ready to go outside for the procession. All over the church, they were picking up icons they had brought from home, or taking them off the wall to hand to the children. Loud Mrs. Murphy, the choir director, gave Abigail an icon of a saint that she didn't know. Abigail really would've preferred the icon of St. Romanos, who had curly hair like her father. But it didn't matter, because she had a poem and it fit perfectly in the gum commercial music:

O little fly
Won't you please rest?
We know you've done
Your very best.
Don't make us get
A big flyswatter,
Or else she'll cry —
Your poor granddaughter!

Abigail hugged the icon of the surprised-looking saint. She felt like the last line about the granddaughter was especially good. Who would want a granddaughter to cry? Who knew a fly even *had* a granddaughter? It was very dramatic and made the poem interesting.

AS THE DOORS OPENED and the chilly air hit the good people of St. Michael's, they began a cautious shuffling walk on the snow-dusted sidewalk. The procession was led by the clergy in front with the subdeacons and altar boys holding sparkling gold fans and candle-holders. After them came the choir and the children from smallest to biggest, clutching their icons in mittened hands. And all the other adults followed behind, some with icons as well. Everyone was walking carefully and singing the processional hymn as best they could, with breath puffing into little clouds in the frosty air.

They didn't even seem to notice when Abigail started singing a different song. "O little fly, won't you please rest?..."

She really didn't think anyone would hear her, but there is something about the crisp air in March that makes certain sounds carry farther than others. A person can hear the clear notes from the first robin or the bright song of a jewel-red cardinal, even if they're a long way off. Or, on this occasion, they might hear the high, clear voice of a little girl.

Before the procession had even gone completely around the church, there were people that noticed that a different song was being sung. Mrs. Garzo and her twin sister looked at each other. Something about a fly? Two flies? A *granddaughter*? Mr. Gillespie and both his daughters turned around. So did a few other people. Abigail's father didn't turn around — he didn't need to.

Her brother Mark, really, *really* wanted to turn around, but didn't.

Still, it might not have been so bad — at least, it might have just been a tense family discussion in the car on the way home — but unfortunately, Abigail got a little too carried away. In the commercial, there was a point where all the people in the orange jumpsuits clapped their hands because the gum was so delicious. Abigail thought that her song could benefit by something exciting like that. So right on the beat of the word "flySWATTER", Abigail neatly tucked the icon of the saint (who really looked *very* surprised) under one arm and brought her gloved hands together with a resounding smack.

In Abigail's defense, she did admit later that clapping was a mistake.

It wasn't that it was loud, but it was unexpected. At the sound of that clap, Mr. Broadmere, who didn't like sudden noises, jumped and almost tripped. Miss Abrigado, who was always very serious about everything — especially icons — thought Mr. Broadmere was going to drop his icon, and so she quickly reached out for it and almost dropped her own icon in a snowy shrub. That made a few people say "Oh!" and "Whoops!" at the same time. Which then made Mark turn around even though he was an altar boy. Which made the procession come to a stop, with some people in front stepping on other people's feet and at least two little toddlers sitting down suddenly in a snow bank.

And that was why Abigail ended up in Fr. Andrew's office after the service, with her mother on one side and her father on the other, hearing a lot about respect and manners and icons.

Chapter two

"Abigail, what were you *thinking*?"

That is a question no ten-year-old wants to hear from her mother. Right after the service, with only the briefest break for some cocoa and a bagel at coffee hour, Mr. and Mrs. Alverson parked Bet with Mark and steered Abigail into Fr. Andrew's office. Her mother had a rather stiff expression on her face that was never good news. Her father's face was blank, but Abigail knew that that could mean anything.

Father Andrew, who was a very gentle man with thick glasses that made him look a little like an owl, seemed perplexed, which he always seemed to be. As the priest, he had been at the very front of the procession and he hadn't known very much about what had caused the disturbance behind him, other than what Miss Abrigado had told him afterwards. Mrs. Abrigado had been upset and not very clear, and he hadn't really understood what had happened. He couldn't see, for instance, what flies had to do with anything.

But now, Abigail's mother was very detailed and left nothing out of the story, because unfortunately, she had been standing near to Abigail and had seen and heard everything. Abigail explained about the fly, but for some reason, that didn't seem like it settled the matter, and her mother repeated everything she knew about what had happened outside.

Father Andrew's expression changed from puzzled to thoughtful to *very* thoughtful, because it's a serious thing to spoil a procession and almost send icons and people tumbling into the snow. He would have been displeased with Abigail, but Mrs. Alverson looked so annoyed that it hardly seemed necessary.

Abigail looked unhappily at her mother. She knew that she wasn't a bad girl. But there was no doubt that her mother had a lot to say and hardly any of it made her sound like a good girl who had just made a teensy little mistake. Her mother told everything that happened and then told it all over again. And then she started talking about other Sundays and other services, which seemed to Abigail to be beside the point, and used words like "inattentive" and "distracted" and "daydreaming." And then she threw in "irresponsible" and took a deep breath as if she was going to start all over from the beginning.

"But I wasn't doing anything *really* bad," Abigail objected quickly. "I didn't trip anybody or push anyone or … or bite them." That seemed important to make clear. Pushing and biting would have been bad, but no pushing or biting had occurred. "There was a fly and so I made up a song about it."

"But Abigail, church isn't the place for songs about flies," said her mother in exasperation. "We have talked and talked to you about this. You can't just keep making things up like this."

"I didn't make up the fly," said Abigail. This also seemed like an important point in her favor. "I didn't put it there."

"Abby," said her father quietly, "That's not the point. There are always going to be things going on somewhere in church, but you have to be able to tune out what doesn't matter so you can pay attention to the services and not distract other people. I know it's difficult for you sometimes, but you have to try harder. I know you can do it."

Abigail sniffed petulantly. In her home-schooling assignments and in her chores, her parents constantly had to tell her to pay more attention or do things over. Even when she really tried to do better, she was always thinking of things that she would rather do than what she was supposed to do. It was something she didn't really know how to fix about herself. And now here she was in Fr. Andrew's office with her father telling her about it again as if she hadn't heard it over and over.

This was the bad part, even worse than hearing her mother have so much to say. Her father usually didn't say much, but when he did, he had a voice that went right to her heart. Abigail loved her mother and knew that she was upset. She loved her father and couldn't stand for him not to be proud of her. But there were things that were possible and things that weren't possible. And she didn't know how to tell him that he was asking her to do something impossible. She looked at him and her mother.

Her mother looked at her father. And then they all looked at Fr. Andrew, who had leaned forward in his chair so that he wouldn't miss anything. He sat back now and inclined his chin down so he could watch Abigail over the top of his glasses.

"Was it a good song, Abigail?" he asked.

The question obviously surprised her parents, but she thought it was the first really helpful thing anyone had said so far.

"Yes!" she said enthusiastically. "The fly was flying up in the dome where it could be in the sunbeams and — " She paused and then the words all tumbled out. "I know it only wanted to get out, but it looked like it was dancing for all the apostles, and so a poem just popped into my head. Or, the first line did, but then when I got to the flyswatter …" she stopped, realizing that the whole story might take more time than it was worth. Especially since both parents were looking at her as if she wasn't making much sense. "But it *was* a good song," she said. "It all rhymed and it all fit in the lines and …" she was going to mention that the granddaughter in the poem made it seem more interesting, but instead, she ended with, "… it made me happy to make it up."

Fr. Andrew nodded, leaning further back in his chair. "That's a good thing, Abigail. We need better songs in our lives. It's a wonderful thing to be able to make up poems and songs and dances. I hope you never stop doing that. But a very wise man named King Solomon said that there's a time for everything under heaven. A time to laugh and a time to be solemn. A time to speak up and a time to be silent. Do you understand?"

"Yes," said Abigail carefully. But she was being polite, and Fr. Andrew seemed to understand that.

"You can do the right things at the wrong time, and then they're not the right things anymore," he said kindly. "Knowing when to do something can be just as important as knowing what to do, and you may have to think about that a little bit. You see?"

She nodded. "Yes, Father." And this time she did understand.

"After all," said Fr. Andrew, "when you clapped your hands, you almost made Miss Abrigado drop her icon. How would you have felt if you dropped your icon? Who is your patron saint?"

"Saint Abigail," said Abigail.

"Ah, Saint Abigail. Abigail? From the Old Testament?"

"Yes."

"That's an unusual saint," he mused. "Well, what if you had dropped your icon of St. Abigail?"

Abigail gave him a blank stare. "I don't have an icon of St. Abigail."

Fr. Andrew's eyes registered surprise behind his thick glasses. "You don't?" he said, glancing at her parents.

"No, Father," her mother apologized. "I picked St. Abigail for her because it was easy to remember and Abigail likes the story. We were new to Orthodoxy and I didn't know it would be so hard to find an icon of her."

"Oh, I see. Yes, sometimes that happens," he said thoughtfully. "Well, Abigail, since you like her story, what would your patron saint have said?"

"Saint Abigail? My Abigail?" He nodded and she pondered a minute. "She would have been kind. She saw inside people."

"Did she?" said Fr. Andrew. "Tell me about your Abigail. She sounds remarkable."

Abigail looked at a spot on the carpet but didn't see it. She was thinking about her favorite book of Old Testament stories, seeing the pictures she had redrawn in notebooks. "Abigail lived in Old Testament times," she said. "She was married to a man named Nabal, but he wasn't wise and she was. And one day, when messengers from King David's army came asking for hospitality ..." Abigail stopped and considered the whole story — how Nabal had been rude to King David's messengers. And how Abigail — her Abigail — had heard what happened and sent servants and donkeys loaded with treasure and rich food to please the king.

Abigail could picture the whole thing. One of the donkeys was loaded with sultanas, which her mother had told her were like raisins, and she had drawn that donkey several times, since she liked raisins. And St. Abigail came to King David with words to make him forget his anger. She had apologized for her husband so well that the king saw that she was a good and wise woman. And later, when Nabal died from pure bitterness after hearing all that had happened, King David came back and married Abigail, and she was one of his wives (because Old Testament people sometimes had more than one wife). She was a rare and intelligent woman, the book had said.

Abigail could see it all — the king and Abigail and the donkey loaded with raisins — but she was unsure how to put it all in the right order and stood shifting from foot to foot while she sorted it all out.

BUT AS SOMETIMES HAPPENS just when you are about to start a really good story, there was a sudden interruption.

"KNOCK KNOCK," said someone, rapping on the door so loudly it sounded like they were using a hammer. Immediately the fluffy blonde head of Mrs. Murphy, the choir director, appeared around the door.

"EXCUSE ME!" she bellowed, making everyone take a step back in the office. "Sorry to intrude!" she said a little quieter. "Emma, I just wanted to remind you about Tuesday!"

Emma, Abigail's mother, looked blank, and Mrs. Murphy said,

"Tuesday? Extra choir practice? And FLOWER COMMITTEE!" She had started getting louder again, as she tended to do, and said the last words loud enough to shake the leaves on Fr. Andrew's houseplant.

"THANK you," said her mother, trying to match her volume. "We'll be there Tuesday."

Abigail's father looked alarmed. "We? Who is 'we'?"

"We," said her mother, gesturing vaguely. "Abigail and I. We'll be there Tuesday."

"What?" said Abigail.

"Of COURSE you will!" yelled Mrs. Murphy, turning to Abigail. "Xenia will be here too, to keep you COMPANY." Xenia was Mrs. Murphy's daughter, who wasn't very good company at all. "And your friend Maggie-May. And Vanessa. And ... WHAT'S HER NAME, the other one. It'll be a regular EVERY TUESDAY Club, like I used to have with my church girlfriends growing UP!"

Mrs. Murphy beamed at Abigail with such boisterous good will that Abigail wished she could think of something to say back, preferably something she could say loudly. But spending a lot of time in the drafty church classrooms every Tuesday while the mothers sang and talked and planned flowers didn't sound very exciting at all. The only one of those girls that she knew well was Maggie, and Maggie usually had to watch a baby, since she came from a large family. That had been fine when it was little Isabella, but lately, it had been Baby Jacob. And Jacob, well ...

With a start, Abigail realized that the room had gotten quiet and Mrs. Murphy's large crystal-blue eyes were focused on her as if she expected an answer. Apparently, Abigail had missed something.

"I *said*," said Mrs. Murphy, with special emphasis, "'isn't that going to BE GREAT?!!'"

"Yes," said Abigail in a small voice, thinking of Baby Jacob. And she was going to say more, but there was another quick rat-a-tat at the door, and Maggie's mother, Mrs. Peasle, stuck her head in. "I'm sorry to interrupt, Father," she said, in her wonderfully gentle voice. "But did I hear — ?" She looked behind the door and saw Mrs. Murphy. "Oh, Donna. I just wanted to remind you about bringing the chairs on Tuesday."

"ME bring them!" sputtered Mrs. Murphy. "I thought EMMA was bringing them!"

Father Andrew cleared his throat meaningfully. "I think that this could be solved outside? And Emma, I believe that Mark is trying to get your attention?"

Abigail's parents turned to see responsible Mark looking tense and holding little Bet, who had grape juice on her shirt.

A small stampede of adults ensued, with Abigail's mother turning back for her at the door.

"I wondered if I might keep Abigail just a bit longer," Fr. Andrew said. "I have something in the church I want her to see."

"Oh," said her mother in some confusion. "Yes, certainly. And Abigail …"

Her mother looked as if she wanted to start all over again with everything she had already said. Manners. Responsibility. Attention. But in the end, she just shook her head abruptly and said, "*Behave yourself*," swinging the door shut with a bang.

Abigail felt like a bee had stung her. Behave herself? She thought she *did* behave herself. It was so hard for her to think of herself as anything but a good girl doing her best, but what did her mother think? Why did she frown at her so much these days and look so annoyed? Things seemed to be changing between her and her mother, and Abigail had a terrible feeling that whatever the change was, it was something small but poisonous that was going to get bigger over time. It felt like time was running out to fix it, but she didn't know how.

She managed to invent a kind of sneeze that allowed her to wipe her nose quickly so Fr. Andrew wouldn't see that she had been about to cry. When she looked over at him, he was studying her intently, and she couldn't tell whether she fooled him or not. But to her relief, all he said was, "Let's take the back way out. It's quieter. I want to hear the rest of the story about Saint Abigail."

As he held the door open for her, he added, "And you can sing the fly song for me on the way over."

Chapter three

"Abigail married King David because in the Old Testament, some men had more than one wife, and then they lived happily ever after. Well ..." Abigail frowned, "not happily ever after, because that's for fairy tales. But they lived ... happy."

Father Andrew smiled. "Well, happy is good." He had looked relieved almost as soon as they got out of the noisy social hall and had laughed merrily on the walkway when Abigail sang her song, even singing it with her once. When they entered the church, Fr. Andrew asked her again to finish the story and listened silently until she was all through.

He gazed into the nearly empty church — a stillness punctuated by the quiet business of people removing candle stubs and straightening chairs. As soon as he had stepped into the building, Fr. Andrew looked more like himself somehow, Abigail thought.

"Saint Abigail was a rare and intelligent woman," said Abigail. It was the last sentence of the story of St. Abigail in her book, and it seemed like a good way to close things off.

"Yes, she was," Fr. Andrew agreed, nodding. "But why did you say before that she saw inside people?"

"Oh. I …" Abigail floundered. She hadn't thought anyone heard that. She had just blurted it out, and she wasn't sure where it had come from. "That's just the way I see her, I guess. She… I think she could see who people really were and…" Abigail paused again. This wasn't going well. "I … I think she could solve problems. With people. People problems."

Father Andrew didn't say anything, so she added, "Problems that other people couldn't solve."

"Solving people problems that others can't solve," Fr. Andrew repeated thoughtfully. "That would be a wonderful gift to have. But you surprise me, Abigail. I thought you only wanted to sing songs and draw pictures."

"I do like drawing and writing stories. But I wish …" She frowned, struggling to pull her thoughts together. "I wish that someone would give me important things to do, too. Everyone has these … problems. I can see that they do. And I feel like I almost could fix them, if they'd let me. But I'm too little to do anything about it."

Father Andrew didn't say anything. He appeared to be thinking of something else and glanced over as some of the loud talk from the social hall came in muffled through the windows.

"It's something I'd really like to do," said Abigail. "I've prayed to St. Abigail to help me." She immediately wished she hadn't said that. She hadn't told anyone about those prayers. If Fr. Andrew was surprised, though, he didn't look it. Instead, he just said, "Wait here," and went up the steps and through the door of the icon screen.

Abigail blinked in surprise as he disappeared, wondering if she had said something wrong. She knew it wasn't a bad thing to pray, especially to your patron saint. But that particular prayer was probably strange. And the problem with doing strange things is that if you didn't realize they were strange —

"How *are* you, dear?" said a flowery voice as a thin arm hugged her from behind.

Abigail tried not to squawk as she was pulled off balance. "I'm fine!" she said with a little desperation. When she could wheel around, she added, "I'm fine, Mrs. Jenkins." Mrs. Jenkins was the church secretary, a thin woman with watery blue eyes.

Mrs. Jenkins smiled down on her with one hand over her heart. Her daughter Photini was almost hidden behind her but looked out with wide eyes.

"I just wanted to check on you. It'll be okay," said Mrs. Jenkins, soothingly. "Father just wants to make sure you treat sacred things with respect, that's all."

"Oh … okay," said Abigail, hoping she sounded polite and not dense. She had no idea what Mrs. Jenkins was talking about. What sacred things?

"The icons," said Mrs. Jenkins, as if she heard the question. "They are *very* special."

Abigail understood and felt her face get hot. This was about the procession and her fly song. Mrs. Jenkins must've thought Fr. Andrew was lecturing her.

"Your family hasn't been Orthodox very long," said Mrs. Jenkins, absently tugging on her head covering. "Photini didn't like the icons at first, but now she has them on every wall and is going to be an iconographer." Mrs. Jenkins put her arm affectionately around her daughter, and Photini looked at Abigail through her blond eyelashes. "An iconographer is someone who paints icons," Mrs. Jenkins added.

"I know," said Abigail in a flat voice. Privately, she wasn't sure that Photini was as perfect as her mother wanted everyone to think. She was very quiet and shy, but Abigail thought she was a little snooty and kind of a tattle-tale. So Abigail might have blurted something out that she would regret later. But as it turned out, Mrs. Jenkins didn't give her a chance. She suddenly swooped down and scooped Abigail into another iron hug. "It's *okay*, dear. I'm sure Father won't be too harsh."

"Sure I won't be too harsh about what?" said Fr. Andrew, thumbing through a book as he lightly stepped down the steps in front of the altar.

Mrs. Jenkins looked back at Abigail with a pinched smile. "I was just cheering Abigail up. I don't want her to be in too much trouble."

Fr. Andrew looked from Abigail to Mrs. Jenkins and her daughter. "Oh. Yes. Everybody makes mistakes, don't they?" and gave Abigail the quickest wink she'd ever seen.

"That's exactly right," said Mrs. Jenkins, missing the wink completely. "Mum's the word. Photini, let's see if there is any more blessed bread left in the hall."

Fr. Andrew's eyes followed Mrs. Jenkins as she swept out of the church with her daughter quick-stepping after her. The door shut with a soft thud, and it seemed to take a minute before the hushed air of the church recovered from her exit.

"I think we were talking," said Fr. Andrew, still looking at the closed door, "We were talking about …" He took a breath and then remembered his book and started turning the pages. "… about helping people," he finished, thumbing through the book's stiff pages.

Abigail looked over at the thick book as he flipped through its pages. It didn't look old, but it was very well-worn, and some of the pages were almost coming out of the binding. "I think there's something here that will help," he said.

Abigail could see that it was a book of icons, with colored images on one side and writing on the other. But there was something else that she couldn't make out, and she reached out her finger to stop him turning past at one point. "What's that?"

"What? Oh … that." Father Andrew looked annoyed. "Those are ink sketches. This book belonged to an iconography student, and apparently he couldn't resist drawing in the margins." He turned to another page where there was a complicated pattern drawn up one side. "Dear, dear," muttered Fr. Andrew. "Abigail, remember that you should never do this to your books. It was very inconsiderate of him."

"These are really good drawings." Abigail traced the pattern with her finger.

"Well, I'll let him know," said Fr. Andrew, smiling. "If I ever see him again, that is. But where's the one I'm looking for? Is it in another book? No …maybe… Yes! Here it is!" He turned the book around with one swift movement that almost made several pages tumble out. "There's Saint Abigail."

Abigail's eyes snapped wide. On the page was a beautiful woman in a green and gold robe. Her brown hair was pulled back in a tight pattern around her face, but stray tendrils were showing on her temples and neck. One hand was raised in blessing, and her large gray-green eyes looked out at Abigail with so much life in them that it was almost shocking.

Abigail felt breathless. "Is this ... a very old icon?" she asked incredulously.

"Yes," said Fr. Andrew. "It's more than thirteen hundred years old, but it doesn't look it, does it? It was on a monastery wall that got bricked up when the monastery was under attack, and no one knew it was there until about eighty years ago."

 Abigail was speechless. The picture didn't look thirteen hundred years old. It didn't look eighty years old. It looked like it had been painted last week, yesterday, this morning. And painted just for her.

Fr. Andrew said, "You talked about being able to help people, Abigail. Being able to solve their problems." She was hearing Fr. Andrew's voice, but she was still looking at St. Abigail — it almost felt like her saint was doing the talking.

"I think that is a gift, Abigail," said Fr. Andrew. "And I think you should pray for it. God hears our prayers and God puts people in our life so we can work out each other's salvation. What people has God put into your life? Who can you help? I think you can put your good intentions to work right now. I don't think you need to wait."

Abigail stared at him, feeling stupid. She wished she could take a minute or two to make sense out of everything. She thought to herself, *I'm only ten. I can't do anything.* She said, "Is this because I made up a song in church?"

Father Andrew chuckled lightly. "No, Abigail. But ... well, maybe it is, in a way. You see things in pictures, don't you? You see stories all around you. You think of poems and you want to hear them sung. I think that most people are trying to tell their story, but sometimes they get lost along the way. They need someone to help them. That's what I think you can help with."

"*Me?*" She felt dizzy. No one had ever asked her to do anything that really mattered. They always seemed to know that she would be careless and disinterested. And she usually was. All the same, she couldn't help feeling a thrill of excitement. This was exactly the type of thing she had secretly longed for — someone asking her to do something serious and important. But how in the world was she going to help people with their life stories all by herself? With no help from anyone? Or ... was there help? Her eyes fell back to the icon. She looked at St. Abigail and St. Abigail looked back.

"Will you do it?" said Fr. Andrew, smiling.

"Yes," she said, in a small voice. And then she lifted up her eyes with an effort and said more decisively. "Yes, I will. If I can get this icon."

The smile froze on Fr. Andrew's face. "*This* icon. This icon is ... it's on a monastery wall in Greece, Abigail. It's on the other side of the world."

Abigail didn't want to give up. "A copy then? Isn't that what happens with icons? New ones are painted from the old ones?"

"Well, yes ... but ..." Fr. Andrew looked at the icon as if he wished it could help him. "You have to hire an iconographer for that. And it takes time. And a blessing from a bishop." He spread his hands helplessly. "Abigail, I just don't see how it's possible. Custom-painted icons are very expensive — they can cost hundreds of dollars."

Abigail didn't want to hear that. She looked at the icon again, unable to believe she was so close but so far.

Fr. Andrew's face fell. "I could make a quick copy of it for you. On the color copier?" Abigail realized he was trying to be helpful and she wanted to nod, but she couldn't. After a quick, searching glance, he said, "But that wouldn't be the same as a real painted icon, would it?" A second later, he answered his own question. "No, it wouldn't."

"Abigail, I'm sorry," he said softly. "I just don't see how we can get you that icon." She nodded, taking her hand from the book. With a sigh, Fr. Andrew closed it gently and laid it down on the pew.

And that would have been the end of it, and this would've been a much shorter book. Abigail thought it was the end. She tried to swallow her disappointment as they walked up the snow-dappled sidewalk towards the hall. But in an instant, everything changed. One minute, they were walking wordlessly, each lost in their own thoughts. And then the next minute, it seemed like there was noise everywhere.

The door of the social hall swung open with a bang. "Oh, FA-THER!" bellowed Mrs. Murphy. "THERE you are. Thank GOOD-NESS! We need to know — "

"Father," said Maggie's mother, with a hard look at Mrs. Murphy, "Didn't you tell me you didn't want any potted plants for Palm Sunday?"

"Wait!" said Abigail's mother, elbowing in. "Let me show Father the plant I found at the nursery."

"It's too expensive!" thundered Vanessa's mother, standing up very tall. "Show me the tag and I'll find it on sale."

A second later, the whole pack had disappeared through the open doorway, but they could still be heard above the other conversation, and their raised voices were building and getting higher.

Abigail blinked in wonder, but the next second she felt Fr. Andrew's hand come down firmly on her shoulder, pulling her back to reality. She couldn't have known it, but Fr. Andrew had been trying to make up his mind for the last minute or two. He had just decided something that she wouldn't find out about for a long time.

"Abigail," said Fr. Andrew suddenly, "I'll tell you what: You go to work fixing problems and I'll get you a copy of that icon by Pascha." His eyes looked a little wild. "Deal?" he said, dropping down a gloved hand.

This all seemed really bizarre. Abigail knew that Pascha was about five weeks away. That wasn't very much time to help people with their problems. But since she didn't have the slightest idea how to do that, what difference would it make whether she had five weeks or five months? So she answered: "Deal." And although she was scared, she knew she meant it. She was going to try to do this important thing Father had given her to do.

The gloved hand grasped hers in a quick tight grip and gave it a single shake. Just as quickly, Fr. Andrew swung away with a billowing of garments and then the hall door shut behind him as if he had been swallowed up.

Abigail stood blinking in the frosty March morning, wondering if things could possibly get any stranger.

But of course, they could.

Chapter four

"... SO NOW I've got to bring extra paper plates because Andrea said that the ones we had are all wobbly from getting dripped on under the sink."

The Alverson family was driving home. When they had piled into the minivan, Mrs. Alverson had a grouchy expression on her face, and Abigail thought for a minute she was going to start lecturing again. But after she had Bet buckled in and got her choir books and sign-up sheets and her purse all settled, it seemed to have slipped her mind and she just started talking about church things like she often did for the first few minutes of the ride.

"And then there's the coffee for the parish council meeting Thursday. Doug says we're almost out and I have to bring it."

"Mm," said Mr. Alverson, looking through the windshield wipers at the slushy road. "Can't you tell them to bring their own coffee?"

"I'd like to." Mrs. Alverson yanked off a glove. "Actually, I'd like to tell a few people to shut up!"

Mr. Alverson shot an alarmed look at his wife, and she closed her eyes tight. She composed herself and half turned in her seat so she could address the back seat.

"I shouldn't have said that. It isn't nice to say 'shut up' and I didn't mean it. I'm just tired, that's all."

No answer.

"Kids?" she said, turning completely around. But Bet had fallen asleep. Mark was playing games on his phone with his headphones on in the back seat. And Abigail was staring vacantly out the window.

"What?" said Abigail, when she realized her mother was talking to her.

"I said …Well, never mind." Mrs. Alverson smiled at her husband, who smiled back. "It wasn't important. So," she said brightly, changing the subject. "You're certainly quiet. Did Father Andrew give you something to think about?"

"Absolutely," said Abigail decisively.

Mrs. Alverson's eyebrows rose. "That's … good," she said uncertainly. "So what was in the church that he had to show you?"

"An icon."

Her mom nodded. "That makes sense. Maybe he'd let you show the girls at the Every Tuesday Club. Was it one of the ones in church?"

Abigail looked out the window at the delicate white flakes landing on the glass and then melting. "No, in a book he had."

"A book?" asked her mother, confused.

"Yes," said Abigail with hesitation. "An old book he had. It was full of pictures of icons and there was this one ..." She saw again the fragile pages, the fine ink sketches. And St. Abigail looking at her with those serene gray-green eyes. "There was an icon of — "

"Books!" exclaimed her mother, smacking her forehead. She grabbed Mr. Alverson's coat sleeve. "Do not let me forget to return the books on quilting. We'll have to pay a fine unless I drop them off at the library tonight."

Mr. Alverson nodded curtly and steered nimbly around a dirty box that had blown into the road.

"Sorry, Abby," her mother apologized. "What about the book? I didn't mean to interrupt."

"That's okay," said Abigail. And it was. But the interruption had helped her make up her mind about something. She had been thinking, and she didn't feel like she could really describe any of it — the book or the icon or the deal. She had noticed there were some things that you just couldn't tell grownups, and suddenly she didn't want to try. Maybe she could tell Mark? Maybe a brother could help?

"So what was in the book?" her mother prodded. "You said an icon?"

"Yes ... a lot of icons. And some drawings ..." How could she talk about those spidery drawings, those delicate patterns up the page margin?

At this point, Mark saved the day, though he didn't know it. He was done with his game and pulled off his headphones. "Can we get burgers for lunch?" he asked, leaning forward in his seat.

"What? No, Mark," sputtered Mrs. Alverson. "You had bagels and peanut butter at church."

"And it's Lent," said Mr. Alverson.

"And it's *Lent*," echoed Mrs. Alverson. "You're giving up red meat this year, remember?"

"Veggie chili then? They have it at Babe's Barbecue. And it comes with cornbread." Mark was a very serious altar boy when he was at church, but he was also a boy, and he was always hungry.

"I want chili!" said Bet, who had woken up and only heard one thing.

And so the subject was officially changed, and Abigail relaxed. She made a snap decision not to mention anything about the deal to Mark. There was something about seeing him drumming the seat and shouting for chili that made her think he wasn't quite the right person to consult in this delicate matter. But she suddenly knew who she could talk to. Something her mother said had given her an idea.

WHEN THEY GOT HOME and stamped off the snow, Abigail shook out her coat. She deposited Bet's bag of toys on the couch, picked up her sketchbook and went up to her room.

Flipping past drawings of her family and some favorite cartoon characters, she opened up a new page. She consulted a book to get her spelling right and then wrote across the top in large, precise letters: *Every Tuesday Girls Club*.

She looked at it for a minute. Why was that the name? It was just something Mrs. Murphy had said — funny how it stuck right away. Mrs. Murphy had a way of making people do what she said even when she wasn't trying to. Abigail shrugged. Everything had to have a name, and this one was as good a name as any.

She had made a deal with Fr. Andrew and she intended to give it her best shot. She wasn't sure how he would know whether she was doing a good job of solving people's problems — that part of it was kind of sketchy. But he was a priest, and priests seemed to know a lot of things. She remembered him looking at her over the top of his glasses. Yes, he would know.

But that meant she would need some assistance, and who better than the other girls in church? They all ended up thrown together on Tuesday nights while their parents had meetings and practices. All of them were left over — too small to go off with the teenagers and too big to stay with the little kids. If they had to spend time together every Tuesday night, the other girls might as well help her get her icon. And maybe she could practice solving problems by helping them. Maybe they could all help each other.

 She picked up an orange marker and wrote the first member of the Club: *Maggie-May Peasle*. Her real name was Magdalena Mary, but she usually got called Maggie or Maggie-May. Maggie was her friend and would definitely be a major help. But then, Maggie was also kept busy. She had five brothers and sisters and so she always had a baby brother or sister to watch. That had been Baby Isabella until last year, but now it was …

Baby Jacob.

Abigail had been doodling flowers in Maggie-May's hair, but she stopped. She had forgotten about Baby Jacob. "Well, …" she sighed. There was nothing to do about it.

She got a purple pen — who else was there?

Xenia Murphy. But Abigail didn't know how to spell it. She knew it had an X, even though it was pronounced *Zee-nee-ah*. So she made a letter X, and then wrote "Zee" just so she'd remember. She looked at the X for a minute and realized she didn't know very much about Xenia. She picked up a green pen and decided she'd come back to her later. Who else? There was Photini Jenkins.

She didn't know how to spell "Photini" either, so she wrote an O for Ophelia. Her patron saint's name was Photini and so it was the name she went by in church. That was probably just as well, because Ophelia seemed like a funny name.

Abigail doodled another flower and realized she didn't know very much about Photini either, other than that she was pale and nervous. But she also cared deeply about the Church — maybe her mother was right and she was going to be an iconographer when she grew up. Abigail looked at her drawing and saw that her flower was tall like an Easter lily. Maybe Photini would come in handy, like having an encyclopedia about church things.

Abigail picked up a black pen. Who was left? *Vanessa Taybeck.*

Oh … Vanessa.

She wasn't certain how to spell it, but she made a guess and actually got it right. V-a-n-e-s-s-a.

Vanessa was older than any of them. And she acted older. It was hard to remember a conversation with Vanessa. Her whole family tended to just keep to themselves. She had a younger brother, Noah, and an older brother James who always looked kind of mean to Abigail, but she didn't like to say so. Vanessa had masses of thick black hair that looked like a lion's mane. Abigail was secretly jealous, because her hair seemed thin and spaghetti-like by comparison, but she had heard Vanessa complain enough times to know not to even mention her hair to her — she didn't like it and could get a little cranky if anyone brought it up. In fact, it was usually a good idea not to bring up anything to Vanessa that she didn't want to talk about — she was very emotional and could be quick-tempered and sarcastic. She was hardly like a kid at all. On the other hand, people tended to treat her with some respect, Abigail had noticed. There was no doubt that it would be a real benefit to have someone older and wiser in the group. But what if she did all the talking? What if she thought the Club was so cool she wanted to be the boss of it?

Abigail had been drawing a lion with a black mane, but she

stopped. It would be a problem if Vanessa wanted to be in charge. But ... no. Abigail didn't want to think about that. There really couldn't be any doubt who was in charge of the Club.

She picked up the purple pen and looked at that letter X again. Xenia was difficult to know anything about. She always had some kind of screen in front of her. As soon as church was over, Xenia would play games on her cell phone or her pink game-player or her tablet. And when she answered questions in Sunday school, the things she said were very strange. How was Xenia at helping people solve their problems? Would she even try?

Abigail sighed again, and next to the letter X, she drew a big question mark.

Finally, she got a brown pen and drew her cartoon version of herself, which usually ended up having dog's ears that hung down. And she wrote *Abigail Alverson — president.*

And under that, she wrote a slogan in gold sparkly ink: *We help people.*

She was *very* excited.

Chapter five

"We're going to do *what?*"

"We're going to help people. That'll be our slogan." The girls were stationed in their usual spot in an out-of-the-way upstairs room usually referred to as the littlest conference room. The upper level of the social hall had been subdivided into a maze of so many rooms that it was just a matter of which one the girls felt like inhabiting for their occasional time together. The littlest conference room had one main table that they could all sit around, but the thing they liked about it most was that it was far enough away from the adults' meetings and the teenagers that they could talk or read or draw in peace.

And that's what they usually did, but of course, Abigail had other plans for that particular Tuesday night. She began by getting their attention, which wasn't easy to do. Vanessa and Photini usually talked together — or rather, Vanessa talked and Photini listened, occasionally remembering to agree. And Xenia, as always, was playing games on her tablet with total focus, her eyes flicking rapidly and her fingers swiping the screen or clicking buttons in fitful energy. With difficulty, she was persuaded to put the tablet down, but she refused to turn the game off and from time to time, she would steal glances at it or refresh the screen just to check on scores.

But once Abigail started in earnest to describe her plan, she couldn't complain about a lack of attention. Maggie always liked Abigail's ideas and turned her chair to face her as soon as the group was together. At first, Vanessa was looking around the room in a great show of disinterest, and Xenia's eyes kept flicking nervously to her tablet. But as Abigail's words flowed, they began to be drawn in. In fact, if anything, they were staring at her a little too much. She started talking faster to cover her jitters. She drew pictures in words for them — the Every Tuesday Girls Club. They would use the time they were left hanging around in church to have meetings. Father Andrew had told her to do it; he had told her it was a good idea. (She knew that was a stretch, but it certainly got everyone's attention.)

She considered telling them about her icon, but realized — with a twinge of guilt — that she didn't want to include that part. Of course part of the reason she was starting the Club was really to help her get the icon, but she realized it was rather selfish of her. Would they go along if they knew about it? Probably not. So she left that out and instead described the meaningful and important Club meetings they would have. She ended with the best part of all — it wasn't just something to do; they would have a mission.

She stopped for breath and realized she was getting blank stares. Maggie's delicate forehead was puckered and Photini's mouth was actually hanging open. Unsure what to do next, Abigail restated the most important part.

"We'll help people with their problems," she said, with imperfect confidence.

There was a moment of complete silence. The girls' parents would have been amazed to know that these four girls could ever be quite that silent, but for a solitary moment, they were.

And then, Vanessa broke the spell — she laughed. And it wasn't a very nice laugh. "Abigail," she said, in a lazy way, "Why would anyone want a bunch of ten-year-old girls to solve their problems?"

Abigail felt a flush of confused anger, but all she could think of to say was, "Well, … *you're* not ten."

"No, I'm not," said Vanessa, in the same bored voice. "But I," she pointed to herself lightly, "am not going to be in your little club."

Abigail was thunderstruck. "We're all in the Club."

"I'm not. I'm too old for things like this. I'm twelve — "

"You're eleven!"

"I'm nearly twelve, and I don't want to be in a girls' club."

Abigail struggled to control her panic. "But we need everyone, so we can solve problems."

"And who," rejoined Vanessa, "would want a bunch of little girls to solve their problems?"

So they were back where they started, and Abigail could only look at her helplessly. But Maggie, who had a courageous heart and never liked to see anyone picked on, turned to Vanessa and said, "I think it's a great idea."

Photini was stunned into speech. "You do?" she asked in wonder.

"Yes," said Maggie staunchly, and hoped she sounded certain. Actually, she didn't feel certain, and if Abigail had told her the idea in private, she would have delicately tried to change the subject. But as it was, she sat up a little straighter and threw Vanessa another glance. "Yes, I do. And I think we can help a lot of people." Even

Xenia looked up at that. Her fingers had been twitching toward the tablet, but Maggie sounded so confident that she couldn't help but pay attention. Maggie realized she would have to say something else.

"I mean," she said, thinking furiously, "We're here anyway. We might as well do something. Why shouldn't we be able to solve problems? We know things, too. If we ... if we put our heads together, and ... join forces..." She was terribly afraid that she had gotten that last part from a TV show, but she was stuck with it now. "We could probably make a difference." That had definitely come from a TV show, and Vanessa raised an eyebrow and gave her an *Oh, really?* look. "Or at least," Maggie persisted, "we can have a little fun." That part was closer to being an original thought of hers, and the others immediately looked a little more interested.

She looked at Abigail, who still didn't know what to say, and then turned back and dropped her eyes. "Besides," Maggie said in a smaller voice, "our parents all want us to stay out of trouble, right? Right now, they think *we're* the problem."

It was as if a little bomb went off in the room that no one could hear. Vanessa's smirk froze on her face. Photini was too struck to be frightened for an instant, and Xenia actually stopped slouching and sat up straight. Even Abigail felt a little shockwave hit her. It was true. Right now, her mother and father seemed to worry about her all the time, as if she were the one bill they couldn't pay. But that couldn't possibly be true for Maggie-May, who was so sweet and pretty that no grown-up could pass her without saying something nice. She looked at her friend searchingly, but Maggie's eyes were still lowered. In a wave of sympathy, she opened her mouth without knowing quite what she should say.

"We should advertise," Xenia said. "On television."

As usual, Xenia had said something so strange that no one was sure they heard her right. But her remark had broken the spell of silence, and Vanessa seemed to have woken up. "Okay," she said, and Abigail was relieved to notice that she wasn't sneering anymore. "So you'll have this ... mission, or whatever. But how are you going to start? You can't expect people to trust you with their problems when you've never done anything like this before."

"That's a good question," said Photini, crinkling her blond eyebrows in thought. She was going back and forth between interest and doubt, trying to make up her mind.

Xenia looked like she was about to say something, so Abigail hurried to answer. She was afraid that one more odd comment from Xenia might kill the fragile spark of life that the Club suddenly had.

"I thought maybe we'd practice first," Abigail said, haltingly. She thought again about what Maggie had said and how much it had affected all of them. "Maybe we can practice on each other."

"On each other," echoed Vanessa with an edge of sarcasm. "We're going to solve all of our own problems just like that."

"Not just like that," said Abigail sensibly. "And not all of them. Maybe just a couple. Maybe just one. Our biggest one — the biggest problem we have. One each, to make it fair." Vanessa seemed to be actually considering it and, sensing an opportunity, Abigail addressed her directly. "Don't you have at least one problem you'd like help with?"

She couldn't believe she had the nerve to talk to an eleven-year-old like that, and Vanessa drew in a quick breath as if she was going to answer with a cutting remark. But to everyone's surprise, Photini's high voice cut in first.

"I do," she declared excitedly. She had stopped wavering all at once — she had made up her mind and suddenly liked the idea very much. "I've got three problems or … no, I've got *four* problems. But I definitely have one biggest problem. And I think this is a great idea. And I want to go first!"

"We should go in alphabetical order," said Xenia, whose mind went immediately to orderly thoughts. But then she realized that a girl named Xenia always went last in alphabetical order, and so she added. "I mean, reverse alphabetical order. With a backwards alphabet."

Abigail was thrilled with the sudden rush of enthusiasm, but she had actually just assumed that as president, her problem would be the first one to be solved. However, she was starting to think that her presidency wasn't quite a settled matter with the Club. Recovering from that mistake, she gathered her wits quickly. "We should all write down what our biggest problem is — the problem we want the Club to solve. And then we'll pick one at random every week and we'll all go to work on it. When that one is solved, we'll pick the next one. That way, everyone gets a chance."

Xenia, who had been looking at the wall, seemed to wake up suddenly. "I know what *my* problem is, and it's *big*. There's this — "

"No, Xenia," insisted Maggie. "We'll write them down like Abigail says."

Xenia set her jaw stubbornly. "When?"

Abigail was flustered, but Maggie merely glanced at her before answering, "Tonight. Now."

The other girls rounded on her in surprise, but she looked back at them steadily. "Well, why wait? Here." She flipped her spiral notebook open to the back and tore out three pages. "We'll all write down our problem — "

"Our biggest problem?" asked Photini, who always wanted to be certain of the rules.

"Our biggest problem," nodded Maggie, tearing the pages neatly in half. "And then fold them in half like this — "she creased a practice ballot to show them, "And we'll put them in … " She looked around. "This baggie." She emptied out a bag with markers in it and held it out.

Xenia was looking lost. "You don't want to hear my problem?"

"*No*, Xenia," said Abigail and Maggie together. Maggie pushed a half sheet across the table at her. "Write it down. Here." She took pens out of Abigail's polka-dotted pencil box and handed them out. "One for me. Abigail. Photini. And …"

"Not for me." Vanessa folded her arms.

They all looked at her. "Why not?" said Abigail.

"Because I don't have any problems," said Vanessa in a strange, flat voice.

Abigail started to feel her temperature rise again. "You don't have *any* problems."

"I don't have *any* problems," repeated Vanessa defiantly. "At least, I don't have any that I want you *girls* to help me with."

She put an emphasis on the word *girls* that made Abigail think she was about to claim she was twelve again. And there was no doubt that right then, Vanessa didn't look like a little girl. She was taller than any of them, and with her head raised, she looked proud and in control. But there was something wrong with that tough stance — there was a sudden tightness to her face and her voice as if she was closer to tears than anger.

Abigail stopped on the verge of making a snappy comeback. She felt confused by what she was seeing. And Maggie, who sensed it as well, said in a consoling tone, "You don't have to put in a problem then. We'll have you pick, because it'll be the most fair. We'll know you're not picking your own."

Filling out the ballots didn't take Abigail long. She just wrote "Icon of St. Abigail" and folded the paper. Maggie was already done, and Photini only took a second longer. Xenia seemed to have a lot to write and was even turning the paper sideways so she could write along the edge. But eventually even she was finished, and all four pieces went into the baggie.

Vanessa had been reluctant to take any part in the Club's business, but she decided to make the best of things. So she lowered the baggie under the table and gave it a shake. Abigail fidgeted anxiously, feeling the tension grow. If her problem was the first one, the whole group could help her figure out how to raise money to get the icon. It was true that Fr. Andrew had said he'd help get it for her. But she was starting to wonder what he really meant by that. In any case, surely it was better to have the group working on fundraising as well. Maybe they'd be able to come up with a way to raise even more money than she needed. And then they could give something to the church and announce that it was from the Every Tuesday Girls Club. And everyone would be amazed and Vanessa would be very, very sorry that she hadn't wanted to be in the Club.

It could all happen, and all she needed was for Vanessa to pick her paper and read her problem.

But instead, Vanessa unfolded a paper that Abigail could see had Maggie's curly handwriting on it. And she read out, "Baby Jacob."

"Baby Jacob?" Xenia looked from one blank face to the next. "Who's Baby Jacob?"

Chapter six

WHEN SHE WAS BACK AT HOME, Abigail had a different sort of Tuesday night.

Tuesdays at the Alverson house generally went the same way. Mrs. Alverson would grab Abigail and go to church for the evening. Mr. Alverson and Mark would head out for their *jiu jitsu* classes, and Bet would be dropped off with a neighbor who had puppies. When they all came back together, everyone else was tired out from their activities and Abigail was sulking from having spent another boring Tuesday night. That's how it was most weeks.

This Tuesday, however, she had a lot on her mind and was glad when it was time to go to bed. But she found that her thoughts were too interesting to let her sleep, and eventually she just clicked on the light.

The Every Tuesday Club was launched — well and truly launched. She couldn't believe it. It had certainly looked a little rough at the start, but everything had turned out better than she could've hoped.

Well, maybe not better.

She sighed, looking down at her turquoise bedspread. No, there had been some problems. Things had gotten — what was the word? *Complicated.* There had been that curious lack of interest at the beginning, which Abigail just couldn't understand. And then Vanessa had started acting strange. On one hand, she was so rude and superior about the Club, but then, she had looked like she needed help after all. It was like somebody singing one song while another one was playing on the radio. Or ... something.

Abigail shook her head. It didn't make any sense, but who could understand the strange ways of eleven-year-olds? She looked around her room for something to keep her hands busy. She didn't feel like drawing for once, so she just started rummaging through things on the floor and separating them into piles.

No point trying to figure out Vanessa. There was the rest of the Club to think about and their first assignment. It had certainly been a surprising evening.

Abigail looked from the clothes to the toys. She was running out of room for piles, so she pulled all the clothes onto the bed and began folding shirts into squares.

The Club had its first assignment, all right. If only it wasn't ...

Abigail sighed. She could hear Xenia's clear voice as if she were in the room.

"Baby Jacob? Who is Baby Jacob?"

Maggie turned on her in disbelief. "*Jacob*? My *brother*." Xenia nodded to cover her embarrassment, wondering why the Peasles always called their youngest one Baby So-and-so. It just seemed a little weird, and she was actually about to say that, which would have made Maggie very upset. So it's just as well that Maggie cut Xenia off before she had a chance to open her mouth.

"You know, Xenia. My baby brother, who is *always* with me? Like, *all* the time? The baby brother I have to watch in church and at home and at the park and *everywhere*?"

Xenia shrank back before the sudden burst of strong emotion, and her fingers stretched out toward her blank tablet screen. At home, whenever her mother or brothers would raise their voices (which they did often), she could take refuge in the comforting glow and cozy logic of a computer game. She was pretty sure she didn't get to do that now, because Maggie was still glowering at her and the other girls were looking uncomfortable. But what Maggie was saying just didn't make sense to her and, drawing up all the courage she had, she said in a little voice, "But you had a little sister with you before, and another little brother before her. Why is this different?"

And what she said was true. As with a lot of big families, the older Peasle children all had jobs to keep the household running smoothly. There were six children, and Maggie was almost the oldest. Once her parents had found that she had a natural way with the littlest ones, she had a Peasle toddler in her care almost constantly.

"So why is it any different now?" asked Xenia again. "Why is Baby Jacob your biggest problem?"

RECOLLECTING IT IN HER ROOM, Abigail shook her head and started nudging toys into the closet with her foot. So typical of Xenia not to notice what was obvious to everyone else. When she had asked, there had been an awkward silence. Photini and Vanessa had looked at each other and Abigail straightened up markers on the table. And Maggie-May had just sighed. "Well ..."

The problem, as any of the other girls could've told Xenia, wasn't exactly that there was anything wrong with little Jacob. He was a healthy, happy and curious baby, constantly delighting in each day's new discovery.

But from the very beginning, he had been a bit of a shock. All of the Peasle children had been exceptionally good-looking, but you

couldn't say that about Jacob. It wasn't just that
his eyes had been a little crossed at first — that
had grown out in time. It wasn't even that his
wispy black hair insisted on sticking straight up
or that his ears were too big or his head was so
very round. For all anyone knew, he would grow
out of all those things as well.

But more than those things, it was the way Jacob behaved that really put everyone on edge. Because he didn't behave like a Peasle. All

 the Peasles had a shy grace and beautiful
manners. They didn't talk too much or
too little. From the youngest to the oldest, they had a natural way of knowing
just what to do and never drew unwant-
ed attention to themselves. Until Jacob
came along.

Poor little Jacob. What could you say? He was a sweetheart, but
he always seemed to be on the edge of disaster. He couldn't keep
his shoes on his feet, but he could get them stuck on his hands. He
could hardly totter about, and yet he managed to send displays
tumbling in markets and drug stores. Wherever he went, sooner or

later heads would turn and people
would laugh, holler a warning or
just shout. He was hopelessly clumsy, but it was almost as if he liked
being a little ridiculous. There was
something of the happy clown
about him — he just seemed to
enjoy getting people's attention and making them laugh, even if it
meant causing a spectacle.

And so, the utter calm that the dignified Peasles knew evaporated into a series of humiliating mishaps. His crazy antics meant that he had to be watched constantly, and even so, all anyone could do was limit the damage and pick up the pieces afterward. For sensitive Maggie, who had gotten used to the approving attention that came from having sweet Baby Nathan and angelic Baby Isabelle, the horrors of trying to mind Baby Jacob were just too much. It was obvious that he was good-tempered and almost indestructibly happy. But every day brought another misery of embarrassment — nerve-wracking carefulness followed by flustered apologies.

She felt terrible, but she had to say it, because she felt like her heart would burst. She loved her family, but Baby Jacob was just too much for her.

"My mother and father are getting so mad at me because I can't keep him out of trouble. But I don't know how, and I've just given up. That's why Baby Jacob is my biggest problem, Xenia." There was silence in the group, and they thought she was done. But she wasn't. "He's my baby brother and I know I should love him …but I don't. He doesn't even seem like my brother."

He doesn't even seem like my brother.

Those words had sounded so cold. They just rang in the air, as if a hammer had hit a big metal nail. It had been Abigail's job after Maggie spoke to conclude the Club meeting, since they could hear from the noise in the hallways that the adults were on the move. But she couldn't think of anything to say, and the meeting ended with awkward words and even more awkward silences. All the same, she found an opportunity to give Maggie-May a warm hug before they split up to get into different cars.

In the quiet of her room that night, the whole situation seemed a little overwhelming. Abigail hadn't known what the Club's first assignment would be, but she didn't think it would be Baby Jacob. She had to admit to herself that she had no reason to expect that they could help Maggie at all with her problem.

"Abigail!"

Abigail whipped around and saw her mother's disapproval dissolve into wonder as she gazed into the room. "I saw your light on. What are you doing up so late?"

Abigail looked around her room blankly. "I'm cleaning," she said. And it was true. For the first time in a month, nothing was on her floor except the carpet.

"Well ..." faltered her mother. "No more cleaning for now. Time for bed."

MRS. ALVERSON looked so stunned when she came to bed that her husband asked her what was the matter.

"Abigail was up late," she said in disbelief, "cleaning."

"Well then," said Mr. Alverson, putting his glasses back on after he had processed this information. "We are living in an age of miracles."

Chapter seven

ON WEDNESDAY, Maggie-May called. At first, they talked about the usual stuff — fieldtrips, movies and the like. But then Maggie sang out something to her mother about getting boots from the downstairs closet, and a minute later, a voice Abigail hardly recognized hissed into the phone. "Abigail, can you talk right now?"

The abrupt change shocked her. "Maggie?" she asked cautiously.

"Of course it's me. Can you talk?"

Had Maggie-May Peasle lost her mind? "We ... *were* ... talking."

"I mean, can you talk in private?"

"Oh! Um ... hold on." She reached out with her foot and swung the door of her room closed. She knew that meant that in ten minutes at the most, Bet would get curious and would want in. But at least she would have ten minutes of privacy. "Okay, I'm alone."

"Did … did you tell anyone what I said last night. About Baby Jacob?"

"What? No." Abigail was insulted.

"You didn't tell your mom or your dad?"

"No! I didn't tell anyone anything. I wouldn't tell what we say at our Club meetings. They're secret." Abigail had assumed that went without saying, but she realized that maybe she probably should have told everyone that.

"Do you promise?" pushed Maggie. "No, wait. Do you swear?"

"Maggie — "

"Do you *swear*?"

"Definitely. Yes. I swear."

There was the sound of a big breath being let out. "Thank you," she said with obvious relief.

Maggie had been nervous all morning. Her father had said something out of the blue about brothers, and her mother seemed to be looking at her. And she was suddenly very afraid that they knew and were mad at her. "I never should have said all that last night," she groaned. "I'm a bad sister."

Abigail was distressed. Maggie was certainly not a bad sister. But before she could tell her, Maggie thought of something and lapsed back into that urgent whisper.

"Omigosh! I said all that in front of Photini. And Xenia. And *Vanessa*!"

Abigail still felt indignant, but maybe she did see Maggie's point. "They won't tell," she said, but she couldn't keep the doubt out of her voice.

"They have to promise they won't. Make them swear," whispered Maggie desperately.

"Make them — "

"*Swear.* You have to call them. I would just die if my parents found out that I had any problem with Baby Jacob. Call them. Will you call them?"

Abigail glanced out her window to see if anyone heard how crazy this was. "Yes, I'll call them."

"Do you promise? No, wait. Do you swear?"

Abigail was about to object to this lack of trust, but Maggie suddenly altered her voice completely and started saying things like, "No, I can't find your boots anywhere, Abigail. I have to go now, Abigail!" It was obvious that someone had finally wondered why Maggie was in the downstairs closet for so long. She said, in a slightly edgy tone, "Don't forget to do *that thing* for me, okay? Bye," and hung up the phone.

CALLING THE OTHERS was problematic. It was difficult getting the necessary levels of privacy. As usual, Bet's sensitive radar had detected that her sister's door was closed, which could only mean that she was doing the kind of totally exciting things that older sisters do when you're not looking. Abigail had to get the other phone numbers off the church directory list in the kitchen and then amble from room to room the whole time trying to appear to Bet as if she wasn't doing anything interesting.

Luckily, the calls went well. Xenia mostly answered in words of one syllable: "What?" "No." "Yes." "Oh." The only difficulty was that she was hard to make out, given that her brothers Randy and Amos were having an uproarious time trading insults in the background. Abigail was just able to extract the promise and oath of secrecy from Xenia before her brothers noticed she was on the phone. Their shouting indicated that they were coming over to hang up the phone, but Xenia beat them to it, and the line went dead. Abigail put down the phone, shaking her head. Her brother Mark suddenly seemed like a really great brother — he never would've done the things that Randy and Amos did.

There was no question of background noise at Photini's house. Mrs. Jenkins was having an afternoon nap because of a bothersome headache, and Photini could only speak in a whisper.

But Photini, as Abigail feared, had a bit of a gossipy streak in her. She was terribly quiet in person, but over the phone she found it easier to converse, and she would've talked at length if Abigail had let her. Photini said she was shocked — but she sounded delighted — at Maggie's confession on Tuesday night. In truth, she would absolutely have told her mother as well as her older brother Jeffrey. She had just been waiting for a good time and planning what she would say. She didn't tell Abigail that, of course.

But to Photini's credit, once Abigail told her how distressed Maggie was, she promised to keep the secret. Photini may have lacked self-control where gossip was concerned, but she was very scrupulous in other ways and gave her promise with only a tiny moment of disappointment.

She vowed to keep the secret, but she wasn't happy about the request to swear that she'd do it. She knew there was something in the Bible about not swearing and just letting your "no" be "no." But she couldn't think where it was, and so after minor objections, she gave in and swore secrecy.

And Abigail, for her part, told her that it would be helpful if she could call Vanessa for her, since she was having a hard time keeping the calls private. That wasn't entirely true, since Bet was distracted rearranging fridge magnets right then, but it served its purpose. Photini would have an excuse to call Vanessa and extract this important-sounding vow of secrecy, and Abigail could finally get off the phone.

Which was just as well; Bet had been getting restless. Abigail looked at her little sister, who had on her favorite rainbow-colored leggings and shoes that she had glued glitter onto. It was true that having a younger sister was kind of a bother sometimes. You had to go out of your way for her and remember that she was little. You had to talk so she could understand and let her win at games, and even then she might get fussy for no reason. Bet could be kind of a pest. Still ...

Abigail sat down on a low stool so she could give Bet a hug, which she liked very much and hugged her back. On the whole, Abigail realized that she was very lucky. Her sister might not have been a perfect angel like little Baby Isabelle was, but she certainly didn't get into as many impossible scrapes as the unfortunate Baby Jacob.

Was the problem with Jacob, though, or was it with Maggie? And could she help her friend to get a break from him somehow? Maybe if her mother talked with Mrs. Peasle ... but no, that would violate the oath of secrecy, and it might not work anyway.

Abigail hadn't realized she was frowning until she felt Bet's little fingers trying to push her eyebrows up.

"Bad day, Babbagail?" she asked fretfully.

Abigail had to smile, and she pushed her eyebrows up and down for Bet to see. "No, I'm not having a bad day. Let's go find Mark."

MARK TRIED TO BE HELPFUL, but he really wasn't. The girls found him at a good time. He had been reading a book for an essay about the way the sun worked, and he wanted a break. So he had actually smiled when they showed up, and he helped Bet get her plastic horse Buddy from under his books.

But he couldn't quite understand what Abigail was talking about. She had to keep all the details vague in order to keep Maggie's secret, and so she tried to make it sound like it was someone else's problem.

"I'm sorry, Abby. I don't know what you mean. Do you think I'm mad at you?" he asked.

"No," she said in some frustration. "But ... I mean, brothers can be kind of a pain sometimes." Mark looked offended, so she hastened to add, "Not you! But sometimes ... sisters don't understand brothers and ..." She could tell she was losing Mark's attention. "... And then it can be a problem for them and ... for the whole family."

"What's a problem for the whole family?" inquired Mrs. Alverson lightly, putting Mark's soda can firmly on a coaster.

Abigail hadn't heard her come in and was too startled to answer. But Mark was happy for the interruption and said matter-of-factly, "Abigail thinks I don't understand her."

Abigail sputtered. "That's not what I said."

"You said you were thinking about brothers and sisters and problems," insisted Mark.

"But I didn't mean *our* problems! I wasn't talking about *you*!"

"Then why did you *ask* me?" There was a kind of boy logic there that Abigail couldn't even begin to answer. But Mrs. Alverson put a hand on both heads and told them not to raise their voices. She followed up with a firm but polite suggestion that Abigail and Bet should leave Mark to his homework and get a cup of something from the kitchen.

Bet picked up Buddy and grabbed her mother's hand, leaving Abigail to trail in after them.

Abigail was still feeling unjustly accused when she got to the kitchen. "I wasn't talking about Mark," she repeated. "I was just thinking about family problems, that's all."

Her mother glanced at her as she filled the kettle. "Whose family problems, Abigail? Are you having a problem with your brother?"

With a jolt, Abigail realized that she had put herself in a kind of a trap. "No," she said with an emphatic shake of the head.

"Whose problems, then?" her mother gently asked.

There didn't seem like any way out. "The Peasles," Abigail answered truthfully.

"The *Peasles*?" Mrs. Alverson was so astonished that she dropped the kettle in the sink. "Why on earth would you think there was anything wrong with them?"

Abigail was torn. Part of her wanted to just tell her mother what had happened at the Every Tuesday Girls Club meeting. But she had promised that she wouldn't. And anyway, her mother probably wouldn't believe her.

"Nothing's wrong, probably. I just … Maggie seemed kind of stressed out on Tuesday. But it's probably nothing, so please don't tell anyone I said anything."

Her mother seemed to think about it as she put the kettle on, but she shook her head. "I won't tell, Abigail. It's sweet that you're concerned about a friend. But I think you're wrong this time. What has Maggie got to be stressed about?"

Abigail was conflicted again. Someone should know. "I think it's hard for her. You know, with Jacob."

"With Jacob? Oh," Mrs. Alverson said absently, scouting the cupboard. "Oh. With Jacob. Well ... yes, he is a handful."

Mrs. Alverson hesitated, a mug in each hand. She thought about little things she had seen. That sweet little toddler who was always having to be herded and tended so carefully. And shy Maggie — so young to have to keep a constant watch over him. But then she saw her friend Andrea Peasle, who was always so calmly and beautifully in charge, without a hair out of place. Mrs. Alverson had to admit that sometimes she was jealous of how easy Andrea made everything look. And the whole family — it always appeared as if they were ready to be photographed for a magazine.

No, it wasn't possible. "Abigail, you worry too much. You can take my word for it," said her mother with finality, handing her a cup. "There's nothing wrong with Maggie. Nothing is ever wrong with that family."

And Mrs. Alverson was certain she was right about that. Until Sunday.

AT THE BEGINNING of the Saturday night service, there was no indication that anything was wrong. There was peace and tranquility in the Peasle family. They had gone to see a steamboat museum, and Baby Jacob was fascinated with the gigantic wheels. He had spent the afternoon playing endlessly with a little wooden steamboat his father bought for him, and he was quiet and well-behaved the rest of the day. Maggie was relieved almost to tears, and Abigail began to think maybe it had all been a mistake. Maybe Jacob had just gotten off to a bad start and would be fine from then on.

But then came the Sunday Divine Liturgy, and it was obvious that nothing had changed. Jacob had a good night's sleep and forgot about steamboats, so he was more Jacob than ever. He wanted to re-arrange chairs and run between people's legs and pull down candle stands. He was taken into the outer area of the church — the nar-thex — for time-outs, but came back with renewed vigor at the end of every break and picked up where he left off. When he was made to sit still, he would talk or sing or make funny noises. He had been taken from Maggie a few times, but most of the time, she had the unwelcome chore of trying to get her brother to mind his manners — *or mind the manners he would've had if he had manners*, Maggie thought bitterly.

It didn't help that Fr. Andrew was away that week. Fr. Andrew had two grown boys of his own, so nearly nothing could distract him from a service. But the second priest, Fr. Boris, was serving, and he and his wife didn't have any children. He was actually a very nice man, but Fr. Boris was notoriously strict during church services. On that Sunday, it almost looked like Fr. Boris didn't hear Jacob's noises and interruptions, but those who knew him best saw that the priest's face and neck were turning red, and he was saying his part of the service very loudly and distinctly.

It all came to a boil when Fr. Boris came out to give the homily. It was the Sunday of St. Gregory Palamas, which was a subject that he loved preaching on. Fr. Boris was determined not to be distracted as he stepped up to the podium and began warming up to the topic, but unfortunately, Jacob began warming up as well, beginning a stream of constant comments, with words he knew or with animal noises or sound effects he made up. He had a lot to say right then, and nothing that Maggie did seemed to make the least difference. She tried to catch her mother's eye, but Mrs. Peasle had to deal with her other children and didn't seem to notice. Maggie was left to sort out Jacob as best she could, and she tried every trick she could think of.

She had tried shushing him and covering his mouth, but finally, as Fr. Boris seemed about to make an important point, she caught Baby Jacob's lips in her fingers and gently squeezed them shut. This didn't turn out to be a good idea. Jacob was delighted with what he thought was a new game, and when he found he couldn't make any sound with the usual amount of air, he puffed up his cheeks and blew enough air into his lips to make a surprisingly loud raspberry that echoed alarmingly in the utter silence.

There was a startled gasp from some churchgoers, and suppressed laughter from others. But the storm cloud of Fr. Boris's temper finally broke, and his heavily accented voice crackled with fury. "Please to remove the cause of dis disturbance."

Poor Maggie could have died right there. No Peasle child had ever been asked to be removed before. She was on her feet in an instant, but her mother swept Jacob out of her arms. She carried him swiftly through the doors into the narthex, leaving Maggie standing with a bright red face and eyes brimming with tears.

"You were right, Abigail."

It had been an unusually quiet ride home for Abigail and her mother. Mr. Alverson was in the van with Mark and Bet, taking a longer route home so he could swing by an office supply store. With just the two of them in the car, there hadn't been much to interrupt the squishy sound of the tires on black, wet pavement. Both Abigail and her mother had been lost in thought.

"You were right to worry about Maggie and her family," Mrs. Alverson said. Considering the words, she added, "Not a lot. But ... maybe a little."

Abigail was amazed. And relieved that an adult knew. "So what do I do?" she asked.

"What do you do?" Mrs. Alverson seemed surprised by the question.

"I want to help."

Her mother took her eyes of the rolling road momentarily and scanned Abigail's face. "That's very thoughtful of you, Abigail. But I don't know what you could do. Just be a good friend to her, I expect. Things are bound to get easier for her when Jacob grows up a little. Meanwhile, just pray for her."

Abigail nodded, but she felt disappointed. "But isn't there something to do?"

"Praying *is* doing, Abby. Didn't you hear what Fr. Boris said in the homily?"

Abigail had to admit that she hadn't. "It was about St. Gregory Pull — "

"Saint Gregory Palamas. I know there was a lot there that you couldn't follow, but do you remember what he said at the end just for the kids?"

"About prayer?" This was tricky — who ever listened to Fr. Boris's homilies? But there had been something, now that she thought of it. "That we should pray this week?"

"He said that if you didn't remember anything else about St. Gregory, you should just pray this week. Not just with words. Pray with your heart. And then — ?"

Abigail could picture Fr. Boris. He always looked so stern, but his voice had gotten surprisingly soft at that point. Pray with your heart. And then ...

"Listen?"

"Yes. Pray and then listen. Because God hears our prayers, but we don't always hear His answers."

THAT GAVE ABIGAIL something to think about. But more than that, it gave her something to do, and she was glad. She had been thinking all week, and she was tired of it. She had also been feeling sad and anxious for Maggie all week, and she had prayed, but all the buzzing thoughts and unhappy emotions seemed to go around in circles.

She drew a picture of the icon she hoped to have soon, and wished very much that she had the real thing there to give her some courage. So she sat by her window when she went to bed and propped the drawing up. She looked out into the night and saw the vague outline of the giant maple tree that always seemed like it was guarding her bedroom. She said the simple prayer she knew by heart called the Jesus Prayer. She just looked out and let herself say it until the words seemed to be saying themselves. "Lord Jesus Christ, Son of God, have mercy on me, a sinner."

The night got so quiet. Eventually, Abigail stopped saying the words, because somehow, they were already there, already in the room with her. She didn't feel sorry for Maggie anymore, and she didn't feel alone.

The only feeling she had was a kind of certainty that everything was going to turn out all right. She didn't have any reason to be so certain, but she wasn't worried about that either. She just knew it was going to turn out all right — she felt just peaceful about it, and after the stress of the last few days, she was very glad to feel that way.

Abigail turned away from the window and could make out the outline of her sketched icon, but the features were hazy in the gray light. Looking around her room, she had the feeling that there was something she had forgotten to do. What was it? Her eyes fell on the book of Bible stories she had on her desk and she pulled it over and flicked on the light.

What was it she was thinking of? She felt as if she would know it if she saw it. Without much idea of where she was going, she flipped to the story of St. Abigail and felt the familiar contentment. But no, there was something else. She turned forward to the next story and the next. And there was an illustration of one of King David's sons who had become a great king — King Solomon.

She recalled that Fr. Andrew had said that King Solomon had written many wise sayings. But she didn't recall the story that was on the page in front of her. She must have seen it before — she had read all these stories many times — but she didn't remember this one. Bold letters at the top of the page read, "King Solomon and the Baby."

Abigail opened the book wide with her elbows and started reading. Then she read it again and began to make notes and draw pictures.

Because this seemed to be exactly what she was looking for.

Chapter eight

THE CLUB MEETING GOT OFF TO AN UNEVEN START on Tuesday night. All the girls were there on time for once, which seemed like a good beginning. But the teenagers declared that they needed the room to rehearse a talent show they were working on, so the girls had to find a new room.

The move was complicated because Maggie was watching Jacob that night. It took time to get all of them settled. But eventually, the backpacks, books and pens were loosely arranged on the wide conference table, talk subsided and heads turned to Abigail, one by one.

Abigail was still in high spirits from the success she felt certain of, so she cleared her throat meaningfully and proclaimed, "Let it be known that today is the third day — or fourth? No, third — of April." Xenia goggled at her, but Abigail sailed on happily, more sure than ever of the great prospects of the Club. "This meeting of the Every Tuesday Girls Club is called to order. A — "

Abigail stopped in momentary confusion. She had been about to say "Abigail Alverson, president," to add the right touch of authority. But she remembered that her presidency hadn't been exactly settled. However, that "A — " was still hanging in the air, so thinking quickly, she barked out "All rise!"

It was such a surprise that the chairs were immediately pushed back and even Vanessa stood up. The problem was, Abigail had no idea what to do next. But she had another flash of inspiration, and turning to Photini, she said gravely, "Club-member Photini, will you please lead us in prayer?"

Photini frowned in thought for a few seconds and then located an icon of Christ. Crossing herself, she said, "Heavenly Father, bless this undertaking of your servants. Bless our dealings with each other. Teach us to act firmly and wisely without embittering or embarrassing others. For all good things come from You, to the glory of the Father and the Son and the Holy Spirit. Amen." And the four girls answered in some amazement "Amen" with little Jacob chiming in with some sort of syllable. Abigail was impressed and asked Photini if she had just made up that prayer on the spot.

"Oh no," said Photini with modesty. "That's the prayer we use for family meetings. Jeffrey taught it to us after he came back from the monastery." There didn't seem like anything else to say, so Abigail merely remarked with dignity, "We may be seated." They all tumbled back into their seats, and then Abigail cleared her throat again and continued.

"LAST TUESDAY, it was decided that we would form the Every Tuesday Girls Club in order to help people with their problems." Abigail was still enjoying herself, though she could tell that she sounded a little pompous. But she couldn't think how to fix that, so she continued along in the same way, "*Furthermore*, we agreed that we would begin by solving each others' biggest problems first, just for practice. And *furthermore*," — Abigail liked the word *furthermore* — "that we would start by helping Club-member Maggie with the problem of what to do about Baby Jacob. And so," she concluded, swinging to her right with finality, "what have we come up with?"

It was a splendid ending, but unfortunately, the person on Abigail's right was Vanessa. And she closed her eyes and answered disagreeably, "Well, I didn't come up with anything, because I think this is *dumb*."

The rudeness! Abigail was caught off-guard, and in a flash of temper she blurted out, "Well, I think — " and would have said she thought *Vanessa* was dumb, just to be spiteful. But at the last minute, she stopped herself and ended with, "I think you're bossy."

Which was much harder to argue with, but Vanessa seemed used to hearing it and didn't act as if she cared. "*I'm* bossy? What about you, Miss All-Rise?"

Abigail was speechless.

"Miss *Furthermore*?" Vanessa pressed.

"Vanessa!" said Abigail, thunderstruck by the impertinence.

"Abigail!" said Vanessa, parroting her tone perfectly.

"May I say something?"

That last question had come from Maggie-May, and the magic of the Peasle voice was still in full force. Although she didn't say it loudly at all, both girls immediately stopped as if they had been shouted down.

Maggie didn't want to cause a fuss, but all week she had been planning a short speech. Having thought about it, she was sure it was a mistake to have told the Club how she really felt. It would be really, really embarrassing if it got back to her parents that she had said that minding her brother was difficult for her. Maggie was planning to convince the girls that she didn't really mean it and that she didn't need any help.

"Okay," she began. "So, um, I know that I might have said some things last week that — " At that point, Jacob tried to put a red crayon in his ear, and Maggie took it from him with a pinched smile and started again. "I might have made it sound as if there was some kind of problem going on or something. But I think I gave you all the wrong idea. Really, there isn't any — " Jacob tried the same trick with a turquoise crayon and Maggie grabbed it. " — *problem*. There isn't any problem." She threw a watchful look at Jacob, and when it seemed like he had other plans for other crayons, she took the whole bunch and closed them up in a plastic box.

Maggie swiped a hand quickly through her hair. "Sorry! I'm sorry. Jacob is just so ... well, you know. Anyway, what I'm trying to say is that I think I made it sound like I didn't love my brother. And I would feel terrible if you all thought that I was the kind of sister ..." Maggie drew a quick breath and was alarmed to find that she felt a sob welling up. She cleared her throat roughly. "I'm not the kind of sister who would say that, because ... I wouldn't. I love Jacob. He's ... *adorable*." The silence that followed was short but awkward. Maggie cleared her throat again and plunged forward. "So what I'd like to say ... I want to thank you all very much — very, very much — but really, we're all just *fine* and I don't need — "

But then, it happened. Jacob managed to get one toe under the lid

of the box and flipped it over, sending crayons and markers clatter-
ing onto the table. Before she could stop herself, Maggie barked out,
"Jacob! *NO!!*" with so much force that the sound reverberated in the
room like a shot.

Jacob only looked up in vague interest, but for the rest of them, the
explosive burst was jarring. Blushing furiously, Maggie let the others help her put everything back in the box while she gathered her
wits. With a mixture of shame and relief, Maggie realized that her
planned speech wouldn't work. So she took a deep breath and simply
said, "I think what I mean is … I'd be very glad to hear any ideas you
have about Baby Jacob."

XENIA HAD INFORMATION that she had looked up at the library. Maggie was touched that Xenia would go to that trouble, but
she became concerned when she heard Xenia talk about consulting
the librarian.

"You didn't tell her … I mean, you didn't mention our names, did
you? I think my mother knows one of the people at that library."

"Oh. No, I didn't tell her about him being a Peasle. I knew that was
a secret. I told her it was about a very important family problem —"

"Xenia!"

"Well, it is. I told her about the time that he got caught in a folding chair, but I changed the names. In fact, I changed most of the
story and told her I knew someone who had gotten stuck in a chair
that definitely was not a folding chair." She paused again. "And then
she gave me a funny look and went and found me this." And Xenia
proudly placed a book in Maggie's hands.

Maggie looked at it and read the title a tight voice, "Help Me!

My Kid is Weird: A Guidebook for Parents of Children with — " she frowned over the hard words " — Social Disorders."

Xenia was beaming, but the others had blank looks. "What are social disorders?" asked Photini.

"Well, it's when you get your head stuck in a chair and stuff, right?" reasoned Xenia. "The librarian said it's important for parents to know they're not alone."

"Xenia — " said Maggie carefully.

"For parents?" interrupted Photini, looking over Maggie's shoulder at the cover. "But Maggie's not a parent."

"Well," frowned Xenia, "They didn't have one called 'Help Me, My *Brother* is Weird."

Maggie let the book fall flat on the table with a loud bang. "Jacob. Is. *Not*. Weird."

Abigail grabbed the book off the table. "Of course he's not! Look, Xenia," she said helpfully, holding up the offending library book. "Look at how angry this little girl on the cover is. Baby Jacob never looks like that. He's really happy all the time." As if on cue, Jacob put both hands in his mouth and gurgled cheerfully. "Besides," continued Abigail, thumbing through the pages, "This is about older kids. Maybe the librarian didn't understand what you meant. Maybe she thought it was for you."

"For *me*?" said Xenia, scratching her head with a pencil. "Why would she think it was for me?"

"No reason," said Abigail hastily. "Anyway, thanks for all that hard work. Photini, what have you got?"

TO NO ONE'S SURPRISE, Photini had found prayers for the occasion.

"Look," she said, ruffling through the sheets enthusiastically. "This one is for Speedy Help in Times of Distress. This is for Help to Do What's Right. And ... ooh ... this is a good one." She opened the book out flat so they could see. "This is For Loved Ones. See? 'Help me and guide me to be a blessing to my — ' and it says 'relative' but you can fill that in."

Maggie felt uncomfortable. "Thank you, Photini, this is great. But Jacob isn't even two yet. He can't read. How would he say these?"

Photini looked puzzled. "Well, he can't. They're not for him, they're for you."

"Me?" Maggie was so surprised she took both hands off Jacob and he fell onto his round tummy. But as usual, he thought that was great fun. "Why would I need to pray to do the right thing? I *am* doing the right thing. It's not my fault Jacob is unfortunate."

"He's too little to pray," argued Photini. "You need to pray for you, and for him, too."

"But he can't help it," said Maggie firmly.

"That's right," nodded Xenia. "He has a social disorder."

"No, he DOESN'T, Xenia," snapped Maggie.

"Well, maybe not *now* — "

Maggie noticed that Vanessa was trying not to laugh, but she didn't see anything funny about it. "You guys are *not* helping," Maggie scowled.

"No, they are not." This was the first thing that Vanessa had said for minutes, but Maggie rounded on her as well.

"At least they *tried*, Vanessa."

"Tried?" Vanessa sneered. "A book for parents and a bunch of prayers? That's the best they can do?"

Photini was hurt and opened her mouth to protest, but it wasn't in her nature to stand up to Vanessa, so all she said was, "Abigail hasn't gone yet. Abigail, what have you got?"

"Yes, Abigail," said Vanessa, packing as much sarcasm as she could into the words, "What do you have? A drawing? A song about flies?"

"No," said Abigail shakily. "A story." Vanessa raised one eyebrow.

"From the Bible," Abigail continued doggedly. Vanessa raised the other eyebrow.

"About King Solomon." Vanessa dropped both eyebrows and rolled her eyes expressively.

Abigail fought to control her panic. This is not how she was hoping to introduce her story. "King Solomon was a great king in Old Testament times. And he knew so many things that people came to him from all over for advice. They even called him King Solomon the Wise."

"I *know* who King Solomon is," said Vanessa briskly. "Your problem is that you think you're Queen Abigail the Wise."

"I do not!" said Abigail hotly. But she had in fact done a quick drawing at home of herself with a crown on. How did Vanessa always know things like this?

Her gaze swept the group. Photini was looking doubtful and Xenia was sneaking one hand toward her computer tablet because that was her natural response to any arguing. But Maggie looked at her with sudden interest, and a thin light of hope in her eyes that touched Abigail's heart.

"I think this story is for you, Maggie. Do you want to hear it?"

"No," said Vanessa.

"Yes," said Maggie, and cut Vanessa off before she could say anything else. "Be quiet, Vanessa. If you're not going to help, then stop arguing and let me hear this."

"Fine!" said Vanessa, with a gesture of resignation. "I'm not saying another word. Let me know when you're through, Queen Abigail." And she opened the nearest book and plumped it down dramatically in front of her.

With Vanessa quieted down, Abigail took a deep breath, pried the tablet out of Xenia's hands, and started again. "Here's the story, Maggie," she said, turning her chair. "As I said, God blessed Solomon with so much wisdom that people brought their problems to him."

Vanessa gave a grunt of scorn, but Abigail ignored her. "There were two women who had a disagreement and came to King Solomon to solve it. They both lived in the same house and they both had babies at almost the same time. But one of the women's babies had died. So she took the other woman's baby and said it was hers. No one could figure out who was telling the truth. The women came with the baby and they each said that they were the baby's mother." Abigail waited while Maggie rescued Jacob from falling off the arm of the chair and went on. "The first woman cried to Solomon and said, "This is my baby!" and the second woman cried even louder and said, 'No, that's not true! King Solomon, she lost her child and she's trying to steal mine. Please help me! Don't let her have my child!'" Abigail had altered her voice to be the two different women, and even Xenia looked interested. Vanessa shoved her nose further into the book.

"What did he do?" asked Xenia, spellbound.

Abigail was glad to get to the good part. "King Solomon said,

'Bring me a sword! Cut the child in half!'"

"What?!" cried Maggie in horror. Photini gasped and looked at Baby Jacob as if he might have nightmares. But of course, he hadn't understood a word, and was only trying to do a kind of somersault off the end of the table.

"But that's not what happened," said Abigail quickly. "Let me finish. When he gave that order, both women freaked out. But here's the important part: The first one said, 'Fine! If I can't have him, then no one can. Go ahead and cut him in half.' But the second one said, 'No, King Solomon. Give him to her, but please don't kill him.' And then King Solomon knew who the baby's mother was, and he gave him to the second woman."

"Ohhh," said Photini appreciatively. "Do you get it, Xenia?"

"No," Xenia sulked. "How did he know the second woman was his mother?"

"Because his *real* mother ... oh, you tell her, Abigail."

Abigail tucked her hair behind her ear and scooted her chair up to the table. "His real mother was willing to sacrifice for him. The argument didn't matter, and she was even willing to see her enemy raise her son, if only he could be alive. Do you get it, Maggie?"

Maggie looked at Jacob quizzically. So small. So needy. There was something about that story, but she didn't know what. Her eyes met Abigail's. "I'm ... not sure."

"But ..." Xenia's voice piped up. "He was going to kill the baby? That's not right. Just because you're a king doesn't make that right."

Photini tried to help. "He wouldn't really have let them cut the baby in half. He just said that so that the fake mother would say what she said."

Xenia was unconvinced. "It just doesn't seem like a very good way to do things."

"Xenia, it's in the *Bible*," said Photini with fervor.

"Okay, look," said Abigail impatiently. She felt like they were getting off the point. She nimbly popped the top off a marker — drawing always helped her put things in order. "Here's King Solomon — " she sketched a man with a crown and a beard. "And here's the first woman and ..." Jacob was sitting on a piece of paper she needed. Without hesitating, she handed him to Xenia so she could grab the paper. "And here's the second woman."

"What are their names?" Xenia tried to look around the top of little Jacob, but he kept moving, so she handed him to Photini. Maggie gave a squawk of protest, but no one noticed.

"Whose names?" asked Abigail. "The two women? They don't have — "

"Rachel and Priscilla," said Photini quickly, pulling her two favorite girl names out of the Bible. She was warily holding Jacob up on tippy toe so he couldn't go anywhere or fall over anything. She was always frightened of babies, and Jacob scared her more than most.

"You guys?" pleaded Maggie, with an eye on squirming Baby Jacob. "Can we — ?"

"Would they sue?" interrupted Xenia, still focused on the story. "Would Rachel and Priscilla take King Solomon to court and sue him?"

"What? *No*," said Abigail, tuning out Maggie's attempts to break in. "You can't sue a king. Look — " She wanted to get back to her drawing.

But Xenia wasn't finished. "How do you even do that — cut a baby in half? What does that mean?"

Photini held up Jacob a little higher so they could see. "Well," she mused, trying to hold Jacob still as he wriggled and fussed, "if you had a sword — "

"But I mean … " Xenia leaned over and drew her finger across Jacob's round belly. "Do you go this way?"

"No, Xenia. Maggie, hold on a minute." Abigail reached over with the marker. "I think you go the long way — like this." And she drew a perfect dotted line down between Jacob's eyes to the bridge of his nose.

Or it would have been a perfect dotted line if Maggie-May Peasle hadn't made a *very* loud noise. And Photini, who was trying to see better, dropped Jacob onto his backside on the table with a solid thunk.

That was enough for Baby Jacob. He took worse falls than that on a regular basis, but the combination of the loud talk, the annoyance of being held up on his toes and the smelly marker on his face was more than he could stand. Within a second of his rump hitting the polished wood, his face started crumpling into the shape that all the girls knew could only mean that a significant wail was going to follow.

Abigail reached for him, but a lightning-fast Peasle hand snaked out and slapped hers away smartly. One other person had had enough — Maggie-May Peasle.

Still drawing in breath, Jacob swung around to Maggie in a fit of tiny distress. He saw the eyes that were always watching out for him, the hands that always helped him, the face he knew better than any other except his mother. He held out his arms as the howl finally broke free and Maggie gathered him up and swung toward the door.

Abigail started to offer help, but Maggie whirled around with her eyes blazing and said in a voice Abigail could hardly recognize, "YOU! LEAVE! MY! BROTHER … *ALONE*!!!" and she was gone. The door swung closed on three very astonished faces and Vanessa still deeply involved in her book.

THE EVERY TUESDAY GIRLS CLUB had a very bad ten or fifteen minutes after that. Xenia grabbed her computer tablet and wouldn't give it up. Photini was in an agony of anxiety that Maggie would run off and tell what happened and froze a minute later when she heard the sound of Mrs. Peasle's voice outside.

"Helen," Mrs. Peasle called down the hallway to someone, "do you have a rag or towel or something? It's for Jacob."

Photini gasped, but Abigail clapped a hand over her mouth as the other woman answered, "What happened? He didn't hurt himself?"

"Oh no," replied Mrs. Peasle with an easy chuckle, walking past the door. "He got some pen marks on his face. Maggie said he was playing with a magic marker." And a second later, her voice got fainter as she went into the kitchen.

Photini almost cried with relief, and even Xenia looked up from the screen with a twitch of a smile. Abigail wanted to feel better, but the realization that she wouldn't get punished only made her notice how very, very bad she felt.

Mad as she was, Maggie still hadn't wanted anyone to get blamed for what happened. But Abigail had to admit that she had acted really thoughtlessly. She almost wished that Vanessa would drop the book and tell her off so Abigail could stop feeling guilty.

In time, the other church meetings broke up and chatting parents came to rescue them from the conference room and the tense atmosphere that had settled over them. The girls left in total silence.

OUTSIDE, ABIGAIL AND XENIA were left together on the curb while their mothers exchanged some last snippets of conversation. Abigail really hadn't wanted to say anything, but her heart was too full, and she had to speak.

"That didn't ... go very well," she said haltingly.

"No," answered Xenia mechanically, and then the silence descended again.

Abigail looked at her mother, but she showed no signs of winding things up. "I don't know what happened," Abigail added listlessly.

Xenia bobbed her head in agreement. "Me neither. But then, I miss a lot of things. You should ask Vanessa."

Abigail snorted. "Vanessa! How would Vanessa know anything? She spent the whole time reading that book."

Xenia gazed at her with her bland eyes. "Not the whole book," she said without emotion. "Just one page."

Abigail felt bewildered. "Just one page? What does that mean?"

"I could see into the book from where I was sitting, and the same picture was always in the same corner." Abigail opened her mouth, but Xenia continued, "Vanessa never turned the page the whole time."

Abigail drew in a breath as she began to see the point, and Xenia looked at the trees. "Vanessa wasn't reading at all," said Xenia. "She was listening to every word we said."

Chapter nine

Unfortunately for Abigail, her bad evening turned into a worse night when she got home. She stayed up late and told St. Abigail everything that happened. Briefly, Abigail considered drawing a new version of her saint that might have a better expression to handle news of the shocking episode, but when she remembered the icon in the book, she knew she didn't want to change anything about it. She wanted her Abigail to still have those wide, peaceful eyes and that look of great understanding. In the conference room, she had felt awful and almost wished someone would scold her, but pouring out her heart to St. Abigail, she realized how much she wanted to hear a gentle word. Abigail held the drawing and looked out the window until she was too tired to sit up, then fell into bed and slept fitfully.

When she got up in the morning, she felt even worse. She sat lethargically in the chair at her desk with her brush stuck in her hair and one sock pulled on. How had everything gone so wrong? She had prayed and listened. She had come across the story of Solomon and the baby, and she had just known it would be the right one. Maybe she made a mistake somewhere. But … no.

Abigail tugged her brush out of her hair and smacked it onto the desk. No, she hadn't been wrong. She had gotten … well, she had gotten kind of excited and hadn't noticed what she was doing, that's all. Couldn't Maggie see that Xenia and Photini needed to have things explained to them? Okay, so using the marker on the baby was bad, but wasn't it obvious that the story was the most important thing? And Vanessa! Abigail threw her shoes down and walked into them. Vanessa was so rude and so bossy. And Maggie ... well, she was just being stubborn.

Abigail rubbed the bleariness out of her eyes with her fist. Now that she came to think of it, there was no doubt — the Every Tuesday Girls Club members were just acting crazy. Except for the president.

Abigail called the Peasles' number as soon as she could, but Maggie didn't come to the phone. Her older sister passed along a message that she was busy. Abigail tried again in the afternoon and Mrs. Peasle answered. "Didn't Maggie get back to you?" she asked in gentle surprise. "Hold on. I'm sure I can find her."

A minute later a glum voice said, "What do you want?"

"Maggie, don't hang up," Abigail said desperately. "I just wanted to talk with you about what happened last night."

"I do not want to talk about it."

Abigail pushed on. "I was just trying to help, Maggie."

"Help?" Maggie snapped. "You didn't even notice what you were doing. You all treated Jacob like he was a rag doll." Maggie didn't know what a rag doll was, but it was a thing her mother said and it sounded right, so she said it again. "You treated Jacob like a rag doll or stuffed animal or something."

Abigail bit her lip. What could she say? "I just got carried away."

"You wrote on him. You wrote on his *face*! With a *marker*!" Maggie had dropped her voice down to a whisper that was almost worse than if she had yelled.

Abigail felt stung, and all the confidence she had that morning evaporated. "I … don't know what to say."

"Then we have nothing to talk about. Don't call me again." And Maggie hung up.

ABIGAIL LOOKED AT THE PHONE, broken-hearted. How could she have been so careless? Why was she always getting caught up in things and hurting someone's feelings? Just a short bit ago, she had felt like all the other girls were wrong and she was right. But with those stinging words from Maggie, her point of view flipped completely. Right now, she didn't think they'd been wrong at all, just her. Only her. Totally wrong. Wrong forever. She would probably be wrong about everything until she died.

She looked at the phone helplessly. Then she had an impulse, and before she could talk herself out of it, she looked up Vanessa's phone number in the church directory. Xenia told her she should ask Vanessa what had happened — maybe she was right.

The phone rang at the other end four or five times before it was picked up and a low voice growled, "What?"

Abigail had never heard anyone answer the phone that way and she wanted to just hang up. But instead she said as politely as she could, "Hello. Is Vanessa there?"

There was a short laugh on the other end. "Who wants to know?"

Abigail hardly knew how to answer that, but she heard someone in the background say disapprovingly, "James, that is not how you speak on the phone." It was Mrs. Taybeck, Vanessa's mother.

Vanessa's older brother James lowered the phone to answer his mother. "It's just one of Vanessa's stupid little friends."

"James! Give me that!"

A second later, Mrs. Taybeck asked in a businesslike voice, "Yes? Who is this, please?"

Abigail was more tempted than ever to hang up, but again she forced herself to answer. "This is Abigail. I wanted to speak with Vanessa."

"She can't talk on the phone right now," Mrs. Taybeck answered crisply. "She's upstairs studying. Goodbye." But as Vanessa's mother was dropping the phone into the receiver, Abigail could hear her call out, "This is not over, young man. James! *James!*" And then a door slammed, and the phone went dead.

Abigail was horrified. She had never heard people talking and shouting like that. Not to each other and not to her. And she couldn't take any more. Abigail managed to make her way up to her room without being noticed. She put her face into her pillow and cried until the tears wouldn't come anymore.

It was such an awful Wednesday that she dragged through the rest of the week feeling sad and tired. If being the president of the Every Tuesday Girls Club was going to be like this, maybe she'd have to think of something else to do to help people.

She overslept on Saturday morning and woke up bleary and low-spirited. But she realized that she just couldn't keep letting this bad mood go on and on. There had to be some way to put it behind her, even if she couldn't figure it out. She felt a prickly feeling in her nose that meant she wanted to cry. But she scrunched her eyes shut to stop it and pulled her icon drawing out from under other papers on her desk. Was Maggie ever going to speak to her again? Was the Club ever going to do anything good? Would she ever own the icon that seemed like the most beautiful thing in the world?

She looked at the drawing and felt like someone was looking at her at the same time.

Don't be sad.

Abigail almost thought that someone had said it out loud, but then she realized there was no one in the room but her.

Don't be sad, little one.

Abigail sniffed one last time. This was what her mother called her small, still voice — that seemed to describe it as well as anything else. It had happened to her, from time to time, for as long as she could remember. And whenever the voice came to her, it always seemed to brighten things up and make her feel just a little more hopeful.

Abigail drew in a deep breath, and when she let it out, she felt some of the awfulness go with it. She had a strong suspicion that there was more that she needed to hear, but it didn't seem like she would ever hear it if she stayed cooped up. There was nothing else for her there in her room, and finally, she was ready to leave.

SHE BUNDLED INTO HER COAT AND BOOTS and said something to her parents about cleaning dead leaves out of the pond. She was sure that the back yard was where she wanted to go. She wanted to be in the place where the giant maple grew and the little pond sat huddled in the rocks, full of icy black water and fallen leaves. The back yard was her quiet place — she always felt better when she could just be there, standing on the pathway or sitting between the tree roots.

If only things could be as simple as they were in the back yard. She couldn't stay out there all day, but what was waiting for her inside? She really should find something to say to Maggie, but she didn't know what. Was Maggie ever going to forgive her?

And what in the world was going to happen to all of her wonderful plans for the Club? How could they possibly survive such a bad beginning?

Abigail glanced down at the straw-colored lawn and tried to imagine it green. When she looked up again, a darting shape caught her eye. She was surprised to find a ruby-red male cardinal perched very close, having just jumped off another twig and sent it wobbling. She could make out the pointed crest on his head and the bright eye in his black face. Abigail noticed with surprise that he was very agitated and making outraged noises at her. But why?

Abigail squinted to recover from the afternoon brightness and as her eyes adjusted, she saw that there was something ahead of her in the tangled shrub over the pond, hidden in the tiny buds that would grow into leaves soon and cover it completely. Just something matted that she couldn't quite make out. But then a quiet black eye blinked in the middle of it, and she realized that it was a bird's nest. And huddled in complete stillness on the top was a female cardinal, with a crest like the male's but her feathers all tan and russet brown.

A cardinal's nest in the bushes. And if the female was staying where she was, it had to be because … there were eggs in the nest.

Abigail breathed in the April fragrance of wet rock and sodden earth. She was surprised how happy it made her to think that even now, there were little speckled eggs that were being kept warm. Tiny little cardinals that were growing inside their eggs where everything was completely quiet. And out here … Well, it wasn't so quiet at all.

She squinted up again at the male cardinal, who was still cheeping in noisy protest.

"All right, all right. You don't have to yell," she said to him, carefully stepping backwards. "I'm going in now." The hopping cardinal didn't seem convinced until she made her way as quietly as she could back to the screen door.

When she put her hand on the doorknob, she became aware that she had a lightness in her heart where earlier it had felt like lead. For the first time since Tuesday night, things didn't seem quite so bad — she even felt like they might be okay. And there was something else she felt, but she couldn't tell what.

She turned back, and the cardinal was still just visible. Another insistent chirp penetrated the crisp morning air. And as it did, Abigail heard something else, speaking in her heart.

It said, *"Do you see, Abigail? Sometimes where there's the most noise, there's life just waiting underneath. Just waiting."*

Abigail inhaled, and when she did, it felt like she breathed in some of the spring and the light. Flipping open the loose screen door, she went inside, leaving a little of the winter gloom outside and bringing inside a little bit of the glittering April sunshine. Now she knew what the other feeling was. It was hope.

She went past the dining room table where her mother and father were going over stacks of paper to file their taxes. Mrs. Alverson spotted her and said, "Oh, there you are. Maggie called."

Abigail stopped in her tracks. "Maggie called?" she repeated.

"Yes." Her mother looked up, vaguely surprised at the response. "Oh, by the way — " She still had a box of receipts in one hand, but she waved the other over the crowded table. "We'll have to just have sandwiches or something for dinner. Sorry about that. And sorry about — well, all of it. I don't like having to put everyone through this every year."

"That's okay," Abigail mumbled absentmindedly. She was thinking about Maggie. Winding her way back out through the piles, she said, "Sometimes where there's the most noise, life is waiting just underneath it."

And she walked out of the dining room leaving both parents with very perplexed looks on their faces.

OUT IN THE KITCHEN, Abigail dialed the Peasles' number and was very glad when Maggie answered the phone. She suddenly knew what she wanted to say more than anything, and she couldn't hold it inside a moment longer.

When Maggie said hello, she burst out, "Maggie, it's me Abigail. And I am sorry. I am just so very, really sorry. I didn't mean to write on Baby Jacob at all and I didn't mean to treat him like a doll rag — I mean a rag doll. It was bad and I'm just … I'm sorry!" And she stopped to catch her breath.

But Maggie broke in at that point, and Abigail could have started dancing just at the sound of her voice, because she sounded normal. She didn't sound furious or freaked out or anything. She had her really nice voice back and she said words that made the last of Abigail's unhappiness go away like magic.

"Abigail, it's okay! I was mad. I was just really, really mad. But I know you didn't mean to hurt my brother — you were just trying to help."

"Yes! I was!" Abigail was so relieved she almost dropped the phone. "Oh Maggie, thank you, thank you. I have been feeling so awful. You're my best friend, and I meant for that story to … oh, I don't know what I meant. I thought the story of King Solomon and the baby would help somehow. I'm just lame sometimes."

"No, you're not!" Maggie never liked anyone be too hard on themselves. "It was a good story and, well … "

Abigail waited for a second, but had to ask "What?"

She heard Maggie sigh. "Well, here's the thing. That story sort of … I don't know … it worked."

"It worked?" echoed Abigail in confusion.

"I mean, it … I don't know." Maggie paused, searching for words. "Maybe it was the story, or that you guys tried so hard to help, or that I just got so mad and suddenly wanted more than anything to keep Jacob safe. But ever since Tuesday night, he doesn't seem like a pain, or a bother. I mean, he does, in a way, but more than any of that, he seems like my brother. Really my littlest baby brother and I … Oh Abigail, I have just been loving him so much!" And Maggie couldn't speak for a second. Abigail heard her sniff and felt her own eyes fill up with sudden tears. Of all the things she thought she might hear, to find out that the story she told had actually helped would have been the least expected. But even that didn't make her as happy as hearing Maggie talk about loving Jacob.

IN TRUTH, Tuesday night made more of an impact on Maggie than she could understand at first. "I was so upset about what had been going on with Jacob," she told Abigail. "It only seemed to get worse and worse, and by the time I got to the meeting, I felt like I was going to explode." She sniffed again at the memory, and then there were a few words she said to someone else. With surprise, Abigail realized that Maggie had Jacob on her lap while she was talking. "And then," Maggie continued unevenly, "I heard that story. I know that it's not like stories people tell now. I know why Xenia and Photini had questions. But to me … " There was a pause while she thought and looked at Jacob. "To me, it was about a king who had wisdom from God that told him that a mother's love for her son is stronger than anger … or selfishness. Or, you know … anything. And then that thing with the marker happened … "

Maggie picked her words carefully. She didn't want to remind Abigail about the bad part of the meeting, but as she said then, what happened with the marker made everything break loose all at once. When Maggie heard her brother let out a cry of real anguish, she felt like her heart was breaking. Out of her quiet spirit, a sudden fire of deep sisterly love burst out and he seemed more important to her than anything, even herself. She and Jacob were bonded together in that moment, and it was only the intense protectiveness of him that had kept her angry at Abigail all week long. She had been changed in a little way that made all the difference in the world, and she couldn't imagine ever feeling again that Jacob was such a terrible nuisance.

It was hard for her to talk about. She wished she had Abigail's flair for language, or even that she could pick up a pen as she did and try to draw it. But she did her best, with several more brief pauses to blow her nose, and Abigail helped her fill in what she couldn't say quite right.

"I just wanted to tell you," she concluded. "You were bound to notice it anyway. My mom has totally noticed. Jacob's still … well, you know. He's Jacob. He still does stuff. But I can't help it — I just think he's the best. My totally great little brother."

Abigail was so amazed she couldn't speak. She felt like she should say something, but nothing came to mind.

However, Maggie knew what to say. "So," she said, with a final sniff. "My problem is solved. What is the Every Tuesday Girls' Club going to do next?"

Chapter ten

What would the Every Tuesday Girls Club do next?

Abigail hadn't even thought of that, since it had seemed so doubtful that the Club would have any future at all. But with Maggie and Jacob suddenly in a much better place, Abigail realized happily that it was worth thinking about. The next problem — what would it be? Privately to Maggie, she could admit that she hoped that the next problem picked would be her own. She didn't tell the great secret of the icon she wanted, and Maggie didn't ask. But glancing at the church calendar in the kitchen, she could see they were already almost halfway through Lent. Would the group have time to help her get the icon before Pascha? She hoped so. It was wonderful that the first problem had worked out well, but it seemed like a bit of an accident. In fact, she still wasn't quite sure how it had happened — it seemed like the Club had made a series of mistakes. *Well, so what?* thought Abigail. All of this was just for practice anyway. They would do better next time. If the problem picked was her problem, and her beautiful icon of St. Abigail was at stake ... well, they would really have to do better.

When Sunday morning dawned, it occurred to her that she might hear something in church today that would help her decide what the Every Tuesday Club would do next. Abigail tugged on her shoelaces and pulled them into a bow. There was always a special theme to every Sunday in Lent — what was this one?

Abigail didn't have a chance to ask before they were all in the van. There was the last flurry of activity while purses and books and keys were found and sorted out. But after the Alversons had pulled out of the driveway and onto the street, she remembered to ask what Sunday it was.

"What Sunday?" asked Mrs. Alverson quizzically, scanning the road ahead for deer. "You mean, what Sunday in Lent? I think it's the third one. Right?" Mrs. Alverson looked to her husband, who nodded. "Yes, the third one."

"But which one is that? What are we going to talk about today?"

Mark's voice piped up proudly. "It's the Sunday of the Cross."

"Yes, that's it," said Mrs. Alverson. "Today's the Sunday of the Cross. Why did you want to know?"

Mark jumped in. "She wants to know if the service is going to be any longer, that's why."

She looked at him indignantly. "No, I don't."

"Yes, she does," he smirked knowingly.

Abigail's mouth popped open. "Mommm," she drawled in innocent outrage, "that's not why I asked! I just wanted to know, that's all."

Mrs. Alverson looked back at the road. "Well, it's the Sunday of the Cross, so we have extra prayers in the service today. And we all know you'll behave yourself this time." But Abigail couldn't help noticing that she sounded doubtful.

ABIGAIL'S MOTHER needn't have worried. This Sunday, Abigail wasn't suffering from the itchy boredom that had bothered her two weeks ago. The church service was longer, as her mother had told her, but there were things that made it pass more quickly.

For one thing, standing near Maggie lifted her spirits. There was no doubt about it — there was something different about how Maggie acted with her baby brother. Jacob was still tough to manage, but Maggie did that now as if it were less of a chore and more of a game. She attended to him and then gave him a smile or a hug. And Jacob looked at his big sister more and was less interested in getting into trouble. He was getting pets and hugs, and that seemed to make it worthwhile to stay put just a little bit more.

What a happy change from the awful tension there had been! Abigail couldn't help looking around at the other girls to see if they noticed.

Photini looked back at her once or twice. She still couldn't believe that someone hadn't gotten in trouble for what had happened. And what was even weirder was that Maggie was getting along with Jacob now. Abigail beamed and gave her a big thumbs-up sign, which Photini was sure you weren't supposed to do in church. But no one was in trouble — that was the main thing. She couldn't help smiling when she looked back at the front of the church. She hoped the prayers she gave Maggie helped.

After trying for a couple minutes to catch Xenia's attention, Abi-

gail gave up and shrugged to herself. Xenia just didn't notice any-
thing, that's all. Then again … Abigail studied her with interest. Did
Xenia notice more than she let on? Hard to know, Abigail thought.
She was hard to figure out.

Turning back, she was surprised to see Vanessa looking their way.
Not just looking — she was staring. Not at Abigail, but at Maggie. At
Maggie and Jacob. In confusion, Abigail turned to them herself to
see if anything was wrong. But no, here was Maggie-May, looking at
Jacob tenderly and he was smiling back at her. The two of them were
so cute that it made you feel good just to see
them. What could be wrong with that? She
glanced over at Vanessa and saw that same
hard, frozen look. Vanessa realized that Abigail was looking at her, and she clicked back
into place and stood perfectly straight.

That seemed strange. But Abigail hadn't
forgotten that she was also there that morning looking for some kind of clue about where
to go next, what God wanted her to do. She
was determined to pay more attention so she
wouldn't miss anything important.

WHEN FR. ANDREW GAVE THE HOMILY, he talked about
the one, true Cross. The way he said it, Abigail was sure that it was
Cross with a capital "C". He told them that a tiny piece of that Cross
was actually preserved in the cloth up at the altar. Then Fr. Andrew
said that the true Cross was present, in a way, in every other cross
they had in the church. He held up his blessing cross and pointed to

the one on the Gospel book. He held up his stole so they could see that the pattern was made up of crosses. He said it was even present when they crossed themselves.

That made Abigail's head swim. Every cross. She started looking and counting, but she lost count. So many, many crosses. And all from one Cross. Then ... what was it, exactly? What was there about that first Cross?

Abigail knew, or she thought she did. She knew about Jesus Christ and that He died and then rose from the dead. She had been told the story, it seemed, almost as many times as there were crosses in church. But she hadn't really thought about it having a lot to do with her. It all seemed so far away somehow. There were some parts of the story she didn't understand. There were other parts that she did understand, but they seemed ... big. Overwhelming. They were too big for your head, like the way she felt when she had seen an enormous blue whale on an oversized movie screen once. It was just hard to take it all in — scary and really wonderful at the same time.

Abigail's eyes strayed up to the dome and the great image of Christ Himself looking down on them all. That image larger than any other, seeming to fill up the sky. One hand was raised in blessing. The other was on a book and on the book, a cross. She seemed to hear that voice again. *Do you see, Abigail? Do you see?*

But she wasn't sure she did see. All these crosses, because there had been one Cross. What did that mean? Her thoughts kept fluttering off like butterflies. But at least they were flitting butterflies and not buzzing flies. It seemed like a definite improvement from how hard she had struggled in church before. Her thoughts were kind of lighter and ... prettier. Wait, could thoughts be pretty?

Abigail shook her head. She was really glad that people didn't know what she was thinking most of the time. These things didn't make much sense to her. She felt certain they wouldn't make any sense at all to other people.

One Cross. Many crosses. What did it mean?

SHE WAS STILL THINKING ABOUT IT as her parents were saying their goodbyes to a cluster of people huddled in the parking lot. One story just seemed to lead to another, and Abigail was beginning to think she would have to go back inside to get warm. But Mrs. Murphy had her story rudely interrupted by her two sons — Xenia's brothers, Randy and Amos. One of them knocked Mrs. Murphy's wool hat off her head, and as she bent over to get it, the other one took her purse and ran off laughing. She should have been angry, but everyone knew she wouldn't be. Both of Xenia's brothers enjoyed pestering their mother and rarely got into any trouble for it. Xenia's father — the quiet and long-suffering Mr. Murphy — didn't look pleased at all. He looked as if he would like very much to deal with the boys sternly. But Xenia's mother merely turned back with an apologetic shake of the head.

"THOSE TWO!" she yelled affectionately (because Mrs. Murphy said everything loudly). "They are definitely MY CROSS TO BEAR!" And she shambled off after them, with Xenia and her father trotting behind.

There was some scattered chuckling in the crowd, but Abigail looked after her thoughtfully.

"Mom," said Abigail, when the Alversons drove away from church, "What did Xenia's mother mean about Randy and Amos being a cross?"

"Being what?" her mother asked. "A cross?"

Her father helped out. "She said they were her cross to bear."

"Oh," her mother said. "Well, they are."

"Yep," agreed Mr. Alverson, smiling. "They certainly are."

"But what does that mean?" Abigail broke in, not wanting them to get into grown-up talk.

Mark thought he could be helpful. "That means they get on her nerves."

That didn't sound right, and Abigail must've shown her perplexity, because her mother asked, "Abigail, why are you asking?"

"Because of the Cross today," answered Abigail. "Everything Father Andrew said about crosses. But I don't get why she said those guys are a cross."

"It's just an expression, Abigail," explained Mr. Alverson. "But it does still have to do with the Cross. When someone talks about something being their cross to bear, they just mean it's one of the things they're struggling with — one of the problems that God gave them to deal with."

Abigail digested that information, frowning. "But how is that a good thing? Isn't a cross a good thing?"

"In the end, a cross is a good thing. But it can start out as a problem."

Abigail frowned even more, so Mrs. Alverson added, "God can use your problems to make good things happen. Understand?"

"So … problems can be good things," mused Abigail.

"Yes. When you ask God to help you with them. That part is important."

"When God helps," said Abigail.

Attention got diverted almost immediately to other things, but Abigail was determined not to forget. *God can use your problems. God can use your problems to make good things happen.*

THE NEXT TUESDAY NIGHT, the five girls straggled into their room to find that it had been cleaned — which was nice of somebody to do — but whoever cleaned the room had moved things around. Photini went and found the chairs they liked and Vanessa brought back a trash can they used to put things on. Xenia had hunched over her screen, but she shut it off of her own free will when everything was in place, and they all exchanged expectant looks.

Well, I guess it's up to me, thought Abigail. And it was.

"Okay," she said, "Let's go ahead and start the Every Tuesday Girls Club. We, um … we don't have to stand up or any of that." She made sure not to look at Vanessa when she said that, but she had made up her mind to avoid last week's mistakes. "But Photini, I liked the prayer you said for us. Can you say it again? Maybe that's a good way to start."

Photini brushed her hair from her face to hide how pleased she was. She started them all off with prayer, and then the topic turned naturally to how last week's problem had turned out.

The happy resolution to Maggie's problem almost went without saying. Maggie still had Jacob with her that night and the difference was so noticeable that even Xenia couldn't miss it. Maggie tried to recount some of what she had told Abigail about just how the change had come about. She had a hard time explaining it, but they seemed to understand, all the same.

"Thanks be to God," said Photini, with feeling.

"Definitely," nodded Maggie, taking a spoon from Jacob. "I'm so happy not to feel so angry all the time. It was wearing me out."

"Amen," said a voice softly, and they turned to Vanessa. She met their eyes and gave a reluctant smile. "I'm really happy that story about King Solomon helped you, Maggie. I have to admit, I didn't think it would, but Photini is right. Thanks be to God." And after a pause, she added. "And good job to you, Queen Abigail."

Abigail was surprised that Vanessa was able to say that she had been wrong. All the same, she wasn't quite sure she liked being called Queen Abigail. Was that more sarcasm? Abigail looked at her and couldn't tell, but she decided to let it pass. It did bother her — a lot of things Vanessa did bothered her. But she was in too good of a mood to spoil it by bickering. And besides, there were more important things to do with their time.

"So," she said brightly, "I guess if we're done with Maggie's problem, it's time to pick a new one." She hoped she sounded nonchalant about it, but it was hard not to feel excited.

"Oh. That's right," said Photini. "Oh … I hope it's mine. Do you still have the baggie, Vanessa?"

Vanessa produced the baggie with a flourish. "Of course I do. Behold the Baggie Full of Problems!"

"Don't shake any of the papers out," Xenia said abruptly. "If we have to put them back in the bag, it's like cheating."

That warning didn't make a lot of sense, but Vanessa handled the baggie more carefully all the same. She was enjoying the effect of the suspense and moved the baggie from one hand to the other while the three girls fidgeted nervously.

"Ohhh-kay," she said at last, when she couldn't drag it out any longer. "Let's have a drum-roll." Maggie obligingly drummed two fingers rhythmically on the table and Jacob joined in with occasional bumps of his little fists. "And the winner is … "

Abigail, thought Abigail. *Me, me, me. Pick my problem.*

Vanessa picked a piece of paper out and held it tight in her hand so none of them could see it. But she looked confused. "Uh, the winner is … " She pursed her lips with effort, and then looked up at them.

"Who is it?" burst Abigail.

"Well … it's Xenia," she said, and Abigail and Photini both slumped in disappointment. "But Xenia, I can't make out your handwriting. Are you saying something about giraffes?"

Xenia nodded so hard her glasses almost shook off. "YES," she said. "Two big giraffes on level two and four little ones on level eight. And the little ones — "

"And … hippos?" continued Vanessa, studying the slip of paper.

"That's right! The hippos are all over the place. And they're really hard to get past. You can't even run when the hippos are there, because they'll wake up. There are nasty flying rats and these things called bugbears. You don't even want to know about them." She shook her head at the sad memory. "That's why I need your help."

Abigail felt like she'd be sorry, but she asked all the same. "You need our help with what, Xenia?"

Xenia dropped both hands to the table in astonishment. "With ZooBlastex," she said as if the answer were totally obvious.

Photini and Abigail had no idea what she was talking about, but Maggie, who saw the games her older sister played, said, "ZooBlastex … that computer game with the zoo animals?"

"YES," said Xenia. "I can't get past level eight and it goes up to level twenty-five. But I have to get past level ten. I *have* to get past level ten."

She stopped abruptly, overcome by thoughts of the difficulties of giraffes and bugbears. No one spoke for an instant, and then Xenia seemed to remember they were there. She looked up at them pleadingly. "I have to get past level ten of ZooBlastex," she said more softly. "And you have to help me. It's my biggest problem."

Chapter eleven

"So ... it's a game," Photini said flatly. "A computer game. But where's the problem in that?"

Xenia looked at her and her face turned expressionless. "I told you. I can't make it past level eight, because of the giraffes. If you don't help me, I'll never make it to level ten!"

"Who cares?" Vanessa said rudely, and Abigail saw Xenia flinch as if she had been slapped.

"I care!" she retorted angrily. "The Every Tuesday Club was supposed to help us with our problems. And we didn't say what kind of problem it had to be. I helped Maggie with Baby Jacob — we all helped with Maggie's problem. And this is my problem, and now ... " she seemed on the verge of tears. "And now ... you won't even ... "

Maggie quickly put her free hand over Xenia's clenched fist. "Xenia, it's not that. We'll do whatever you want. Isn't that right, Vanessa?"

Vanessa turned sharply to Maggie, obviously meaning to argue. But something in her look made Vanessa's self-righteousness wilt.

Reluctantly, she muttered, "That's right."

Maggie continued soothingly, "It's just that I don't know if we can be much good. Photini doesn't play any games like this, and the rest of us don't play many. I know it's a good game for older kids — my sister Violet plays it sometimes. But I've never played it at all."

Abigail sensed that Maggie might be on to something that could get them out of the situation without hurting Xenia's feelings. "Maggie is right," she nodded. "ZooBlastex sounds like a lot of fun. But I think it's just too hard for us."

"But … " Xenia looked from one to another, and gave her nose a last swipe to banish the sniffles. "But it's not hard. It's easy."

And she vaulted out of her chair so abruptly that Photini barely escaped being bumped. "What are you doing?" Photini asked in alarm.

"You can all play it and see," came the muffled voice as Xenia rifled through her backpack. "On my little game-player. And then I've got a tablet and a smart phone and another game-player — they've all got it loaded on them. You can all play."

"But I don't want — hey!" protested Photini as she saw her book bag get tossed aside. "Be careful!"

Photini rushed over to prevent further damage. Watching them, Maggie shifted Jacob to one arm and said softly to Abigail, "How are we going to help?"

"Never mind *how*," growled Vanessa. "*Why* are we going to help?"

Abigail felt the familiar flush of irritation at Vanessa's remark, but there was no chance to answer. Xenia had rounded back to them with her arms dripping cords and gadgets. As she happily handed out the devices and clicked them on, Abigail wracked her brain for what to do next.

Maggie had told Xenia that the game was too hard, and Xenia hadn't been convinced. Vanessa had argued, but that had just made her unhappy. What hadn't they tried?

Abigail tapped the screen of the tablet Xenia had given her and said listlessly, "It's not working."

Xenia peered over as she untangled the cord on Photini's hand-held device. "You have to wait until it powers up. Stop tapping — it can't hear you yet."

"Can't hear me," Abigail repeated. "The computer can't hear me." *That's what we didn't do,* she thought to herself. *We didn't listen to her.*

"Are we ready?" Xenia inquired eagerly.

Abigail mentally grabbed hold of the first thing she could think of — a detail that had stuck in her mind. "Xenia, why do we have to get past level ten?"

Xenia's shoulders slumped at this new show of slowness. "I *told* you. The hippos — "

"I know about the hippos," said Abigail, turning the device over as it lit up. "But didn't you say this game goes up to level twenty-five? So what happens past level ten?"

Xenia's eyes took on that dull look all of the sudden and she dropped her head. "We win."

"How?"

Her voice got so quiet they could hardly hear it. "We beat Randy and Amos' best score."

Vanessa frowned. "Randy and Amos — your brothers? They play this?"

Xenia nodded without lifting her head. "All the time. Randy started playing it first and then Amos started next. They play all the time and beat each other's scores. I just started playing to see what they were doing. But I can't get past level eight, and that's not even close. They tell me I'll never be any good at it because it's a game for geniuses and I'm just a doofus. But I'm not a doofus. I want to win, but to do that I have to beat their best score. I have to get past level ten."

An astonished silence fell (except for Jacob, who latched onto a word he knew and happily exclaimed, "Ten!").

Maggie was torn between sympathy and exasperation. "But Xenia, it's a game for older kids. Isn't there something else you could beat them at?"

"No," said Xenia gloomily. "I'll never beat them at sports or school stuff. I never win any arguments with them because they're really good with words and I'm not."

She had been getting quieter and she finally stopped talking completely. The girls exchanged looks, but Xenia noticed them doing it and glanced from Vanessa to Photini to Maggie. At last her eyes rested on Abigail, and she seemed to Abigail to be pleading.

"I'm not a doofus. I just … I want to win." Abigail couldn't look away. And she couldn't let her down. She thought of quiet Xenia with her two rough brothers and her loud mother. Quiet, odd Xenia who no one listened to, with two older brothers who teased her all the time. Xenia never reacted — it was always as if she didn't even hear them. But apparently, she did.

"Well … " said Abigail, tapping the screen to refresh it, "I think we should play ZooBlastex. So Xenia, how does this work?"

ABIGAIL THOUGHT she had made the right decision — one look at Xenia's grateful face had told her that — but for the next twenty minutes or so, she wasn't so sure. It was all very well to want to help Xenia, but Maggie hadn't been lying about how difficult the game was. It was incredibly complicated. Your character was constantly running, jumping, kicking and shooting. You also had to dodge obstacles and enemies and find extra credits and lives. And the whole thing went at rocket speed — it had music and sound effects and there were bright things zipping by all the time.

It hadn't been so hard at the beginning. The game had a complicated plot about Mogrons from the planet Zazzonk who had landed at the zoo and would turn all the animals into monsters unless you saved them. Photini liked the part about saving zoo animals, but she just couldn't understand why you had to shoot them with laser blasters to do it. Xenia shrugged and showed them all how to bring up the Reptile House, which was the first level. Even Photini, who was hopelessly bad at figuring out how to navigate, was able to manage getting up one level. But none of them could seem to move fast enough to keep up very well as the game went on.

Xenia tried to help them out, but one by one, they all ended up watching her play rather than playing themselves. When Xenia played the game, she almost made it look easy. She wasn't unsure or hesitant the way they had been, and she didn't let anything get her mad or agitated. Where their characters had constantly tripped or gone down the wrong way, Xenia's character zipped and skipped and flitted from room to room and past vampire bats and the giant Mogrons. She knew exactly when to jump or duck or shoot, and she was able to keep up a running commentary at the same time.

"Wow," said Maggie feelingly when Xenia nimbly shot seven bug-bears and kicked down a door to end the third level.

Abigail fist-bumped Xenia as the game paused between levels. "You're really good at this. I don't know why your brothers tell you you're not."

"Abigail is right," smiled Vanessa. "You shouldn't let them get away with that. You should tell them off."

Xenia had been beaming at the compliments, but her face fell at this last comment. "I can't do that."

Photini shook her hair back. "No, she can't. They are still her older brothers."

"That's right," Xenia said sadly "And they're mean."

Vanessa snorted dismissively, and Abigail was offended on Xenia's behalf. "They are," argued Abigail, "I've seen it. They're always playing tricks on her and making fun of her and stuff."

"Big deal," shrugged Vanessa. "That's what brothers do. My step-brother James does all that." There was an awkward pause. Abigail wanted to reply that James was definitely mean, because she thought he was. But she couldn't say that, so she didn't say anything. Vanessa also seemed to be at a temporary loss for words, but she shook her head and muttered to Xenia, "Anyway, I still think you're exaggerating. They are your brothers, after all."

Xenia fingered the screen and sighed. "They're my cross to bear."

"Your what?" asked Maggie, deftly taking a cord out of Jacob's mouth.

Abigail stared at Xenia. "That's what you heard your mother say about them, right?"

"It sounds disrespectful," mumbled Photini.

Abigail answered, "It's not, really. It's just a thing people say. It just means that they're a problem for her."

Photini clucked disapprovingly and Maggie also looked a little uncomfortable, but Abigail was thinking again about what her parents had told her. Her cross to bear. And a cross is a problem, but God can use it to work things out.

But how could Randy and Amos be both the problem and the solution?

She realized that Maggie was talking to Xenia and telling her a little bit more about how things had changed between her and Jacob. "I know that's just me, Xenia, but I don't think you should think of Randy and Amos as your cross to bear. After all, they're still — "

And Maggie would likely have repeated that they were her brothers, but we'll never know for sure, because the door suddenly swung open and a lanky sandy-haired teenager thrust his head inside.

"Hey, doofus!" he called out. It was Xenia's brother Randy, and chunky Amos was by his side, as always. "Mom says that if you can gather up your stuff, maybe we can leave early tonight."

XENIA STARED AT HIM as if he had popped into the room by magic. None of the girls could quite believe the boys' sudden entrance at just the time when they had been talking about them. Randy glanced around at the shocked faces, but wasn't interested in the strange behavior of little girls. He pushed into the room to make sure Xenia had understood him. "Hel-loooo," he said, waving a hand in front of Xenia's eyes. "Earth to Xenioid." (This was their name for Xenia, and Amos laughed appreciatively at his humor.) "Come innnn, Xenioid — Hey!"

Randy had happened to glance over and saw the tablet that Photini was holding loosely in front of her. She suddenly felt guilty and, blushing furiously, she held it close to her so he couldn't see the screen. But Amos had seen the tablet as well, and he chimed in. "What's the deal? Are you playing computer games in here?"

For some reason, Photini felt compelled to give a truthful answer. "We were playing ZooBlastex."

Both brothers burst out laughing. "Oh, no! The Brownie Brigade is playing a serious game?!" Amos whistled in disbelief.

Vanessa shouldered her way to Xenia's side and looked at them squarely. "We asked Xenia if she'd show us, so she did. What's wrong with that?"

Randy pointed at his sister, grinning broadly. "How can a numbskull teach a game she can't even play?"

"Maybe she could," Vanessa snapped, "if her numbskull brothers would stop ragging on her all the time!" Photini gasped and blushed even more. The brothers just chortled merrily.

"Whatever, tough girl," Randy said. "But seriously, Xenioid, be ready at eight o'clock, right? Then we get to leave early."

Behind him, Abigail was thinking frantically. It was too much of a coincidence that they had shown up just when the girls were all talking about them. Randy and Amos were part of the solution somehow, but how?

With a jolt, she realized that the two boys were looking at her in amused perplexity. "You're in the way?" said Amos, indicating the door behind her. She looked back at them, still thinking, and Randy tried again, gesturing as if she was slightly deaf.

"You're blocking. The. Door."

"Will you teach us to play ZooBlastex?" burst Abigail.

The boys' mouths both dropped open and several girls said, "What?" at the same time. Without much idea of what else to do, Abigail just repeated the question. "Will you teach us to play Zoo-Blastex?"

Randy recovered from his shock first and turned to Amos in mock amazement. He certainly would've come up with a suitable put-down for the occasion, and a resounding answer of "No." But Vanessa had been watching them with a crafty look in her eye, and she hissed to Abigail when his back was turned, "Get Maggie to ask them!"

Abigail was too confused to do anything but stare. However, Maggie had heard the suggestion, and even though she didn't understand, she obediently piped up as Randy turned back: "Um … please? Could you teach us ZooBlastex, please?"

Both boys turned to her in surprise, and Randy wasn't smirking any more. Vanessa chimed in immediately. "That's right," she said sweetly. "I think Maggie's sister Violet said you were really good at this game."

Amos still looked completely lost, but Randy seemed to be weighing those words with keen interest. Suddenly, he came to a decision. "Right!" he said briskly, "Let's go." And without another word, he pushed Abigail aside and disappeared down the hallway.

Amos trotted after him, followed by all the girls. "Where are we going?" Amos inquired huskily. Randy was several inches taller than him and keeping up with his long strides wasn't easy.

"Well, we're going to teach the Xenioid's little friends a few things about ZooBlastex, aren't we?" Randy answered in high spirits. "But we can't do it on her junky tablet. We need a bigger screen, and I know where to find one."

There didn't seem like any answer to be made to this, so Amos shambled along in silence and the girls sprinted after them, straggling down the narrow hallway and trying not to lose sight of them.

Maggie had a harder time keeping up than the others because she was carrying Jacob. He enjoyed the bouncy pace immensely, but was still a hefty boy to carry on such an adventure. In spite of the effort, Maggie took the opportunity to ask about something that was bothering her. "Vanessa," she said breathlessly, "Why did Randy change his mind?"

Vanessa was distracted with the excitement of the hallway chase they were having. "Huh? Oh, that. He changed his mind because he has a total crush on your sister Violet."

"He what?!" Maggie was so shocked that she stopped walking and the others swept around her. Muttering something rather unkind about Randy Murphy not being good enough for her sister, she took a deep breath and then headed off after the trailing girls again.

In the meantime, Xenia picked up her speed so she could yank on Abigail's sleeve. "We're going to get Randy and Amos to teach us? Why?"

Abigail took a second to glance over and almost hit a doorway. "Because you said it yourself. They're your cross to bear. But if they're your problem, maybe they can be part of the solution."

Xenia shook her head in disagreement, arms flailing as she marched. "No, they can't. They never help me with anything. They think I'm a numbskull."

Vanessa rounded on Xenia as they all navigated a tight corner. "No, they don't. It's like I said. They're only kidding. You've got to just stand up to them once in a while."

"I don't know how to do that," said Xenia pitifully.

Vanessa was running out of breath, but she called back over her shoulder. "That's nothing. I can show you how." And ahead to the boys, she chided, "Where are we going? Kansas?"

"No, we're not going to Kansas, little smart-mouth," Randy yelled back. "We're going to the nearest real computer we can use. No way am I going to try to show you how to play ZooBlastex on a junky little tablet or something. Annnnd ... here we are!"

And with a dramatic flourish, he opened the door and they all spilled into a big room with a comfy couch, a large desk and abundant bookshelves.

It was Fr. Andrew's office.

Chapter twelve

Exactly two minutes after they had left the littlest conference room, Photini and Maggie came rushing back in. Maggie came through first with Jacob and barely got through the door before Photini bolted in after her and shut the door with a bang.

"Oh ... my ... goodness!" Photini collapsed into a chair. "That was just awful!"

Maggie was distracted. "Have you seen my bag?"

"No," answered Photini, without looking. "I mean ... it was awful."

Maggie rifled through backpacks until she found the striped cloth bag she was looking for. "I know," she mumbled to Photini.

"We were *not* supposed to be in Father's office," Photini continued. "I just know it. But *nobody* would listen to me."

Maggie checked the contents of the bag. "Everyone was listening, but Randy said that Father Andrew told him he could use the computer any time he wanted."

"Ha!" said Photini contemptuously. "I don't believe it. And then he turned on Father's computer and got onto the internet so he could play that silly ZooBlastex game!"

"I know," repeated Maggie, handing the red bag to Photini. "I was there, remember?"

Photini was still overexcited at the recollection of such bad behavior. "Well, I bet he's going to get into a lot of trouble. You could tell that even Amos was getting nervous about it. I think Randy was just showing off. Why would he do that?"

"Hmm. I don't know," said Maggie carelessly, trying not to think about Randy and her sister Violet. "Anyway, let's go."

Photini noticed the red striped bag for the first time. "Let's go where?"

"To the changing station in the bathroom? I can't change Jacob here. That is why we came back, remember? Jacob needs changing."

"Oh!" said Photini. "But … well, I just said I needed to come with you because I couldn't stand to stay there anymore. I'm … I'm not really very good at things like that."

Maggie was a little irritated, but there was no time to argue. "Suit yourself," she shrugged, and taking the bag and Jacob, she left the room.

PHOTINI PEERED out into the hallway meekly, wondering if she should have gone with Maggie. But she had never changed a diaper and the idea really didn't sound very appealing. All the same, there wasn't much to do in the littlest conference room. She picked up a book or two halfheartedly, but it was difficult to concentrate on anything, knowing that there was a big adventure going on in the other side of the building. She was trying to gather up her courage to go spy on the others when a loud noise distracted her. It was an explosive cry — almost like a loud bark — but too far away to make out clearly.

She decided to go investigate and had just started off in the direction of the noise when she heard someone coming rapidly down the hall. A second later, Vanessa appeared around the corner, running and giggling. When she saw Photini, she waved her back and said, "Back in the room! Get back!" Photini fled as if all the Mogrons of Zazzonk were after her, hearing Vanessa slam the door behind them and fall into a chair. Vanessa hid her head in her arms, gasping and laughing. "Oh man!" she choked out at last. "Ohhh man!"

"What happened?" squeaked Photini fearfully.

For a frustrating minute, Vanessa didn't answer and could only catch her breath between giggles. "Oh man!" she finally said again. "That Randy. He's mad now."

Photini eyes opened wide. "Did *he* make that noise?"

"Oh yes, he did," exclaimed Vanessa gleefully. "He thought he'd just start that game up on Father's computer, but he kept pushing the wrong buttons because it's a PC and not a Mac."

Photini furrowed her brow. "I don't know what that means."

"Neither do I," admitted Vanessa. "All I know is that when he finally brought up the game on the internet, he was still hitting wrong buttons. And Xenia tried to tell him not to do something. She was all, 'Don't hit Okay. Don't hit Okay.' But he didn't listen to her. He told her not to be a doofus and then he hit Okay and guess what?"

"What?" gulped Photini. She had heard people talk about crashes and meltdowns on computers and envisioned melted plastic strewn all over Fr. Andrew's walls.

"He zeroed out all their scores!" crowed Vanessa. Seeing Photini's blank expression, she explained, "Randy and Amos have played that game for months and months. That's how they've gotten these mega-high scores that they're so proud of. But the computer asked him if he wanted to start a new game for their team, and he hit Okay. So he and Amos and Xenia have a score of zero, as if it were the first time they were playing the game. That was when he made that noise," she ended, slapping the table for emphasis. And as an afterthought, she said, "And that's why I had to run back here."

Photini blinked at her. "Why?"

"Because I just couldn't resist. He was being such a smarty-pants to Xenia that I just couldn't let it go. So I'm all, 'Way to go, Randy. That was a good one, Randy.' And then I had to run for my life, because I think he would've thrown that computer at me if Amos hadn't been in the way."

She giggled again and then rested her chin on her hands with a sigh.

"Oh man," she said again. "That was fun."

IN FATHER'S OFFICE, Abigail wasn't having any fun at all. She wished very much that she had made up an excuse and left like Maggie and Photini, or even that she had just run out when Vanessa did. But she hadn't and now she was stuck. None of this seemed to be going well. It just couldn't be right for them to be in Fr. Andrew's office. But Abigail didn't want to leave Xenia alone, and Randy wouldn't be talked out of his plan. It almost seemed like making that last mistake and zeroing out all their scores had made him more stubborn. Even Amos pulled on his sleeve, but Randy shook him off.

"We came here for this and we are going to play this game," he growled. "We are all going to play ZooBlastex."

He started playing the game from the first level, Reptile House, since they all had to start over from the beginning. Abigail couldn't see the screen from her angle, but she could tell from his frequent flinches and exclamations that it wasn't going very well.

Looking over his shoulder, Xenia said blandly, "Go left. You need to go left or — "

Randy made an explosive noise and smacked his forehead.

"I told you," said Xenia, in the same flat voice. "Next time you do it, go left."

But Randy suddenly whirled around. Vaulting out of the chair, he held it out for Xenia. "Here!" he barked. "You do it."

Amos objected loudly with a single "Dude!" but Randy insisted. "If anyone is going to get junk scores online, let's have Xenia do it."

Abigail thought they were all acting crazy, but Xenia climbed calmly into the chair and began a new game. Abigail had heard enough of the sound effects when she had played to realize that Xenia wasn't running into walls or getting eaten. Unlike Randy, she was completely composed and her fingers nimbly clicked buttons and moved the mouse with precision. The boys were hunched over her and counting off the levels as she passed them. Level two, level three ...

But Randy was getting increasingly restless. He started making more and louder remarks and trying to get Xenia to slip up. "Come on, get eaten or something," he grumbled. "I want to get on now."

It was all just too weird to keep looking at, and besides, it was boring when you couldn't see the screen. Abigail scanned the bookshelves and knick-knacks, and her eyes fell on an icon of Christ on a white shelf. It made her think about church, and she sighed. What were they doing here? Xenia had said she had a problem, but did that really have to do with this computer game? Wasn't it more about Randy and Amos?

A sudden cry in front of her snapped her out of her thoughts. Randy and Amos were both making whooping noises, which had to mean that Xenia had finally made a mistake. Sure enough, Randy almost yanked her out of the chair in his rush to sit down.

"You jiggled my elbow!" Xenia protested.

"All's fair in love and war, doofus," Randy remarked poetically. "Now show me all the keys to play the game on this computer. I don't want to mess up again."

As a hurried session followed with Xenia petulantly pointing out which keys to use, Abigail's eyes strayed back to the icon. Xenia and her brothers. Xenia's cross to bear. But why wasn't any of this working? Abigail had asked them to teach the game because she had some idea that she was supposed to. But nothing seemed to be going well. What had her mother said? Abigail tried hard to remember. God can use our problems, but we have to ask for His help.

It was something like that. Abigail looked again at the three people in front of her. Randy had settled himself triumphantly in the leather office chair and Amos had come in so tight that Xenia was squeezed out and had to peek in between them. Her face was still flushed, but she stayed meekly behind them. Out of the way and away from the action.

There was something a little frozen about it to Abigail, as if it were a snapshot. There was something wrong, something missing. She looked toward the icon, but didn't know what to do.

"God, will You help us?" she said under her breath. "Help Xenia, and help Randy and Amos … I don't know what to pray." Those were the only words she could think of, and they didn't seem like a very good prayer. She wished she had Photini there, because she seemed so good with prayers. Abigail tried to think of something better, but her attention was diverted by two things that happened almost at the same time.

In front of her, Randy announced grandly that he would now be a star at ZooBlastex. And behind Abigail, a noise. From outside in the hallway. Getting closer. Voices.

She made a kind of "um?" noise, but no one heard her. Randy had begun tapping in earnest and Amos was already cheering him on. And behind her. Not just any voices. Wasn't that … ?

"Uh … guys?"

She didn't have time to say anything else. The door behind her opened and the mild voice of Fr. Andrew stopped mid-sentence as he saw the three Murphy children at his desk. And behind him, neatly framed in the doorway, and looking very, very surprised, Mr. and Mrs. Murphy.

THE MINUTES in the littlest conference room had passed rather slowly until Abigail returned. Maggie had come back and gotten the update from Vanessa on what had happened. They talked all that over, and were trying to decide what to do next when they began to hear clear signs of some kind of ruckus going on from down the hall.

Vanessa was all for going on a scouting trip, but Photini didn't want to budge now that trouble had definitely arrived to Father's office. In the end, it was agreed that Vanessa alone would go try to gather some information, but just then Abigail walked in quietly and sat down.

Abigail wasn't a person who went out of her way to cause a sensation, but if she had been, she couldn't have gotten a much better effect or a better audience. The girls gathered round and wanted to know every detail of what had happened. Abigail told them everything, right up to that awful moment when the door had opened to reveal Fr. Andrew and Xenia's parents. Photini could hardly speak.

"Oh ... my ... " and she started coughing so badly that Maggie slapped her on the back a few times to help. But as soon as Photini caught her breath, she desperately wanted to know what mattered most. "Did they get in trouble? Are you in trouble?" And then, after a horrified instant, "Wait. Are WE in trouble?"

Abigail started with the last part first. "We're not in any trouble, Photini. You guys definitely aren't, and I don't think I am, either. Just before I left, Father Andrew said — "

"Wait!" said Vanessa urgently. "Never mind what he said at the end. What happened next? What happened right after they showed up?"

"I think we heard yelling," said Maggie fretfully. "Was there yelling?"

"Oh. Yes."

"What did they do?" persisted Vanessa.

"It all happened so fast," said Abigail. "Of course, Father Andrew was surprised to see those guys at his desk and Randy on his computer. He just said, 'What are you doing here?' But then Mrs. Murphy burst in the way she does, you know?"

The girls nodded knowingly. They all knew that Mrs. Murphy entered a room like a whirlwind. If she was really worked up, it was hard to imagine how explosive she would be.

"So she burst in," continued Abigail, "and she saw the game on the screen, and … " Abigail winced at the memory. "Wow, was she mad."

Photini wanted details. "What'd she say?"

Abigail pursed her lips in thought. "Well, she was like, 'I know you are NOT playing THAT STUPID GAME on Father's COMPUTER!!'" All the girls tittered, which embarrassed Abigail. She hadn't meant to make fun of Mrs. Murphy, but in telling the story it seemed natural to talk like her, and it was a fairly good imitation. She pressed ahead.

"Anyway, Fr. Andrew just wanted the facts and stuff, and he might actually have gotten Mrs. Murphy calmed down. But Randy started kidding around like he always does." She shook her head. "It was a bad idea. I guess he thought he could just treat the whole thing like a joke and sweet-talk his mom and all that. But this time, she just didn't want to listen to him. And she turned around … "

Abigail drew in breath at the strange occurrence, and all the girls leaned in closer. "She turned around, and there was *Mister* Murphy. Mrs. Murphy said something like, 'Well, what do YOU think?!' And … and he told her. He had been right in front of me and he was shaking like a leaf, and when she actually asked him for once, he said, 'I have had enough.'"

Vanessa didn't understand. "Enough? Enough of what?"

"Enough of everything. Enough of bad manners. Enough of disrespect and trouble-making and breaking rules and … I don't remember. He went on for a while. But he had really, really had enough of computer games. He is taking away every computer game for six months."

She stopped, and the girls digested the news in shock. "Six months?" said Maggie.

"Yep."

"No computer games for six months?" Maggie repeated. "But I've never seen Xenia without some kind of screen in front of her, except when she's in church. She's always playing computer games."

"I know," said Abigail pensively. She couldn't help thinking of how Xenia looked, peeking out from behind her brothers. When Mr. Murphy had said those words, she thought Xenia would've looked shocked or angry or horrified. But to her surprise, Xenia hadn't registered shock. In fact, she almost seemed a little relieved. That was strange.

Vanessa had a question. "Did Mrs. Murphy try and argue about it? She's always making such a fuss over Randy and Amos. Didn't she say anything?"

Abigail hadn't thought of that. "Nnno," she said, after reflecting. "She really didn't. I think … she looked almost happy to have Mr. Murphy actually put his foot down for once."

There was a pause. "Well, that's that," said Photini. "Poor Xenia."

"Where is Xenia, anyway?" asked Maggie, glancing over Abigail's shoulder.

"Back there, maybe. Or maybe they all went home. I don't know. Father Andrew finally got around to asking Xenia what happened, and she mentioned me. I really don't think they had noticed I was there until then. And Father Andrew said something dignified like, 'I think the Murphy family might prefer to discuss this privately.' So I just came on back and … and here I am." She left out that Fr. Andrew had watched her carefully as she was leaving, as if he was still curious about her part in things. It didn't seem like a good thing to mention, since it might make Photini nervous all over again.

There was more to say — the whole thing had been quite an adventure. But they could all hear the clear sounds of movement and chatter in the hallways. As always, that signaled that the meetings and practices were at an end, and the four girls got their things together, promising to finish up the rest of the conversation by phone later.

IN THE CAR on the way home, Maggie Peasle was distracted almost immediately by family chitchat. But she hadn't forgotten everything that she had heard, and when her older sister Violet needed help with a crossword puzzle and asked what a five-letter word was for "annoying trouble-maker," Maggie immediately replied, "Randy." And then she looked at her sister meaningfully.

IN THE JENKINS' CAR, Photini was wishing very much that there was a way she could tell everything that had happened, because she thought her mother would be really interested. But Photini realized that she was in a difficult place — hadn't they all agreed not to tell what went on during the Club meetings? It was terribly annoying, and she tried to come up with something nice to think about Randy and Amos to make up for the irritation she felt. But nothing came to mind. She saw it was starting to rain and sulkily thought that that suited her fine.

IN THE TAYBECK CAR, Vanessa sat in the back seat with her little brother Noah, listening to her mother and father argue about the usual subject. She had been in high spirits when she got into the car and, unlike Photini, she felt no qualms about telling about the evening's adventure. But her parents were already bickering when they got in, and her heart seemed to dry up inside her as she heard the same old words being exchanged. She was glad when the rain started because it gave her an excuse to turn towards the window and hide her face from Noah so he wouldn't see that she was crying.

ABIGAIL'S MOTHER was busy trying to go over one part of a song for choir and didn't want to talk, so Abigail could retreat into her thoughts. There were a lot of impressions that played out in her mind like images from a photo album: Xenia's pleading look when she said, "I just want to win"; Randy taking them all on a mad dash through the hallways at church; Father's somber office with three Murphy faces all lit up by a computer screen. The frozen looks on everyone's faces when Father and Xenia's parents showed up. And the moment when Father's eyes met hers as she was leaving. So much had happened so quickly. She would need time to figure it out.

She leaned her head against the window as her mother kept trying to get one line of the song right. Raindrops had started falling, hitting the window and being drawn out in streaky lines as the car moved through the night.

"Did I do the right thing?" Abigail found herself thinking, addressing the question out into the black trees and shrubs that sped past. "God? Did I do the right thing?"

There was no answer. Just the thrum of the car's wheels on wet pavement and the delicate tapping of the rain.

Chapter thirteen

Throughout the week, Maggie, Abigail and Photini found snatches of time to call each other. Vanessa had become strangely quiet — when pressed, she reverted to her old rudeness and told the others they were being ridiculous and needed to grow up.

"How do you think Xenia is doing?" Abigail asked, when Maggie called her on Friday. "Have you heard anything from her?"

"Not a thing. Amos is always texting Sammy." Sammy was Maggie's older brother. "But this week, there hasn't been anything. I wonder if they all got their cell phones taken away."

Abigail sat down unhappily on the kitchen stool. "I hope not. I don't care what their parents do to Randy and Amos — those guys are tough. But Xenia loved computer games more than just about anything. It's not really fair to punish her when her brothers were the ones who messed up."

"I don't know," said Maggie doubtfully. "Xenia didn't have to go along with them. Maybe Vanessa is right and she needs to stand up for herself more. It's up to her mom and dad, I guess. But I have to go now. Are you coming to the yard day tomorrow?"

"I'm not sure. Probably."

Maggie said, "Well, if you are, I'll see you there. Bye for now."

"Bye." Abigail hung up the phone and looked at it glumly. *What am I supposed to do now?*

SHE WAS STILL WONDERING about it on Saturday as the family pulled up to the church to help with yard work. Several trucks had already arrived with bags and tools, and two more cars pulled up when the Alversons did.

The St. Michael's Yard Day was a spring tradition for the church. There were people that looked forward to it, but Abigail wasn't one of them. She didn't mind yard work, but the church grounds were extensive, which made for a long day. It took a lot of time to get the gardens and landscaping repaired and clear out winter's damage to the forested parts of the property. Teams would begin close to the building and the workday would start with a lot of talking and singing. But as the morning turned into afternoon, the high-spirited banter tended to die off and everyone worked a little harder to get things done while there was still enough light. Even in mid-April, the days were still short — once the sun sank behind the trees, it would soon become too dark and cold to work well.

When the afternoon began to turn cool, Abigail could have gone inside and warmed up, but she preferred the idea of a little solitude. She drifted off to the place where the forest came right up to the lawn and the ground was strewn with fallen branches and dead leaves.

Mrs. Abrigado was pleased to see her and handed her a rake and a heavy bag to scoop leaves and weeds into. She gave Abigail some quick instructions on how to turn over the sodden leaves so some of the plants could get better light, and then she trailed off along the tree line to supervise someone else.

Abigail was glad to have the time to herself. It was satisfying to gently rake the blackened leaves away and see green blades of new life that had managed to push up toward the light. One of the sunnier patches had a few healthy plants that were sporting cheery purple blooms. Mrs. Abrigado had told her that they planted crocuses there last year, so that must be what they were. It was nice to see blossoms in the dark, wet edge of the forest and Abigail squatted down so she could look at them up close.

They didn't have any fragrance, but they were a lovely purple color and the small petals were raised up so that they looked like a cupped hand. Abigail put down her rake and touched them lightly, delighting in the smoothness of the delicate flowers. Her mind started wandering to flowers in general, and what it would feel like to eat a flower, or to be a flower. Then she thought about other purple things, and about the word "purple" and what an unusual word it was. Was there anything that rhymed with "purple?" She found a patch of grass to lay in and tried to think of one, determined that she could make a good song about the crocus, if only she could find a rhyme to start with.

So Abigail was feeling like her old self, and she would have liked to keep laying on the grass a little longer, but she could hear the sound of conversation coming nearer. She reluctantly stood up and looked out with her hand shading her eyes to see if she could spot the newcomers. A quick laugh told her that one of them was Fr. Andrew's son Nate, and as he crested the hill, she could see that Fr. Andrew was with him. Nate had a shovel slung over his shoulders, but he swung it down and leaned on it when he saw Abigail.

"You came all the way out here to rake? Mrs. Abrigado must love you. Looks like you're doing a great job."

Abigail beamed at the compliments and turned to look at her progress. Nate had just gone into college this year and he could have ignored the younger children like the teenagers usually did. But he was one of the nicest people she knew and seemed to enjoy talking to everyone.

"It's an excellent job," agreed Fr. Andrew. "But we're starting to lose the light, so let's make our way back in to get some soup and clean up before Vespers. Nate, why don't you go on ahead with the rake so Abigail doesn't have to carry it?"

"Okie doke," said Nate agreeably, taking the rake and starting back over the hill in long strides.

"He didn't have to do that," said Abigail. "The rake's not even heavy."

"Well, it'll give us a chance to talk for a minute. Let's take the long way around so we have time to chat."

That didn't sound promising, and a little alarm bell went off in Abigail's head. "Is this about what happened with Xenia?" she asked. She thought maybe if she asked a direct question, it would make him feel awkward and give her a chance to think.

But Fr. Andrew wasn't thrown off. "Yes, it's about that," he answered mildly.

Abigail looked up at him sideways. "What did happen to her? Is everything okay?"

Fr. Andrew seemed to think about answering, but then changed his mind. "We'll get back to that in a minute. But first I want to get caught up on what has happened in the past few weeks. Tell me about the Club."

Abigail was a little shocked. It wasn't what she had expected him to say, and for a time she couldn't think quite how to answer. She quickly considered denying any knowledge of a club, and just as quickly dismissed the idea. But how much did he know? Was he mad?

"The Club?" she asked, hoping to get more information about what he was going to say to her. But Fr. Andrew's face was unreadable.

"The club that you have with four other girls," he said. "The Tuesday Night Club — isn't that what it's called?"

"The Every Tuesday Girls Club," she corrected, and then realized that she could no longer pretend she knew nothing about it. Darn! How much had Xenia said? Didn't she know the meetings were supposed to be secret?

Fr. Andrew nodded judiciously. "That's a good name. But Abigail, what is it? Xenia told me you started it and said that I told you to."

"I never said that," Abigail countered automatically. But … had she? She wasn't sure. "I … don't remember saying that," she said haltingly. "But I just wanted everyone to see how great it would be."

Fr. Andrew didn't say anything. They just listened to the wind and distant lawnmowers until she felt like talking again.

"The Every Tuesday Club is … " She still didn't quite know how to explain. "It's what I came up with to help me."

"Help you with what?"

"With our deal," Abigail replied. Father Andrew looked puzzled, so she continued, "The deal we made on the Sunday with the icon procession."

Father Andrew said, "Ohhh ... " softly, so he must've known what she was talking about. But he didn't say anything else, and she was starting to feel nervous.

"You said that if I would go to work helping people, you would get me a real copy of the icon of St. Abigail."

Father Andrew seemed to consider this, and he said, "I did say that," as if he were talking more to himself than to her.

"Did you forget?" Abigail asked, struggling to keep the disappointment out of her voice.

That seemed to snap him out of his private thoughts. "No, Abigail, I didn't forget. I have been working on getting you that icon. I got Bishop Paul's permission to have an icon done from that print in the book. And I've been trying to get in touch ... " Father rubbed his eyebrow impatiently. "Uh ... get in touch with the iconographer who owned that book. But Abigail, what does the Club have to do with any of that?"

Abigail was flustered. "Because in the Club we help people."

"You help people?" Father Andrew looked lost.

"Well, for right now, we're just helping each other. Because we need the practice. We can't just start in on other people."

He looked even more puzzled. "What other people?" This time it was Abigail's turn to look confused, so Fr. Andrew followed up with a more direct question. "Abigail, why would you think you needed to help with *everyone's* problems?"

The stress he put on the word *everyone* made her feel suddenly uncertain. "Well," she said, "you said you wanted me to help —"

"Yes, with the people nearest to you — with your family. That's all I meant."

Abigail was shocked. "With … my family?"

Father Andrew could see that his words had struck her, and he went on more gently. "Abigail, your family members are the ones that God puts in front of you — your parents, Mark, Bet. I would never have told you that you had to try to solve everybody's problems. Or even just those other four girls' problems."

Abigail felt terrible. She had misunderstood. She had made a mistake and started something because she didn't know she was wrong. But … it hadn't felt like it was a mistake. She had really liked what they did together. It had meant so much to her to have something to do that felt really important.

She suddenly realized she hadn't said anything in a while and looked up to find Fr. Andrew looking down at her in that searching way he had. "How did you go about solving each other's problems?" he asked solemnly.

"Well … " She felt like she didn't want to talk about any of this, but she forced herself to answer. "We all wrote down our biggest problem, and then we drew one out."

He nodded sagely. "And Xenia was the first?"

"No, Xenia was the second. Maggie was first."

He frowned. "Maggie was? So why aren't you all still working on her problem?"

Abigail shrugged wearily. "Because we solved it."

"You solved it," Father repeated. That seemed to surprise him. "What was her problem?"

"Baby Jacob." Abigail saw Father's eyebrows go up, so she added, "I mean, trying to get along with him was her problem. To take care of him. It was really stressing her out."

His eyebrows went down again. "But it's not stressing her out now?" Abigail shook her head no, and he pressed, "How did you do that?"

"Well, it wasn't just me," Abigail replied truthfully. "It was what Xenia looked up in the library. And it was Photini's prayers. And … " She knew the next part would sound crazy, but she decided to say it anyway. "And it was King Solomon and the baby."

She didn't know what Fr. Andrew would say to this. But after the merest pause, he suddenly looked past her to where a group of people had gathered together. Cupping his hand to his mouth, he called out, "Nate!" His son turned toward them. "Can you bring us out some soup and rolls? Oh, and bring spoons and napkins, too."

Nate might have been surprised, but he just called back a hearty "You got it!" and sprinted toward the church.

Fr. Andrew turned to Abigail and motioned her to a nearby picnic table. "I think we're going to be here for a bit," he said. "Abigail, let's start at the beginning."

AT FIRST, Abigail was too embarrassed to know how to talk about it. She blushed and stammered and couldn't meet Fr. Andrew's eyes, now that she realized the mistake she had made. But the priest listened as intelligently as he always did, asking a few specific questions to lead her along but otherwise letting her take as long as she needed to tell the story.

It was even more helpful that as she went along, Fr. Andrew's mood seemed to improve. He looked less serious. When she got to the part about telling the King Solomon story and drawing the line on Baby Jacob, his concerned expression tightened up momentarily and then he exploded in a burst of laughter.

"Oh my," he said, pinching the bridge of his nose. "Poor little Jacob! He didn't know he was helping you act out a Bible story. Well, well. But go on … what did Maggie do?"

As Abigail told the next part of the story — how Maggie had blown up at all of them but then been changed by the deep need to protect her brother from harm — his face went from mirth to calmness and then to wonder.

"That is quite amazing," he mused. "Of course I had noticed the change — a lot of people have, including Maggie's parents — but no one knew why it happened. Maggie is a very sweet girl, but it's rare for any of us to have a real change of heart so suddenly. Did you have any idea that it would work?"

Abigail had to think. "No … well, not really. Except, I did have the feeling that God was helping me, but I didn't know how, exactly.

I told you about my mom telling me to pray and then listen, right?"

"Yes," he nodded. "It sounds like you made a good start on a kind of prayer that the Church values very highly."

"And then did I tell you about seeing the cardinal on its nest?"

"Yes, you told me about that too. 'Sometimes where there's the most noise, there's life waiting just underneath.' That's very interesting." He didn't say anything for a bit and she thought maybe he had retreated into his private thoughts. But he roused himself and rubbed his hands to warm them up. "Your soup is getting cold," he said, "and I still haven't heard about Xenia. I know more about that so maybe I can just ask you some questions and that'll give you a chance to finish up."

Abigail was glad he had noticed. She hadn't wanted to be impolite, but the steaming soup had been sending off a deliciously savory smell and she hadn't had much chance to dig in. She was happy to let Fr. Andrew relate as much about Tuesday night as he knew. It was obvious that Xenia had told him what happened in the strange way she always had, so he was unclear about some of the facts. But he was good at asking the right questions, so Abigail was able to explain things to his satisfaction before she had reached the bottom of her bowl.

"One thing I don't understand, though," he said, brushing crumbs off the picnic table. "Xenia said it was your idea to ask her brothers to help teach you that computer game — what's it called?"

"ZooBlastex," mumbled Abigail, once her mouth wasn't full.

"ZooBlastex, yes," he said, smiling. "But what made you think to ask the boys?"

Abigail munched on the last bite of her roll, which gave her a moment to consider things. Once again, she knew the truth would sound a little strange. But she didn't like to lie, and Fr. Andrew seemed to be okay with what she had told him so far. So she answered, "Because they were her cross to bear."

"They were her what?"

Naturally, that led to another minute or two of explanation. Father Andrew seemed quite pleased to know that what he had said during the homily about the Cross had made her start thinking. "You have no idea how good it is to hear that people are listening sometimes," he said honestly. "There's a lot more to the Cross of Christ than you understand right now. But then, there's more to the Cross than any of us understand. It's certainly more than just that expression about someone being your cross to bear. And the crosses God brings into our lives aren't just bad things — they're the things that can save us."

Abigail looked confused, so Fr. Andrew made it easier. "What your mother told you is right — God can help us with our problems, if we ask Him." He considered for a minute, glancing idly at the cups and spoons. "And it ended up being a good thing that you got Randy and Amos involved at that moment. As it turned out, it meant that the whole family had to deal with something that had become a bigger and bigger problem."

"So … how is Xenia doing?" Abigail carefully asked again.

He looked at her intently for a minute and then began to stack bowls. "Hmm," he said distractedly. "I suppose you'll have to find out tomorrow, won't you?"

That seemed like an evasive answer, but his eyes twinkled as he said it, so Abigail wasn't sure what he meant. Before she could ask, though, his expression became a little more studious and he added, "Next time, you'll have to be more careful."

"More careful?"

"So far — with Maggie and Xenia — things have worked out all right and nothing has backfired. But the next time the Club tries to solve someone's problem, you might not be so lucky."

Abigail tried to look chastened, but really she had only heard one thing. "Next time?" she echoed. "So … we can keep meeting?"

Father Andrew smiled, and he had a very nice smile. "I see no reason that the Every Tuesday Girls Club can't keep meeting," he said. This led to an explosive squeal from Abigail and a squawk of mock protest from the priest as she hugged him as hard as she could.

"But Abigail," he cautioned, "I want you to fill me in from time to time about what is going on. It's important that I stay informed."

Abigail was still ecstatic, but she couldn't help asking him why she had to give reports. She had rather liked having the Club meetings stay private and secret.

"You have to tell me," insisted Fr. Andrew, "because you've started something by accident that really might have some serious consequences. Once you get involved with people's lives, you can stumble onto things that can be quite terrible if they aren't handled right. I wish that you girls' young lives could be perfect and peaceful, Abigail, but sometimes they're not. Especially these days. People's lives can be quite complicated."

Abigail wasn't quite sure she knew what he meant by that. But while she was still weighing those words, he continued on another track. "And there's also this issue of you looking for God's help and thinking that you know when you're getting an answer." He saw her alarmed look, so he was quick to add, "It is a good thing for a Christian to want to know the will of God, Abigail. It's a very good thing. But what if you had made a mistake? It's very easy for we Christians — even older Christians, or priests or monks — to think we know the will of God and be mistaken. That's why the Church considers spiritual discernment so important. Have you heard that word before? 'Discernment'?"

She shook her head no, so he took one of the napkins and wrote on it with the pen he always carried. "D-i-s-c-e-r-n-m-e-n-t," he said, spelling as he wrote. "Discernment. It means knowing right from wrong. That can sound very simple, and it is when it's as easy as whether to hit someone or steal something. But as you mature in faith, it can become much more difficult." He tore off the written word on the napkin and handed it to her. "I want you to let me know if you hear or feel anything that confuses you, especially when those things affect your faith."

Abigail took the napkin from him with mixed feelings. But Fr. Andrew wasn't finished yet. "By the way," he said, "you didn't tell me what Vanessa's problem was."

"She doesn't have one," Abigail mumbled. She still felt a little stung by Fr. Andrew's warnings. "Or at least, that's what she said."

"Really?" He looked curious.

"Yes," she replied. "When we started, she didn't want to have anything to do with it because she said we were being stupid and she didn't have any problems."

"She said that, did she?"

Abigail was about to answer, but then she saw that he didn't really mean it as a question. Still looking thoughtful, he stacked the bowls and handed the garbage bag to Abigail.

"That's very interesting," Fr. Andrew said.

Chapter fourteen

ABIGAIL WAS ANXIOUS to get to church on Sunday, which surprised her mother. But Mark had noted her interest last week and decided to get a jump on it.

"Don't you want to know what week it is this week?" he asked when they were pulling out of the driveway.

Abigail had been lost in her thoughts and could only ask "What?"

"Well, you wanted to know last week," said Mark. "So I looked it up. It's the Sunday of John Climacus."

Abigail realized that she had walked into a trap. Mark found out something she didn't know, which made him look smart and bothered her. It hadn't occurred to her to wonder which Sunday it was, but of course, it had mattered last week. Maybe there would be something in church this week that would help her as well. But what Mark had said only left her curious. Not wanting to give Mark a chance to look any smarter, she addressed her question to the front seat.

"Mom, who's St. John Clinnitless?"

"St. John Climacus," corrected Mark emphatically.

"He's also called St. John of the Ladder," said her father. "That's easier to say."

"He was a monk," explained Mrs. Alverson, "but we don't really know much about him. We know he wrote a very great book called *The Ladder of Divine Ascent*, about the way that monks could achieve greater and greater holiness through a series of steps, like climbing a ladder. And the book is so famous that he's called St. John of the Ladder because of it."

Abigail was silent, trying to think of any way that might help her figure out what to do for Xenia. It didn't seem very likely. Maybe she needed more information. "Can I read that book?" she asked.

Her mother made a startled squawk, but then smiled at Abigail. "We might have to wait a few years for that one, Abigail. It's a really difficult book — most people these days can't manage it."

"Oh," said Abigail. There didn't seem like much else to say. She wasn't sure how St. John of the Ladder was going to help her if she didn't even get to read his book. Maybe she could try and borrow it from the library. Maybe it had pictures in it. If it was too hard to read, maybe she'd just look at the pictures.

IT SEEMED LIKE A GOOD PLAN, but as it turned out, Fr. Andrew didn't talk during the homily about St. John of the Ladder, and she ended up forgetting the idea. Instead, he took his subject from the Gospel reading. It came from the Book of Mark (which she noticed because Mark always looked proud when they read from his patron saint's gospel book).

The reading told of a time when a man came up to Jesus because his son was possessed by a demon that threw him into terrible convulsions. Jesus told the father that his son could be healed if he believed. Christ said, "All things are possible to him who believes." And the father said, "Lord, I believe! Help me in my unbelief!" And then Jesus made the demon come out of the son, and the boy was healed.

That was amazing, Abigail thought. She had a pen with her and so she drew a quick picture on the church bulletin so she wouldn't forget the story. She sketched the father in terrible distress holding both hands out in front of him. And over his head was a talk bubble. Abigail consulted the Gospel reading in the bulletin and then carefully wrote out, "Lord, I BELIEVE. Help me in my UNBELIEF." The man told Jesus that he believed, because he really wanted his son to be healed. But he also asked Jesus to help him, because he knew that maybe he didn't believe enough. Believing and unbelieving. Having faith in God and asking God for more faith. Having faith, but asking for mercy. Fr. Andrew said that that was the point where miracles could happen.

"What is it that you want from God?" he asked.

For Abigail, it wasn't a hard question. Just for today, she really wanted to know how Xenia was. She was surprised to find that she cared — a month ago she rarely even gave Xenia and her family a second thought. But she felt responsible for what had happened, and she just wanted to try and see how she was doing.

Abigail looked for opportunities to glance around in church, but she couldn't see them anywhere. Of course, Xenia's mother Mrs. Murphy was up at the choir stand, but Abigail couldn't see anything different about her. She was still as flamboyant as ever, waving her arms and making faces to encourage the singers to keep up the pace. It was possible that Mrs. Murphy was smiling a little more and scolding Mr. Broadmere (who always sang too slowly) a little less. But Abigail wasn't sure. And where were Xenia and her father? Why weren't they standing in their usual place?

"What do you want most from God?" Fr. Andrew asked again. And this time he looked at Abigail, or very nearly. He seemed to look just past her, and feeling a bit puzzled Abigail looked over her shoulder and saw Xenia in the row right behind her, gazing placidly ahead.

So they must've come in after her and she hadn't seen them. Xenia and her father were standing with Randy and Amos, who usually loitered around in the back of the church and tended to take a lot of breaks and go out in the narthex so they could talk and joke around with each other.

The boys were both looking quite sullen and gloomy — apparently, they didn't think much of the new arrangement. But mild-mannered Mr. Murphy was giving off clear signs of being in charge and determined to stay that way. His jaw was set and he shot looks at them from time to time as if he was just waiting for them to step out of line.

And Xenia looked ...

Well, not the same. But what had changed? Xenia still stared straight ahead, as if her mind were far away. But at least she looked like she had a mind — she didn't look so much like a robot. Whether it was because her hair wasn't in her face as much or because her eyes were a little brighter and more curious, she was different ... more there.

Abigail shook her head. Was she right about that? Maybe she was wrong.

She might have thought so, until the service was over and it was time to go forward and kiss the cross in Fr. Andrew's hand. As people jostled into a kind of line, Abigail heard Amos mutter to Xenia, "Come on, move it, doofus."

And Xenia muttered back, "You move it, chowderhead."

Definitely, *something* had changed.

"IT WASN'T about ZooBlastex, exactly."

It wasn't until Tuesday night that Abigail and the other girls could fully satisfy their curiosity. Xenia didn't have any gadgets or game-players with her now, and when she spoke to them, she wasn't as twitchy. But she was still Xenia, and getting answers out of her was a little frustrating.

She told them that she and her brothers had their computer time cut back, and all the games were taken away until November. And she added that Fr. Andrew had talked to the whole family together for a while and then the parents by themselves another time. But she was maddeningly vague when it came to giving any kind of personal information.

"How do you feel?" asked Photini finally.

Xenia looked at Photini quizzically. "I feel fine," she said, as if it were a silly question.

"She means how do you feel about having this whole thing blow up," explained Maggie. Xenia turned to Maggie, but still plainly didn't understand what was being asked. "About having your parents take away all your games. Especially ZooBlastex."

Xenia blinked. "Why would I care about that?"

That was too much for Vanessa. "Um, hel-looo?" she chimed. "You said it was your biggest problem?"

"I did?"

The girls didn't even need to answer. Their looks of amazement said it all.

"Oh," said Xenia. "That's right. I did."

She frowned and concentrated, as if she really hadn't thought of that. "But … " she answered at last. "It wasn't about ZooBlastex, exactly."

The other girls were too surprised to reply, but Abigail recovered first. "No, it wasn't," she chimed in. "It was about Randy and Amos, right?" Now that it was obvious that things had gone well, Abigail thought she deserved a little credit for having known what the problem really was. But if she expected Xenia to agree with her, she was disappointed.

"No, it wasn't about that, either," Xenia replied.

"Well," Abigail said testily, "Then what was it about?"

"Um." Xenia paused, and then she paused some more, while the question hung in the air.

Xenia was right that it wasn't exactly about the computer game, or even about how her brothers teased her. It was just that her mother and brothers tended to be very boisterous and melodramatic, and Xenia took after her father — they were both quiet and withdrawn. The more loud one side of the family became, the quieter the other side became, until they had started to live almost like two different families rather than one. Her mother and father had been growing apart from each other, and it was only when they were all forced to talk in Fr. Andrew's office that they were able to see how bad things had gotten. Mrs. Murphy hadn't realized she was forcing her husband away, and Mr. Murphy hadn't realized that by detaching from the family, he left her alone to try and deal with the two boys, who were always too much of a handful for her.

BUT THAT WASN'T EASY for Xenia to tell them. She was a very private person and didn't like talking about her family. So there was only a part of the story that emerged that night. There were parts of it that Abigail had to just guess at, and other parts that she wouldn't know for years. But, after Xenia had said all that she wanted to say, she abruptly changed the subject. "So I guess we're ready."

"Ready for what?" asked Photini.

"Ready for the next problem. Because mine is solved now."

"Oh!" exclaimed Photini, brightening suddenly. "I suppose it is." She hadn't forgotten that her problem was one of the two left in the baggie.

Vanessa looked skeptical. "That's not really true, though. We were supposed to help you get past level eight or ten or whatever, and — "

"No, you weren't," answered Xenia with precision. "That's not what I wrote down. All I said was that I wanted to get the highest score at ZooBlastex."

"Yeah, but — "

"And I did."

Vanessa looked ready to argue, but Abigail understood right away. "Because you guys played the game in Father's office?" she asked. Xenia nodded.

Abigail tried not to look smug when she turned to the others, but she did love knowing something they didn't. "When Randy got on Father's computer, he accidentally reset all their scores to zero. And then when he tried to play, he made all kinds of mistakes and didn't get very far."

Xenia shook her head with pity. "What a chowderhead."

"But when Xenia got on," Abigail continued, ignoring Xenia's remark, "she did really well. She went past level four — "

"Level five," said Xenia.

"Level five," repeated Abigail. "And Randy didn't have a chance to play again before Father Andrew and the Murphys came in. So … if you look online right now … " Abigail was guessing, because she didn't know a lot about playing games online.

But Xenia finished the thought for her. "That's right," she said, with a quirky smile, "My score is much higher than theirs, and we won't be able to play again until November. I have the highest score." She dropped her eyes to her hands as she mulled that over for a second, and then she looked up again.

"I won," she said softly.

It was more emotion than Xenia tended to show, and Maggie couldn't help smiling. She really wanted to give Xenia a hug, but it was obvious that Xenia was ready to change the subject.

"So it's time for the next problem. Where's the baggie?"

VANESSA HAD TO ADMIT that she had the baggie, but she didn't want to. She had been getting more and more annoyed, and she didn't know why. She should have been happy for Xenia — Maggie had been. Photini was happy, too, but then of course, she was hoping her problem would get solved next. And Abigail was obviously happy, but then she had gotten just what she wanted, after all. Abigail looked like some kind of hero. She had helped them fix Xenia's problem, just like she had helped them to fix Maggie's problem. Vanessa found that the whole thing was becoming very irritating to her. Everybody seemed like they were getting just what they wanted, and what was she getting? She wanted to take the baggie out and throw it in the trash. But if she had, she would have had to explain why she did it, and that would just lead to a lot of questions that she didn't want to answer.

All of this was going through her mind as she fumbled in her purse for the folded baggie with its two little pieces of paper in it. She didn't know that her annoyance was obvious, but after she had tossed the contents of her purse onto the table a little too forcefully, she noticed Maggie looking at her strangely.

"Oh-kayyy," said Vanessa with as much enthusiasm as she could muster. "Two problems left. Whose will it be? Let me get a drumroll, please." Maggie rhythmically tapped her fingers, and after a second Xenia dutifully joined in.

Vanessa shook the bag around. "Who will win?" she said with artificial gusto. "Everyone wants to win." She tried not to think about it — everyone all smiles, and her hurting. "And the winner is — "

She lifted one piece of paper out, but just as it was coming up to eye level, she dropped it again. "Whoops!" she said, with a tight smile.

And picking the other piece of paper out, before any of the girls could protest this strange maneuver, she cheerily read aloud. "The winner is Photini!"

Abigail was stunned.

"Hey!" Xenia said righteously. "That wasn't fair!"

"What wasn't fair?" asked Vanessa innocently.

Xenia pointed at the baggie. "You picked up one and then — "

"I just dropped it, that's all," Vanessa replied. "And I picked it right up again, didn't I?"

"No," said Maggie gravely. "You picked up the other one."

"I did?" Vanessa feigned surprise. "I thought I — well, what should we do? Photini, do you think we should go again?"

Photini couldn't answer. She had been overjoyed to hear her name called. She knew the right thing was probably to do it all over again, but the words just stuck in her throat.

Vanessa looked across the table. "Abigail?" she said brightly. "What do you think? Should we do it again?"

Abigail felt her face flush. Had Vanessa known that the first piece of paper was hers? It was almost like she had dropped it on purpose. But, why would Vanessa do something so mean? It must have been an accident. But ... if Vanessa had stuck with the first piece of paper she picked, Abigail's name would've been called. The group would've started on her problem and the next time she saw her drawing of the icon, she would know that she was actually getting closer to the real thing.

And now ... No, there was only one answer. Whether it had been on purpose or not, it didn't feel right. She opened her mouth to demand that Vanessa do it over. But then she caught Photini's eye, and the strength seemed to drain out of her. Photini's pale face was pinched by misery. Of course, she thought she had won, and now everyone was saying it was unfair.

Abigail answered Vanessa's question, but her voice sounded hollow in her ears. "We should just leave it the way it is," she said.

Maggie had watched the struggle evident on Abigail's face, and she was dissatisfied. "Oh, come on, Vanessa. You know we need to do it again."

Vanessa tossed her head. "Seems like it should be their decision," she said, jerking her thumb at Abigail and Photini. "And they're okay with it. Right?"

Maggie struggled to come up with a good argument, but Vanessa took the opportunity to swing around to Photini. "Congratulations!" she exclaimed. And seeing Photini's uncertain expression, she lifted up the paper and continued, "And it says 'solo on Holy Saturday.' I know Holy Saturday is the day before Pascha, but what solo are you doing?"

Poor Photini. She had been hoping for weeks that her problem would get picked, but now that it had, everything seemed kind of spoiled. And now, instead of being happy for her, the girls were all sitting there with odd looks on their faces. Photini thought sadly that she should be strong and insist on a do-over. But she was running out of time. There weren't that many weeks left, and she didn't know what to do.

"Solo on Holy Saturday," prompted Maggie, when the silence grew awkward. "What kind of solo?"

"Maybe she's flying solo in an airplane," offered Xenia helpfully. "My uncle did it when he was getting his pilot's license."

All the girls' heads swiveled to her. "Xenia," said Vanessa, "Why would Photini be flying a plane?"

Xenia frowned. "You don't have to be a grown-up to fly a plane.

You can take flying lessons if you can reach the controls. My uncle told me. Any of us could learn to fly a plane."

"On Holy Saturday?" Vanessa frowned.

Xenia didn't see what difference the day had to do with it, and she would have said that. But hearing these wrong guesses shocked Photini out of her silence. "Singing a solo!" she blurted out. "A song. I mean, a hymn. By myself. At the service on Holy Saturday morning."

The effort seemed to have cost her, and she dropped her folded arms onto the table as if she were exhausted.

Abigail was intrigued in spite of herself. "But … what's wrong with that?"

"Everything!" whimpered Photini, and dropped her head into her arms.

THE PROBLEM WAS that Photini was painfully shy. Photini explained that her mother heard her sing around the house and thought that people in church should get to hear Photini's beautiful voice. The easy thing would have been to allow her to start singing in the choir, because the choir director was always looking for new voices. But her mother didn't think that was good enough — she campaigned to get Photini a chance to do something special. The readings at St. Michael were always done in a singing voice called chanting, and the reading they had picked for her on Holy Saturday was a lengthy story of three young men saved from a fiery furnace and King Nebuchadnezzar's rage. It was from the Book of Daniel and the end of the reading included a song that would be picked up by the clergy and then by the choir. All in all, it was one of the special events of the service on the morning before Pascha, and this year, Photini was supposed to do it.

"How can I?" groaned Photini. "I don't mind singing if I'm all alone, but I'm terrified of having to stand up in front of people."

Abigail knew what she meant. She had done readings in church a couple times herself. She wasn't nearly as shy as Photini was, but she had to admit that when she heard her voice all alone in the church with everyone listening, it was hard to keep her hands from shaking. And the other girls seemed to be considering the matter as well. It was Xenia who broke the silence.

"So maybe you could sit down." Xenia got blank stares. "I mean, if you're afraid of having to stand up in front of people — "

Photini was plainly exasperated. "That's not what I mean! It doesn't matter whether I'm standing or sitting. There will still be people. There will be so many people! I'll be scared stiff!"

Xenia never did well in the face of strong emotion and looked like a turtle wanting to go back into its shell. Maggie came to the rescue, leaning in so that Photini couldn't glare at Xenia. "It'll be okay, Photini," she assured her. "There aren't usually as many people at the morning service. Maybe just ten or twenty — "

"And the clergy. And the altar boys!" argued Photini. Before Maggie could reply, she continued in rising agitation. "But that's not all. My mother invited my aunt from Kansas. And my grandparents from Nebraska. She's always trying to get them to come to church and they said they'd be here. That's why she won't let me out of it now. I told her that the whole idea scares me to death, but she won't listen to me."

That wasn't hard to believe. Mrs. Jenkins didn't seem like she would be an easy mother to talk to. And if there were now aunts and grandparents involved, it seemed useless to hope that she could change her mind.

All the same, Abigail did feel as though Photini might be exaggerating things just a little bit. And also, wasn't Photini putting a bit of a silly problem before the Club? If Abigail had gotten to talk to the girls about the icon of St. Abigail, they would have been working on something that would mean something to her for the rest of her life, rather than just a one-time performance at a church service.

So Abigail might be forgiven if her tone was a little bit surly when she said, "Photini, it probably won't be so bad. A person always has the words right there when they do a reading. What could go wrong?"

Photini seized the question immediately. "What could go wrong?" Apparently, she had been thinking about this in some detail. "Remember last month when Alex Popascu read? He got so nervous he dropped the epistle book and lost his place."

Abigail had forgotten about that. But now that Photini mentioned it, she could recall that the little altar boy's face was beet red as he scrambled on the floor to retrieve the epistle book. Yes, that had been pretty embarrassing for him. "Well, yeah but — "

"Or Mrs. Shemassy during a special feast service?" continued Photini. "She was reading a psalm about God's mercy watering the desert, and she said that it watered the dessert."

Abigail felt lost. "Dessert?"

"Dessert, dessert! With two s's," exclaimed Photini. "Like cakes and pies and stuff. Instead of 'desert' with one 's' like the Sahara Desert. She said God's mercy watered the *dessert*, and it made some people giggle! In church!"

Abigail tried to think of some way to regain control of the conversation. It didn't help that Vanessa now recalled the incident Photini had described. "That *was* pretty funny," Vanessa said, and Maggie had to hide a smile.

Abigail turned away from them and tried again to address Photini's qualms. "Well, okay so — "

But Photini wasn't finished. "And what about Jeffie Sanders at the Presanctified Liturgy last week? They gave him a reading that talked about a broom tree — "

"What's a broom tree?" interrupted Abigail.

Photini waved her hands. "I don't know. It's a kind of tree they had in Old Testament times. But he was supposed to say 'broom tree,' only he doesn't say his r's very well when he gets nervous and he ended up saying 'boom tee.'"

Xenia nodded vaguely. "It sounded like 'boompty.'" She looked thoughtful, but her mouth was starting to twitch upwards in a quirky grin. "He said, ' … with burning coals of the boompty.'"

This time there was definitely a stifled snicker from Maggie and Vanessa. Abigail was afraid she might break out laughing herself, but she struggled valiantly to stay serious. "But, your reading, Photini … I mean, it doesn't have any hard stuff in it, does it?"

It had been the best thing Abigail could come up with. Unfortunately, she had guessed wrong, and Photini jumped on the question. "It does, though. It's got names. You have to say King Nebuchadnezzar. And Shadrach. And Mishak. And — "

Abigail cleared her throat in an effort to sound stern. "But really, Photini, I think — "

Photini had one more. "You have to say 'sackbut.'"

A shocked silence followed.

Abigail wasn't sure she had heard right. "You … you have to say 'sack butt?'"

Photini suddenly realized how that sounded. "No, not — It's spelled s-a-c-k-b-u-t. It's an old word for a musical instrument. It's 'b-u-t.' Not — "

"Sack butt!" roared Vanessa. And this time, it was impossible not to laugh. Abigail couldn't help it, and the other three girls didn't try. Photini really did try, and even said, "C'mon, you guys" in a plaintive way a time or two. But in the end, she was giggling worse than any of them.

It would be nice to be able to report that they all remembered to act ladylike and be moderate in their mirth. But sometimes there's nothing funnier than saying something silly in the middle of a quiet place, especially if the discussion has gotten tense. Every time they started to regain their composure, one of them would come up with an inventive way to use the word "sack butt" in a sentence, and they would almost fall out of their chairs laughing.

All in all, it was five or ten minutes before the giggles had totally

subsided and they could all settle down again.

They were still sniffling and snorting when Photini sighed and looked at them sadly. "But ... you see? That's what I mean. What if I mess up my reading and make people laugh?"

Then she thought of something worse and looked at them all, aghast.

"What if *I* laugh?"

Chapter fifteen

IT SEEMED that they were back where they started. Photini felt better than she had felt for some time because she was a very nervous girl and didn't usually get a chance to laugh that much. It had done wonders to improve her outlook. But the group had to admit that they really hadn't done much to help her.

Abigail took the opportunity to re-establish a little control. Now that the Club had an idea what Photini's problem was, Abigail proposed that they take turns and give their best idea of what would help. Then maybe Photini could pick one and try it out.

Abigail had come up with that on the spur of the moment, and she thought it was pretty good. For one thing, it gave her a chance to think, because she wanted to try to remember what she had heard in church on Sunday and how it might fit in. She was sure that if she could just do that, it would be the right solution.

Another advantage to this idea was that it put things back where she thought they should be. She was still the Club president, after all, and things didn't go along nearly as well when the meeting turned into a big free-for-all.

Vanessa apparently had a different opinion. "Phooey!" she scoffed. "We don't need to take turns and all that. Listen, Photini, I know what you have to do. All of you just need to listen to me."

Abigail and Maggie felt like they should argue the point, but Vanessa was adamant. "No, really! I know all about singing. My mother was a professional singer — "

"But *you're* not," snorted Abigail. She was surprised she had the nerve to talk to Vanessa that way — maybe she was still lightheaded from all the laughter — but Abigail was really getting tired of the way that Vanessa undermined her. "It seems to me," Abigail went on loudly, "that it should be Photini's decision whether we do it my way or not. That's how it seems to me."

Maggie and Xenia both looked uncomfortable, and Photini was horrified at having to make the decision. "Um ... I guess it would be nice to hear from everyone. I mean — " Photini glanced up furtively at Maggie and Xenia. "I mean ... if you guys think so ... right?"

Xenia just goggled wordlessly, and Maggie sighed, "I guess."

Vanessa looked from one to another and then slumped back in her seat melodramatically.

"Fine," she grumbled. "Do it your way."

Abigail couldn't let the remark pass. "Thank you," she chimed sarcastically.

Vanessa glared at her. "Oh no. Thank *you* ... Queen Abigail."

"Don't call me that!" Abigail snapped.

Vanessa's expression was instantly transformed to one of angelic innocence. "Gee, why not ... Queen Abigail? You are so wise!"

"Well, I'd like to go first!" Maggie blurted. She didn't really, but she couldn't think of any other way to stop a fight from starting.

Good grief! Maggie thought. *I feel like I'm babysitting Baby Jacob and his friends.* She hadn't really been prepared to say anything, but there was one thing that had been on her mind.

"Photini," Maggie said, "I think that if this is really important to your mother, you should just make the best of it. I know it scares you to stand up and all that, but your mom is really paying you a compliment by wanting you to sing. And she's even getting other members of her family to come in and hear you?" Photini nodded jerkily and shuddered. "But that really makes it kind of a special occasion. It shows your mom believes in you."

Believes in you. Abigail started at the words. She had been trying very hard to remember what it was she heard in church, and Maggie had triggered her memory. It was about believing. But what, exactly?

Maggie's advice didn't appear to help Photini much — in fact, she looked as if she felt ill. Abigail was still fighting to recall the rest of the message from church, so she gestured vaguely at Xenia.

"How about you, Xenia? What do you think?" she said. There was a stifled noise from the other side of the table, and Abigail realized that really she should have asked Vanessa to go next, since she was sitting right next to Maggie. It would have been the natural thing to do, but she hadn't been paying attention. Having said it, however, she didn't feel inclined to take it back. And after looking blankly at Abigail and then Vanessa, Xenia spoke up reluctantly.

"I don't know."

An embarrassed silence followed.

"I really don't," she added. "I mean, if it were me, I would be sick that day or something."

No one really wanted to ask, but it was impossible not to. "How can you be sick on purpose?" inquired Abigail wearily.

Xenia blinked in thought. "Well," she said, "you could maybe yell and yell until your throat was so sore you couldn't sing."

Abigail tried to change the subject, but Xenia had a new thought. "Or you could eat something you really, really don't like. And then maybe that would make you look sick."

"That's dishonest," Photini frowned.

Xenia lifted her shoulders expressively. "Well, that's what I would do."

"Thank you, Xenia," Abigail sang out. She felt like she had been very patient, but their meeting time was running out. "Do you know what I'd do?"

Photini was surprised. "Oh. Is it … your turn … ?" She inclined her head meaningfully to Vanessa across the table, but Abigail pretended like she didn't understand.

"Do you know what I'd do?" Abigail repeated.

"What would you do?" asked Maggie dutifully.

"I would believe!" Abigail declared.

No one knew what to say to that.

"Believe … what?" Photini politely inquired.

"Just … believe!" insisted Abigail. "Like the man whose son had seizures. We heard about it Sunday. And he said, 'Lord, I believe. Help me in my unbelief.'"

The pause this time was even longer than before.

"So … that's what you need to do." Abigail shuffled her fingers nervously. This had all sounded better in her head. "You have to believe as much as you can that you can do this. But then, you, um … you have to ask God to give you more faith."

"Oh," murmured Photini. She tried to think of something else to say. "Thank you."

There was another awkward pause before Vanessa cleared her throat. "Are you through, your majesty?"

Abigail bit her lip. "Yes," she replied, with as much dignity as she could manage.

Vanessa nodded with satisfaction. "Good!" She scooted her chair up to the table and leaned forward so she could look Photini in the eye.

"Okay, here's the thing, Photini," she said. "What Queen Abigail said isn't totally wrong." (Abigail said "Hey!" but Vanessa kept talking.) "But she's not totally right either. You need two things. You need to learn to be a better singer, and you need confidence. The first part isn't even that hard. Reading in church is easy — I've done it a bunch of times. Like I said, my mom was a singer and she's given me all kinds of voice exercises to do. I could teach them to you in ten minutes. You just practice them whenever you can, and you'll sing better."

"Really?" intoned Photini. For the first time that night, she looked hopeful.

"Absolutely! And second, you have to believe you can do this."

"Like Abigail said?" Photini asked timidly.

Vanessa rolled her eyes and sighed. "Sure — yes. Like Abigail said. I don't know about the part where you ask God for more faith — "

"I liked that part," said Photini quietly, much to Abigail's satisfaction.

Vanessa sighed again. "Okay, so do that, then. But you need to do a reading in church before the big one on Holy Saturday."

Photini's hopeful expression vanished. "What?!"

Abigail tried to scoff but she didn't know how, and it just sounded like a cough. "So Photini was nervous about one reading," she snorted, "and now you think she should do two?" Maggie frowned at her.

Vanessa, however, was unfazed. "Yes," she answered calmly. "But she'll do it with a safety net."

"A what?"

"Like circus performers use so they don't fall," grinned Vanessa. She obviously liked the effect she got. Even Xenia was gazing at her in rapt attention. "You'll have to do the reading with a safety net."

Maggie leaned in. "Vanessa, what does that *mean*?"

"It doesn't mean anything!" Abigail said angrily, pulling her book from under Maggie's elbow.

"It's a trick my mother told me," persisted Vanessa, without acknowledging Abigail's comment. "It's a way to help a singer sometimes. It's almost like magic."

The words had an immediate effect on Maggie, Photini and Xenia. Their eyes opened wide and they obviously wanted to know all about the marvelous trick from a professional singer. Abigail could tell that she'd never get them to take her seriously again as a president if something didn't happen fast. So when she heard a door slam somewhere down the hall, she leapt up from her chair.

"Oh, too bad! Looks like our time's up!"

"What?" Xenia looked at her watch. "No, it's not. We've still got a couple minutes. I want to hear this."

"Too bad," Abigail repeated, stuffing pencils into her purse. "We'll just have to wait until next week. Time to go!"

And she managed to hustle and nudge the girls into putting their things together and leaving the room. She knew she was being childish, but she felt like she'd rather die than let Vanessa hog all the attention right then. Abigail tried not to notice Maggie's disapproving looks, but that didn't bother her half as much as catching Vanessa's expression as they closed the door. Abigail had thought that she would look angry or resentful, but she didn't — Vanessa looked smugly triumphant.

IT FELT like a very long ride home to Abigail.

As Mrs. Alverson drove the car easily over the hilly roads, Abigail started recalling some of the things she had said, and she cringed. She never acted like that. What had made her do it? One word seemed to be the entire answer, and Abigail latched onto it.

Vanessa!

Abigail clenched her teeth as she remembered how she had tried to get even with Vanessa by being rude and interrupting her. And what good had it done? Vanessa wasn't offended in the least, and Abigail had come off looking like a sore loser ... and a bad president! She shook her head. No, it just wasn't right that she had gotten caught up in her anger and hurt feelings. She thought of the way Maggie-May had looked at her, and she felt ashamed.

Abigail kicked at a gum wrapper on the car's floor mat. *Should I ... apologize to Vanessa?*

She winced. That would be really hard to do. But maybe it was a good idea. She hated the itchy way she felt and wanted to do something to make it go away. More to the point, she didn't want to try and compete with Vanessa any more — there must be some way they could be friends. But what if Vanessa sneered at her — she seemed to do that a lot. Or what if she pretended to accept Abigail's apology just so she could make fun of her in front of everyone?

Abigail sighed and kicked the floor mat again. She didn't know what to do.

"You're quiet tonight," commented Mrs. Alverson. "Is everything okay?"

No, thought Abigail.

"Yes," she answered glumly. "I'm just thinking about stuff."

"Good stuff, I hope."

Abigail didn't know how to answer that, but luckily her mother didn't notice. She started singing songs from choir practice again. Abigail suddenly realized that she been hearing that more often for a few days. "You've been singing a lot lately," Abigail observed. "Are you happy?"

"I *am* happy," Mrs. Alverson smiled. "I've had a good week, and you're part of the reason why."

Abigail wanted to hear more about that, but Mrs. Alverson only smiled again and said mysteriously, "I can't tell you now. You'll find out later this week."

Abigail's curiosity awoke all at once. Her mother had a secret? About her doing something good? She pressed for more information, but Mrs. Alverson just deflected her questions with a wave of her hand and said, "You'll find out later."

IT BECAME OBVIOUS as the week progressed that her father was in on the secret, but both her parents were maddeningly good at keeping all the information to themselves. There were whispered conferences and gentle laughter, but Abigail couldn't make out a word of what was said.

To make things worse, both parents barricaded themselves in the kitchen after Mr. Alverson came home on Thursday, and they set Mark to guard the door.

The kitchen rang out with banging pots and pans, silly laughter and other mysterious noises. Bet and Abigail both accosted Mark, but he took his duty very seriously and refused to budge.

"What's going on?" demanded Abigail as Bet tried stubbornly to pry Mark's fingers from the doorknob.

"I told you, I don't know," he replied testily. "They didn't tell me. They just said to keep everyone out until dinner."

"Have to see, have to see, have to *seee*," whined Bet, pulling on Mark's fingers.

Mark's resolve wavered, but luckily for him, he was spared from further temptation. The kitchen door opened and there stood Mr. and Mrs. Alverson, weighed down with bright pots and dishes giving off delicious smells. There was also a very intriguing gift bag slung over Mrs. Alverson's arm — Abigail noticed it and wanted to ask about it, but no one would have heard her over Bet's squeals of delight.

"Dinner ... is served," said Mr. Alverson, with great dignity.

IT TURNED OUT to be quite a feast. There had been a lot of leftovers from a big potluck the church had put on, and Mrs. Alverson was encouraged to bring home as much as she could. There were stuffed grape leaves and fluffy potato pancakes and crispy triangles of pastry called samosas. There was a large bowl of Mrs. Tamar's homemade hummus sprinkled with paprika, and Mrs.

Alverson had picked up fresh pita bread at the farmer's market. Abigail's dad had made up his special shrimp fried rice for the occasion, and there was an unopened box of sticky-sweet baklava cut into triangles and rectangles.

When they had said grace and dug in, there was a quick bustle of noise and chatter as dishes were passed, followed by the kind of contented noises and happy talk that a good meal inspires. In time, her father called for attention by tapping a spoon lightly on his glass.

"No doubt, you are wondering, good Alverson children, what we are celebrating. Well, it just so happens that we have had good news that all came at the same time. For one thing, we're going to get a bigger rebate check on our taxes than we thought."

Mrs. Alverson burst into spontaneous applause. "Hooray!" she said in a comically loud voice. It had been a really difficult year and the extra money, Abigail knew, would be welcome. "Hooray!" echoed Bet enthusiastically. She had no idea what was going on, but she loved applauding.

"Thank you, thank you," grinned her father, with a slight bow. "We're also quite blessed to have three lovely children who have done magnificent things. What things, you ask?"

He paused dramatically, while Abigail and Mark exchanged looks. She couldn't think of any magnificent thing she had done, and Mark seemed puzzled as well.

"Our young man Mark has brought honor to the household by an essay he wrote for the state's Young Scholar competition. I am pleased to announce that his essay on the Russian czars earned him second place —" Mr. Alverson paused for applause. "And $50 in prize money." This brought even louder applause. Mrs. Alverson handed him an envelope with cash, and digging into her gift bag, she produced a new pair of headphones to go with the money. Mark was all smiles and accepted the gifts and some hearty pats on the back.

Abigail was hoping that she would be next, but smiled anyway when her father intoned solemnly, "Miss Elizabeth P. Alverson." Bet squealed in pure excitement and wriggled on her chair. They never used her full name unless it was something very good or very bad, and she was bursting with anticipation. "Miss Elizabeth, I am told, has done her chores this entire week without having to be told, and she has done a splendid job. Fabulous job, Bet." She was still looking at him expectantly, so he ended with "Hooray!" and she added

"HOORAY!" so loudly that the whole family joined in. It was some time before they could stop laughing enough to pull something out of the gift bag for her, but her giggles subsided into awed silence when she saw a fine stuffed bunny with a

floppy hat. She accepted the toy animal from her mother with reverent care.

"What's its name, Bet?" asked Mark.

Bet took mere seconds to contemplate the raggy bunny with its purple hat. "Doppler," she announced solemnly.

Everyone in the family knew that Bet had a gift for giving interesting names to her toys. Abigail was still reflecting on this last one when she heard her mother clear her throat.

"And as for our Miss Abigail," Mrs. Alverson began, "It has been brought to our attention that she has started a girls club at church." Abigail's mouth dropped open.

"Not only did she give the girls something to do while they had to stay around church every week, but she actually organized them into a group that has been working to help each other with their problems."

"Huh?" said Mark, screwing up his expression. "It's a girls club. That helps people? How does that work?"

Abigail felt shocked. She knew that Fr. Andrew was going to tell her parents what she had been doing, but she still felt a little horrified to know that the secret was out. It was hard to stay upset though, when her mother and father were beaming at her with such obvious pleasure.

"They talk together and work together to try to fix their problems," explained Mrs. Alverson. "That's why she's been paying so much attention in church. Father Andrew told us they have had some real successes. That certainly seemed like something to celebrate."

At the word "celebrate" Bet roused herself from playing with Doppler to shout "Hooray!" and set off a proper round of applause as

Abigail was ceremoniously handed a new box of watercolor pencils in a fancy cloth-covered box.

Abigail was stunned. "That is so awesome," she said, fingering the embroidery of the box.

"Amazing art supplies for awesome Abigail," quipped her father, handing her the last piece of baklava.

ABIGAIL THOUGHT THE HAPPY GLOW would last all night, but when she was ready for bed, she found that there was still something nagging at her. After trying to fall asleep, she sat at her desk by the window and turned on the light. There were some pictures set out to dry — new experiments with the watercolor pencils that had been lightly brushed with water to see how the colors would run together. They looked pretty good, Abigail thought, examining them with her head on one side. Imagine getting such great new art supplies for no special reason.

But then, there was a reason: the Club. All this time she hadn't wanted to tell her parents what she was doing, and it turned out they thought it was awesome! They thought *she* was awesome. Awesome Abigail. Maybe that could be like a new nickname.

She put the pencils down, smiling to herself. That was silly. Or … was it? Hadn't her dad called it "a magnificent thing" she had done? He was sort of kidding, of course, but still, they had obviously been really pleased. What had Fr. Andrew told them, exactly? Maybe he said she was awesome. It didn't sound like his kind of word, but if he did, maybe she really could get everyone to start calling her that. "Here comes Awesome Abigail," they'd say. Everyone except …

Abigail sighed and her smile faded. "Vanessa," she said.

That was what was bothering her. She felt like things were still un-settled about what had happened last Tuesday. They couldn't go on with the meetings if she and Vanessa were going to snip and snap at each other. She would've liked if Vanessa would just show her some respect as the president of the Every Tuesday Girls Club. But it was starting to look like that just wasn't going to happen, and Abigail didn't know what to do.

Is Vanessa jealous of me?

That was a strange question. Abigail wasn't quite sure where it came from. But now that she came to think of it, maybe ... well ... maybe she was.

Abigail stopped coloring in the pattern and started doodling on another pad — a pointy jeweled crown. Wouldn't it be cool if she could be a different person, if she really could be awesome all the time? Then people wouldn't think she was silly and look down on her. Maybe her parents would be proud of her more often and Fr. Andrew wouldn't look over the top of his glasses at her so much. Maybe Vanessa wouldn't be able to hurt her feelings. What would it feel like to be Awesome Abigail? Maybe it was time she found out.

Should she apologize to Vanessa?

"No." She was going to be a new person — more cool, more confi-dent. Apologies were kid stuff. Awesome Abigail didn't bother with things like that.

"Besides, I don't need to." Abigail replaced her pencils to the box and snapped the lid. As she did, she uttered the words that have kept many, many feuds alive.

"She started it."

Chapter sixteen

ABIGAIL SLEPT WELL THAT NIGHT. She awoke refreshed, feeling on top of the world. It was great to stop feeling so unhappy and guilty. She was past that now. The old Abigail was always doing silly things, singing and dancing for no reason. But Awesome Abigail wouldn't do that. She looked at the drawings on her desk and decided she needed to get a book so she could draw and paint like a great artist. She used to like drawing whatever was in her head, but they didn't look like what grownups did. She would have to do better.

Abigail talked to Maggie on Friday and she was sure her friend could hear the difference. She shared a little of the new attitude she had about Vanessa.

"I'm not going to let her get to me anymore," she told her.

"Oh good!" Maggie said with obvious relief. "Seriously, Abigail, that was all so weird on Tuesday night! I know Vanessa was kind of ... well, she's ... "

"I know," Abigail finished, tossing her head in a way she was trying to master. "She's a bad person."

Maggie was shocked. "What?"

"Well, maybe not bad," Abigail relented, "but she's certainly not a good person. It's not her fault, though. It's her family. They make her do bad things."

"Abigail!" Maggie cried in dismay.

"It's okay though," Abigail assured her, "I'm not going to let her make me mad anymore. I don't care about bad people. The Club is about good people."

"Oh … "

"You and Xenia are good people. Photini is a good person. I want to concentrate on helping her. Don't you?"

There was a long pause. "I guess," replied Maggie, without conviction.

Abigail felt good when she finished the phone call. She felt strong. Maggie had been pretty impressed, she thought. Maybe she could tell what a handle Awesome Abigail had on the situation. She was determined to help Photini with her solo on Holy Saturday, and when people congratulated her, Photini would say, "I never could have done it without the Every Tuesday Girls Club. They helped me so much!"

That moment seemed so glittering, so grand. Abigail climbed the stairs to her room, and thought how it would sound to hear that. It was all so clear. All she had to do was figure out how to help Photini with her solo, and then the Club would have another victory. And this time, Abigail would make sure that people found out about it. And if Photini was too shy to give the credit to the Club, Abigail would have to step in. She would have to get just the right word in at just the right time. Maybe the old Abigail couldn't do it, but the new Abigail — Awesome Abigail ...

Abigail stopped. She could see part of her reflection in the mirror on the back of her closet door. She reached out and closed it and there she was. She paused and a kind of unpleasantness seemed to sink in. There was something all wrong with Awesome Abigail.

"I don't like her," Abigail sighed. She fell back on her bed. It was fine to feel bright and smart, but there was almost nothing about how she'd been that day that had really felt right. She didn't want to try to be Awesome Abigail, Cool Abigail. She liked just being herself. But just-plain-Abigail wasn't enough, or at least Vanessa didn't seem to think so. Why was that important to her?

Well, Abigail thought, *that's not hard to figure out.* Unless she could work out what was going on with Vanessa, she just wasn't going to really be the president of the Girls Club. And that mattered to her. The Every Tuesday Girls Club mattered — she didn't know why, but it did.

Abigail heard a buzz on her computer and saw that Maggie had sent her a message. Neither the Alversons nor the Peasles liked for the girls to send a lot of instant messages, and they only did it under rare circumstances. This one was short and simple, which probably meant that there were people around and Maggie had to type fast.

"r u okay?"

Abigail was glad to have a reason to get off the bed. She scooted up to the computer and typed, "I'm fine." She thought a minute and added, "I'm sorry."

The computer was quiet for a minute and then it buzzed again.

"why?"

Abigail sighed. She wasn't a very fast typist and it would take too long to explain completely. "about vanessa," she typed carefully. "I didn't mean it. she just makes me mad that's all."

"I know," Maggie replied almost immediately. "I wish she wd stop tryin 2 act tough."

Me too, thought Abigail. But she didn't want to go into that. She considered a minute and then typed slowly "what shoud I do?" Now that it was on the screen, she was pretty sure that "should" wasn't spelled like that. But Maggie must've understood anyway, because the answer came back in a few seconds.

"I don't know. :-(Just be nice 2 her, I gess?" Abigail was still looking at that when the computer buzzed again. "gotta go. see u Sunday?"

"yes," Abigail answered. "bye till then."

Just be nice to her. That was an answer, but it didn't seem like a complete answer. It was a good thing that the weekend was coming up. Maybe there would be something in church that would help her understand how to deal with things.

Abigail turned the computer off, but missed one last message from Maggie and didn't find out about it until much later. The message read: "P.S: you're right that something is going on with Vanessa tho. Remind me to tell you about something I saw. It has been bothering me."

AFTER A THREATENING SKY, Sunday dawned coolish but delightfully clear. The frosty mornings that had been leaving the dew crunchy had subsided, and the tulips and narcissus that the church yard team tended were up and blooming.

Standing in church, Abigail looked idly at the flickering candles and let her thoughts wander. She had tried to spend time on Friday and Saturday praying about Photini's problem and looking up Bible stories. But she didn't feel like anything had really helped, and now they were just a few days from the next Club meeting. How could you help a shy person sing in church? Could the saint of the day give her some clue? It hadn't seemed very likely. When she was riding to church, she asked her mother what Sunday it was, and this time, Mrs. Alverson knew exactly what she meant.

"Is this for the Club? Well, so it's the fifth Sunday. Mark, any guesses? What Sunday is it?"

"Uhhh..,"

"It's Pam Sunday!" cried Bet.

Her mother was impressed, but shook her head. "Good try, Bet, but Palm Sunday isn't 'til next week. This week is the last Sunday in Lent and it's … ?"

"Saint Mary!" Mark answered, with understandable smugness. But his mother wasn't totally satisfied.

"Yes, Saint Mary. Of … ?" Mark looked puzzled, so Mrs. Alverson asked the question differently. "Where did she come from?"

"Oh … " Mark looked unsure. "Jerusalem?"

"Nnnno … Abigail, want to guess?"

"Um. Spain?" That didn't sound right, but Abigail felt like you saw a lot of saints' names in Spanish, so she thought she would give it a try.

"Nnnno … " said Mrs. Alverson. "Any last guesses?"

"Kannas City!" piped Bet. She had been born in Kansas City, and whenever there was a missing place name, she tended to supply that one.

"Nnnno … " replied Mrs. Alverson, smiling. "Saint Mary of *Egypt*." Mark smacked his head as if he had known the answer, but Abigail thought that might not have been the case.

Her mother explained that St. Mary was a woman who had grown up in a large city in Egypt many, many centuries ago. Eventually, she came to live all by herself in the desert for 40 years. No one would have known she was there if a monk named Zossima hadn't come across her and asked her to tell him her story.

"So what was her story? Why did she live by herself for 40 years?" questioned Abigail.

"She needed the time to repent. She told Zossima that she had lived a very bad life until something happened that changed everything."

Abigail quite naturally wanted to know what had happened, but her mother just said that Fr. Andrew would probably tell the story better than she could. Abigail was curious to know what she would hear about this saint who had lived alone in the desert for such a long time.

ALL THE SAME, she reflected as the service got underway, it was hard to think of how any of this could apply to Photini. Abigail let her eyes wander up to the dome as the choir ended a song. Saints' lives and what apostles wrote and what Jesus said — it had all happened such a long, long time ago. But then, she had to admit that her own saint, Abigail, had lived long ago, too — even longer in the past than St. Mary. And yet, she felt a kind of connection to her. It was as if she and St. Abigail knew each other in a way that made the years unimportant.

Abigail suddenly realized that the church had gotten quiet. Usually one thing followed another without a lot of gaps, but things had become oddly silent. People turned around to the middle of the church, so she turned as well. To her complete surprise, she saw that Photini was standing with the epistle book open and Vanessa was standing behind her. With a shock, Abigail realized that Photini was doing the reading for the week. How had Vanessa ever talked her into it? And why was she standing behind her?

"Wisdom!" sang Fr. Andrew.

For a second there was no answer. Abigail knew that it was time for a short chanted line or two called the prokeimenon, but to her horror, Abigail could see that Photini was in no condition to chant anything. She was as rigid as a statue — her face was turned down toward the book and looked ashen. *She's terrified,* thought Abigail desperately. What was Vanessa thinking? How typical of her to force Photini to do something she wasn't ready for!

The silence grew awkward and then Photini gave a pitiful little cough and started singing, chanting on one note as readers did. As soon as she did, Vanessa joined in, lending her confident voice to Photini's trembling one and putting her hand gently on Photini's shoulder. And with that touch, the voices rose together — it was as if Vanessa was lending Photini her strength. *"Pray and make your vows before the Lord, our God,"* Vanessa and Photini sang together, although Vanessa's voice was much clearer and stronger. Abigail exhaled as the choir picked the line after them. There was one line done, anyway.

The next one went a little better. There was no pause at the beginning, and Abigail could make out Photini's voice this time when they both sang. *"In Judah, God is known. His name is great in Israel."* Vanessa left her hand on Photini's shoulder, and the two voices came out again almost as one. Vanessa even varied the pitch on one or two notes, and Photini changed her notes to match. Abigail thought that was clever, and it sounded sort of pretty.

The choir sang the refrain again and the third line from the girls was a distinct improvement — instead of mostly hearing Vanessa, the two voices were blended together almost equally. *Hang in there, Photini!* thought Abigail. She had sung the prokeimenon with Vanessa's help, but how would she do on the reading?

"Wisdom," Fr. Andrew sang again.

That same little nervous cough, and then Photini weakly chanted, "The reading is from Saint Paul's letter to the Hebrews."

Father Andrew sang, "Let us attend."

There was another momentary pause, and Abigail could see that Photini's hands were shaking. As with the prokeimenon, Vanessa's voice came through first. Looking over Photini's shoulder so she could see the words, she read, *"When Christ came as high priest of the good things to come …"* And when she had done a line or two, Photini joined in and they read together. And then Vanessa got quieter, until Photini was doing the reading all by herself. It had happened so naturally that Abigail wouldn't have noticed if she hadn't been paying attention. Photini finished the last line of the reading and remembered to draw out the last few words so that it would be obvious it was the end.

As the reading ended, Abigail relaxed and let out her breath. There was only one thing left to do. A reader still had to sing another couple lines back and forth with the choir singing alleluia three times each time.

Father Andrew started by singing a blessing, "Peace be to you who read."

It was clear, however, that with Vanessa standing behind her, Photini had become used to the sound of her own voice, and she sang the response all alone and without any pause. "And to your spirit — alleluia, alleluia, alleluia!"

The choir repeated the three alleluias as a beautiful short song with harmonies, and it was Photini's turn again. The second line that Photini sang was more surprising. Rather than just chant on one note, she altered what she was singing so that it would match what the choir sang. Again they replied with their three alleluias in the same way.

The last line that Photini sang was the one that got everyone's attention. Like a bird that has tested its wings, she finally trusted her voice, and pure, flute-like notes seemed to come out of nowhere. It seemed that Mrs. Jenkins might have been right after all — Photini had a really pretty voice. She matched what the choir was doing even more closely than the last time and held and swelled the last note until the choir took over jubilantly: "Alleluia, alleluia, al-le-lu-ia!"

The church actually went dead silent. Neither the priest nor anyone else could quite recover, and Abigail could feel the hairs on her arm all prickly. It had been a small wonder. Photini, who had begun so timidly that she could hardly be heard, had ended with a quality in her voice that was actually quite amazing.

As Fr. Andrew remembered his place and began the prayer before the Gospel reading, Photini walked calmly to return the epistle book to its stand, her posture erect but no longer rigid. She looked as confident as Abigail had ever seen her. But by the time she got back to her family and the next prayers were being sung, she almost fell into her mother's arms with relief. There was a little flurry of hugs and well-wishes.

Abigail sighed blissfully and turned forward. The happiest of happy outcomes for Photini's problem. She still had to do the reading in a few weeks, of course, but it seemed very likely that she would be able to do it now — she might even find that she enjoyed doing readings.

THE SERVICE CONTINUED, but Abigail had a hard time refocusing and didn't hear very much of the Gospel reading. She was thinking about how well Photini had done. That was so great! Talking things over in the Club had helped after all. Abigail tried to catch her eye, but Photini was paying attention to the Gospel reading, her arm linked lightly to Vanessa's. Abigail's smile faltered.

Vanessa. Oh.

Father Andrew finished the Gospel reading and motioned everyone to sit down for the homily.

"Well!" he exclaimed, when the shuffling had subsided, "It

certainly is difficult to follow up a rock star performance like that epistle reading." There was appreciative laughter and murmurs of agreement. "Many thanks to Vanessa Taybeck and Photini Jenkins for doing such an excellent job." More murmurs and even a little scattered applause.

Abigail felt a curious prick of jealousy. She couldn't help but look back at Photini again and saw that she was looking at Vanessa with an expression of utmost gratitude. That gave her another flutter of bitterness that she couldn't shake off. Vanessa! Why did Vanessa always have to grab the spotlight?

Abigail tried again to forget about it and listen to what Fr. Andrew was saying, but the feeling came back stronger. She wanted to be happy for Photini, happy for her success, but ... Vanessa! Of course, Vanessa had helped. Abigail could see that standing behind Photini and helping her, even putting her hand on Photini's shoulder, had been the "magic" — the safety net — she had been talking about. It had given Photini the confidence she couldn't find on her own. So Vanessa had been right after all. She would get all the glory now, and she would be even more smug and conceited than she already was.

Abigail stopped, confused. That was an awful way to think, and it didn't even make sense, she told herself. Vanessa hadn't done most of the work, Photini had. And the only reason the trick had worked is because Vanessa *hadn't* been conceited — she had been humble enough to get quieter so that Photini could take over and really sing by herself. It would be fair to at least notice that. But Abigail's emotions were tumbling about like a little storm inside her, making it difficult to think reasonably. She didn't want to be fair — she was just plain mad!

Vanessa! she thought angrily. Everything always goes wrong when

Vanessa is involved. I can't be myself and end up getting all mad when *Vanessa* is around.

"And why is that?" asked Fr. Andrew, startling Abigail back to attention. She had apparently missed quite a bit of the homily. Fr. Andrew asked his question again another way.

"Why would the Orthodox Church reserve the last Sunday in Lent every year for a woman who nearly died unknown — a hermit who lived by herself and died alone in the desert?"

He must be talking about St. Mary of Egypt, thought Abigail. It was good to have an excuse to leave the troubling thoughts behind, and she sat up a little straighter to help her pay attention.

"What happened to turn this sad, desperate young woman into one of the most revered saints in the Orthodox Church?" he asked. Abigail had been wondering the same thing. This was the part of the story that her mother had wanted her to hear from Fr. Andrew.

He explained that Mary told the monk Zossima that when she was a young woman, she had joined up with a group of men who were going to Jerusalem to see the Cross of Christ. In those times, all those centuries ago, the Cross was displayed in Jerusalem on special feast days and people came from all over just to see it. Mary found out that others from her city were going to see it, and even though she was a very wicked young woman at the time, she wanted to go where everyone else was going. When she arrived at the church in Jerusalem, she joined a great group of people packing into the church

"She told Zossima that she was in the habit of pushing and shoving with her elbows to get through a crowd and this is what she did on this day," said Fr. Andrew, demonstrating by jabbing his elbows out at his sides. "Apparently, she was a very rude and pushy young woman."

Huh. Just like some other people I know, Abigail thought. And then she was a little ashamed of herself and tried harder not to be distracted.

Father Andrew continued. "But at that point, a strange thing happened — Mary couldn't get through the door of the church. Other people were going in — she could see that. But some kind of invisible force kept her from being able to cross the threshold of the church where the Cross was. Here is what she said … "

Father Andrew lifted a thin book to read from. The book had the account of her encounter with Zossima that had been written in the seventh century. Abigail thought it was thrilling, because you didn't usually get to hear from saints in their own words.

Father Andrew read:

"But when I stepped onto the doorstep which everyone passed, I was stopped by some force which prevented my entering. Meanwhile I was brushed aside by the crowd and found myself standing alone in the porch. I again began to work my way into the crowd. But in vain I struggled. Again my feet stepped on the doorstep over which others were entering the church without encountering any obstacle. I alone seemed to remain unaccepted by the church. It was as if there was a detachment of soldiers standing there to oppose my entrance. Once again I was excluded by the same mighty force and again I stood in the porch."

He glanced at the congregation over the edge of the book. "This happened to her repeatedly, until she was too exhausted to go on, and was outside by herself while everyone else went inside the church to see the precious Cross." He continued from the book:

"And only then with great difficulty it began to dawn on me, and I began to understand the reason why I was prevented from being

admitted to see the life-giving Cross. The word of salvation gently touched the eyes of my heart and revealed to me that it was my unclean life which barred the entrance to me. I began to weep and lament and beat my breast, and to sigh from the depths of my heart."

"Do you see?" Fr. Andrew asked them, lowering the book. "She had been thinking of the Cross as just some kind of circus attraction — it never occurred to her that it was something holy. But with a heart unprepared, the way was barred for her. When she saw that — really saw what kind of life she had led and considered what it meant to be barred at the door of the church — she repented. There outside the church was an icon of the Mother of God, and Mary poured out her heart. She confessed and made a vow that if she could be allowed to go inside and see the Cross, she would turn her life around and go wherever she was directed."

The church was quiet as Fr. Andrew paused. Many of the parishioners had heard this story often, but everyone was in rapt attention all the same. "And her prayers were answered," the priest continued. "She was able to go into the church without any hindrance. She saw the Holy Cross and attended the service, and when she came out and went back to the icon to give a prayer of thanks, she heard a voice from heaven tell her 'If you cross the Jordan, you will find glorious rest.' That is exactly what she did. She left and bought a few loaves of bread. She crossed the Jordan River into the desert and was there for forty years working out her salvation alone until the time that Zossima found her.

"It wasn't easy. In spite of how we sometimes want to think of these things, a person doesn't change completely because of one promise made in one instant. Mary had to fight many of her own demons."

Fr. Andrew went on in this vein because there was more of the story to tell. But Abigail didn't hear it — she was busy thinking about what had happened to St. Mary and how amazing it was. Imagine having such a bad heart and then coming to that realization and changing your life. Abigail looked over at the icon of St. Mary in the center of the church, and then at the cross in Fr. Andrew's hand.

This is what she had been supposed to hear this Sunday; Abigail was sure of it. She looked at the doodles she had made during the homily, and was pleased with them. She was sure they would help her recall the story. But what did it mean? Who was it for? Did she know anybody in that kind of situation? Abigail felt as though maybe answers would come to her in time, if she could just be ready to hear them.

THE REST OF THE SERVICE passed quickly for Abigail. Father Andrew gave an announcement at the end — something about how the schedule for confessions was going to be different this year — but Abigail was restless at that point and looked around to see if she could see where Photini had gone.

" … so that's it," said Fr. Andrew. "I regret that Father Boris and I will have to be hearing confessions closer to Pascha than usual, but as I said, there have been some unusual circumstances. And you all know that you will need to give confession before Pascha. So I'm counting on you to work within this schedule and not leave it too long."

Yes, yes, thought Abigail impatiently. She had gotten an idea, and it was making her anxious to leave. It occurred to her that the situation with Photini was very close to what she had been thinking about earlier in the week. Photini had made a big impression on everyone, and some people would probably be talking to her about it — wouldn't that be the perfect time for her to start mentioning the Every Tuesday Club? And if she was too nervous, Abigail could do it for her. But where was she?

"And of course, we'll be having an overnight session here at church for the children," added Fr. Andrew. "It's an excellent way to give them some instruction on confession and get them prepared. Father Boris and I will hear their confessions at the end of that time. That will happen next week on the day after — "

Abigail saw a girl who looked like Photini from the back and was about to make some little noise to get her attention, but when she turned around it was a visitor. Abigail craned her neck and tried again to see where she had gone, but the service was over and everyone stood and started shuffling forward to venerate the cross. Bet took Abigail's hand and started pulling on her.

"Oh … phooey," Abigail muttered, and let herself be dragged forward.

ONCE CHURCH HAD LET OUT, there was the usual steady increase of conversation and movement, and Abigail resigned herself to having to find Photini during coffee hour in the social hall. It seemed like a good plan, she reflected as she stood in the food line. She had glimpsed donuts at the food table and hoped she'd get there before the chocolate ones were all gone.

"Well, THERE she is! What a STAR!" boomed a voice in the crowd to her left, and it was followed with Mrs. Murphy's explosive laughter. Abigail turned around in time to see Mrs. Murphy and a few other people gathered around Photini.

"Phooey!" said Abigail again. This was exactly the moment she had been waiting for. It was very irritating to lose her place, but she made a split-second decision and stepped out of the food line.

The throng of people didn't make it very easy to get over to where the group was gathered, and the entire DeMarco family chose just that moment to cross in front of her. Abigail felt like she was waiting for the end of a train at a railroad crossing, but at last all of the toddlers, aunts and grandmothers had gotten out of the way and she could get by.

And just as the path before her cleared, she heard Mrs. Peasle asking Photini with great sincerity how in the world she had managed to conquer her shyness. Photini made some quiet answer that Abigail couldn't hear — undoubtedly she said something very timid and humble.

Well … fine. That would make it easier to mention the role the Club had in this great performance. But as Abigail stepped around the last person and stood where she could finally join the conversation, she looked up and saw Vanessa, who had been there the whole time.

"It's really not hard," Vanessa said to Mrs. Peasle with a brilliant smile. "It's a trick that my mother taught me. And I gave her my vocal exercises. My mother was a singer — did you know that?"

To Abigail's real annoyance, Mrs. Peasle said that she didn't, and Vanessa settled in to provide all the information anyone would ever want about her mother, the singer. No word of the Club or anyone else's help. As if Vanessa and her mother had done this all by themselves. Abigail turned away in disgust.

By the time Abigail got up to the food table, the chocolate donuts were all gone.

THE DRIVE HOME gave Abigail a chance to seethe in private. She buckled in and folded her arms and let her boiling temper overflow. It was unbelievable — really, really unbelievable. The Every Tuesday Girls Club had very likely achieved its third victory — three out of three! — and all Vanessa could think of was herself!

Abigail said the word "unbelievable" to herself again. It was satisfying to find just the words to express her righteous indignation. There was no way around it; she would have to start dealing with Vanessa head-on or there wouldn't be any Every Tuesday Girls Club left soon.

Maybe she could bring it up at the next meeting?

Abigail smacked her forehead. Of course! The next meeting! With Photini's problem solved, there was only one ballot left in the baggie — hers! Even Vanessa couldn't get around that. And Abigail would make certain that this time there was no distraction and none of Vanessa's annoying interruptions. Abigail would act like a Club president — she would even dress like one. She would wear the navy blue sweater, because it made her look older and more important.

"Mom," she said, leaning forward, "is my blue sweater back from the dry cleaners? I want to wear it Tuesday."

Her mother had to think for a minute. "Mmm, I think so. But what's on Tuesday?"

"The Club meeting."

Her mother looked confused. "But … we're not doing any of that this week or next, Abby. No one is having any meetings in church this close to Pascha."

Abigail felt a flutter of panic. "Well then, the Tuesday after that."

Her mother shook her head and glanced at her in the rear view mirror. "The week after next is Holy Week — the week before Pascha. There will be services every night."

Abigail looked at the back of the seat, trying to think fast. "Maybe we could … meet … anyway? This Tuesday, I mean? If maybe you'd drive us ?"

She was aware what a big favor that was to ask. Her mother shook her head again, but not for the reason Abigail thought.

"But you can't. Didn't you hear Father Andrew? There's an overnight session for the kids on Tuesday so you can give confession. Sorry, Abigail, you won't be able to have any more Club meetings until after Pascha."

Abigail felt the way she did that one time when she accidentally stuck a knife into the toaster — an electric jolt that left her breathless. She needed to get the icon of St. Abigail by Pascha — she always thought that somehow she would. She knew that Lent was going on and the time was getting short, but somehow she believed that it would happen. But now it wouldn't. The Club wouldn't meet again until Pascha was over, and she would have failed.

Unaware of the effect her words had on Abigail, Mrs. Alverson shrugged. "Oh well," her mother observed with a wry chuckle. "Maybe you can use the extra time to think about what you want to confess."

Chapter seventeen

What she wanted to confess?

Abigail had days to think about it, and the days didn't help. She felt angry, betrayed, disappointed, unhappy. She moped sometimes and stormed at other times. It was so unfair.

When Tuesday came, she had no idea what she was going to say when she went to confession. She listened to classes and did activities and tried not to think about what was really going on. *What do I have to confess?* she thought. *I'm not the one who has been acting rude and stuck-up.*

On top of everything else, it just didn't seem important right then. She had to try to think of what was going to happen to the Club. Would it still meet? Would the other girls see the point of it? How would they all get together? And was there any way to get Vanessa to stop ruining everything?

Abigail tried to participate in the activities with a good heart, but she felt pulled in different directions. She could tell that she was being short-tempered in the study groups, and she had a hard time behaving herself. Worse, there were groups where she and Vanessa were thrown in together, and she had a difficult time even being polite. She found ways to interrupt when Vanessa was talking, or distract everyone from what she was saying. Abigail had the feeling that glances were being exchanged between the different instructors, and eventually the two were put into different groups. Abigail was a little embarrassed about that, but she also felt a grim satisfaction. The less she was around Vanessa, the better.

At last, the event was nearly over. All she had left to do was give confession, and then she could go home and sulk in private. She still hadn't really thought of anything particularly good to confess.

Maybe Father Andrew can help me, she thought when her group was called into the church nave. They sat in pews waiting to go up one by one while different children read psalms. That covered the sound of voices and made the confessions private. At the front of the church, Fr. Andrew was on one side and Fr. Boris on the other. Both were in front of stands with a book open on it. In front of the stands were large icons to look at, if you wanted collect your thoughts. Abigail sighed and wondered how long until she got to go — she would have to wait her turn, but she was still feeling restless.

Maybe he'll talk with me and we can sort everything out. Maybe Father Andrew can tell me what to do so Vanessa stops getting everything her way.

That didn't sound like something Fr. Andrew would help her with, but it sounded even less like something that Fr. Boris would help her with. And unfortunately for Abigail, when it was her turn to go up, it was Fr. Boris who was free.

Abigail groaned to herself. It was never easy to talk to Fr. Boris. He had an accent, for one thing. But also, he wasn't nearly as friendly as Fr. Andrew. If only she had thought to switch places with someone else. But it was too late now. Father Boris's dark eyes were resting on her expectantly. He didn't bother to gesture, since he had his hands neatly tucked into the large sleeves of his vestments, but his heavy eyebrows lifted in a kind of silent request.

He looks like a cat, she thought, and then realized it wasn't very respectful to think a priest looked like a cat. Maybe that was something she could add to her confession, just to make it more interesting. No, probably not. Crossing demurely to the stand by Fr. Boris, she glanced up at his heavy features and decided that he wouldn't deal well with that last-minute addition.

CONFESSION BEGAN, as she knew, by reading the prayer out of the book on the stand. Which was a good start, Abigail thought. But then came that awkward time when you got to the blank place — at that point Fr. Boris settled his hands even more comfortably into his sleeves and prepared to hear the sins Abigail was confessing. Abigail looked at her fingers and at the icon and began telling Fr. Boris the bad things she was prepared to talk about. She told him about little spats she had

with Mark and times when she had been disrespectful to her mother and father — usually her mother — or not done what she was told. She wound it up with the time she had cheated in a card game with Bet. Father Boris listened to these things studiously and counseled her quietly, directing her with a few comments.

When Abigail thought they were done, Fr. Boris surprised her with a question. "Is there anyone else you not at peace with?"

With Fr. Boris's accent, sometimes Abigail didn't understand what he was saying. But this time it wasn't too hard. Anyone else she wasn't at peace with? Abigail thought that was a rather strange question, and didn't really want to answer it. But just to be polite, she paused as if she was thinking carefully, and then shook her head.

A kind of small grunt came from the depths of the priest's thin black beard. "What about Vanessa?"

Abigail stared at him in total surprise. "Vanessa!" She glanced around and lowered her voice. "Vanessa Taybeck? I'm fine with Vanessa. Why wouldn't I be?"

Father Boris shook his shaggy head very slowly. "I have seen. Vanessa and you — you and Vanessa. You are angry. Why is dis?"

It was no good. She could have kept fibbing if he hadn't asked her directly. But her emotions were too strong to hide, and she didn't want to. "She's so *bossy*," Abigail sputtered in a low whisper. "And she's *rude* to me all the time. I started a girls club on Tuesday — "

"Dis I know."

"You do? Oh."

"Yes. Father Andrew tell me. You start a church club for the girls, which is a good ting. But you do it for you, to get you a special icon. You don't tink dis is selfish?"

Abigail looked at him blankly, and after a second, he gave up the point. "No? Well, never mind for now. But tell me what happen with Vanessa?"

Abigail was still a little unsettled, but again her feelings boiled to the surface. "Well, she keeps trying to take the Club away from me. Vanessa always gets everyone to do what she says and — " Abigail floundered for a minute, realizing that the story of Vanessa pressing Photini to sing in church was too long to tell. "Well, ... I'm the president, that's all!"

Abigail wasn't sure that was a very good stopping place, but she was out of breath and she wanted to collect her thoughts a little better. Fr. Boris asked her another question, but it was so quiet, she had to ask him to repeat it.

"I say, do you tink you jealous?"

Jealous! Abigail's mouth dropped open in disbelief. What kind of a thing was that to say? Weren't priests supposed to be helpful?

Father Boris regarded her mildly. "Jealousy is very strong, Abigail. Do you know what de Bible say about jealousy? King Solomon, he say in the Book of Proverbs, 'Anger is cruel and fury overwhelming, but who can stand before jealousy?'"

King Solomon again! Abigail was annoyed. Why did he always follow her around?

"I'm not jealous of Vanessa," she protested. "I can't be. I try to be good, and she doesn't. She's ... she's like Mary before she prayed!"

The heavy eyebrows lifted in perplexity. "Mary before she pray?" he repeated in confusion.

Abigail suddenly wished she hadn't said that, but she had to answer the question. "Like Saint Mary of Egypt. Before she repented and went off into the desert. She pushed people around with her elbows, but she couldn't get into the church. Vanessa is like that."

Father Boris's throat rumbled disapprovingly. "Be careful what you say, Abigail. Dis is a very serious ting. It is very bad to say other people more sinful dan you. And you say dis at confession?" He tutted in deep consternation.

Abigail's gaze fell to the carpet, but she wasn't ready to give up her point. "But it's true," she glowered. "She calls me names. She calls me Queen Abigail the Wise just to make me mad. And she cheated with the baggie and ballots that we — well, she just cheated. And then, last week after church, she was bragging — I heard her." As briefly as she could, Abigail sketched out the conversation she overheard last Sunday.

Father Boris closed his eyes as if picturing what had happened. "So you try to get to Photini …" he said.

"Yes, but I couldn't get through in time. People kept getting in the way. And then Vanessa — "

"So den," Fr. Boris said, opening his eyes, "You sure that *you* aren't like Saint Mary before she pray? Like you say, Saint Mary couldn't get through the crowd because her heart too hard. You sure is not how *you* were?"

Abigail felt stunned. She wanted to be insulted, but Fr. Boris's question took her breath away. Was she like that? Was she the one who had been hard-hearted?

"But Vanessa is always so mean to me," she said feebly.

"And you are always nice to her?"

Abigail made herself look Fr. Boris in the eye. She was unsure if he wanted an answer, and she felt suddenly ashamed. He was looking at her expectantly.

"No," Abigail replied truthfully. "I did try to be nice at first, but she made me feel stupid and immature."

"Dis is hard," Fr. Boris admitted. "But still, is not right to say someone else is bad and make up tings."

Abigail almost nodded automatically, but she stopped herself. "Make up things? What things?"

Father Boris took a hand out of his sleeve to wave dismissively. "When you say Vanessa is cheating and so."

"But — "

"We will say no more of dis. Read two chapters of the Book of Proverbs — dis is how you make a penance. Remember to say you prayers every night. And most of all, remember dat jealousy is very bad ting."

And before she could utter another word, Fr. Boris laid his stole over her and solemnly began the prayer of absolution in his deep voice. "O Lord God, salvation of your servants, gracious, bountiful and long-suffering… "

ABIGAIL LEFT the confessional stand feeling dazed. It had been very irritating for Fr. Boris to think that she had lied about Vanessa's cheating. But when she searched her heart, she had to admit that it wasn't what Fr. Boris had gotten wrong that bothered her the most — it was what he had gotten right.

What if you are like St. Mary before she pray?

Abigail's halting steps slowed and then stopped. Near the door was an icon of the Theotokos — the Mother of God — that glittered in the candlelight. Abigail stopped beside it, her eyes still fixed on the carpet. The murmur of voices in church soothed her — the low sounds of others giving confession and an altarboy reading a psalm that she heard often in church. She heard the words of the psalm without really trying to understand them. *"Create in me a clean heart, and renew a right spirit within me."*

All week, Abigail had been angry about the ways Vanessa had offended her, but now Abigail couldn't help remembering things she had said and done. Fr. Boris had asked if starting the Club just to get what she wanted had been selfish — maybe it was. And she had been acting so snippy and unkind to Vanessa lately. How embarrassing it seemed, now that she came to think about it. Maybe Fr. Boris was right — maybe she was jealous. Abigail didn't like feeling ashamed, but she had to admit that it was still better than feeling cranky and superior. She was glad to be free of the itchy, angry feelings that had been bothering her, but Abigail knew she still needed to figure out how to do better. If she didn't do something to change how she and Vanessa acted around each other, she would end up arguing with her again and again. Sighing, she pushed open the door and left the somber nave.

THE LIGHT AND NOISE of the narthex took a moment to adjust to. Square windows over the door let in white sunlight that made rectangles on the carpet. People moved about by themselves and in groups — cleaning, chatting, gathering — doing any of the other little jobs that always needed doing. In a way, it didn't seem quite real. And it seemed even more unreal when Vanessa came in from one side and stood facing forward, standing on tiptoe to see into the bookstore. Imagine the one person that Abigail had been thinking about just being there like that.

Talk to her.

Abigail was sorry that her still, small voice chose that moment to say something. Talk to Vanessa? She was so ashamed of herself, she didn't feel like she'd know where to begin. Searching for inspiration, she noticed a glint on the floor and stepped forward to find a quarter.

Abigail looked at it in surprise when a motion caught her eye and she saw another quarter drop behind Vanessa and land noiselessly on the thick burgundy carpet.

Well, that solves the problem of what to say, Abigail thought with relief. Vanessa was still focused on what was going on in the bookstore, so Abigail stooped to pick up the second quarter and tapped Vanessa lightly.

To her shock, Vanessa gave a gasp and clutched at the notebook she was holding. "I'm sorry!" Abigail blurted, holding the quarters out in front of her. "I wasn't trying to scare you. You dropped these."

Vanessa gaped at them as if she had never seen quarters before. "They're not mine," she said, biting the words off through tight lips. "You keep them."

Abigail looked at the coins in confusion. "What? No, they're yours. They fell out of your purse," she said helpfully, pointing to the green leather bag that was sticking out of Vanessa's spiral bound notebook.

Vanessa grabbed at the purse suddenly, but the abrupt motion dislodged the slick bag entirely. It flipped out of the notebook and landed on Abigail's foot, spilling another quarter and a few dollars. Abigail hastened to tell Vanessa that it was okay as she stooped down. It was kind of a relief to know that Vanessa sometimes had clumsy days, and Abigail gathered everything up quickly so Vanessa wouldn't have to feel awkward.

The purse was a funny square-ish thing with a white eagle on it, but Abigail tried to think of a compliment as she held it out. "That's a nice purse. It's a cool color." Vanessa didn't move, and Abigail struggled for something else to say. "The zipper is broken, though. I think that's why money is falling out."

Staring at Abigail intently, Vanessa took the purse in a slow, steady motion and put it firmly under her arm. "Thanks," she mumbled. She still seemed unable to move and Abigail detected again that distress she sometimes noticed in Vanessa. Maybe giving confession had been difficult for her as well. Fr. Boris had said that both of them were angry.

"Vanessa," Abigail heard herself say, "I kind of … I want to apologize. I don't think I've been very nice to you and — "

"That's okay," Vanessa interrupted quickly, glancing around.

"I'm sorry, though." Abigail felt as if she had to finish.

Vanessa had still been standing and looking around, but she suddenly snapped into motion. "Not a problem!" she said, pivoting to elbow through a cluster of people. A moment later, Abigail saw a quick slice of white daylight as the side door opened, and Vanessa was gone.

Not a problem? What a strange thing to say. But in any case, she had done it — she had apologized, and she felt better for it. The narthex didn't seem like a very interesting place to be in, especially since there was some agitated conversation breaking out in the bookstore. Abigail threaded her way through the fussy crowd and popped open the front door, feeling the cool, fresh air on her face.

Abigail squinted up at the afternoon light. The rains and frosts of April had let up at last, and the sky didn't have that flat, iron-gray look to it. Abigail's gaze followed the path of three geese that were flying over the trees. Maybe it would be sunny for Palm Sunday.

And it was. But as it turned out, Abigail wasn't there to see it.

Chapter eighteen

It started on Friday evening. Abigail was drawing and Mark checked homework while a television show was on. Abigail's father remarked how quiet it was, and Mrs. Alverson put down the check-book and agreed. "It's almost too quiet," she said. "Why does it feel like that?"

Mr. Alverson shrugged and they glanced idly around the room trying to figure out what was different. It was Mrs. Alverson whose perceptive eyes lit on the answer first. Little Bet, who would usually have been running around, getting in front of the TV, crawling on laps and asking questions, was just sitting in her chair with a dull expression on her face. Abigail's mother took in the glazed eyes and slack jaw thoughtfully and rose from the couch.

"I'm going to make some cocoa and marshmallows," she said lightly. "Who wants some?"

Abigail and Mark immediately registered interest and added requests for extra marshmallows and a favorite cup. But Bet was still just blinking heavily at the television.

With her concern slightly raised, Mrs. Alverson drew closer to her. "Bet? You want cocoa?"

Bet stirred sleepily and shook her head. "No," she replied. "Too hot."

Mrs. Alverson got down on one knee so she could feel Bet's forehead and cheeks with the back of her hand. "You are warm. How do you feel?"

At this point, Abigail left off her drawing. Mark and her father watched Bet consider the question solemnly. "Mm. Okay." Bet answered. And as an afterthought, she added, "But when I swallow, it's all rough."

Mr. Alverson sat forward on the couch. "It hurts when you swallow?"

Bet nodded with grave, round eyes. "Yeah."

Her parents looked at each other. Mark and Abigail looked at each other. Everyone knew what that meant.

Sure enough, even with children's aspirin for the fever and fruit popsicles to cool her throat, Bet was worse the next day, and it was obvious that she had picked up a bad cold. Her temperature went up and she alternated between lying limply in bed and ambling around fitfully without being able to settle anywhere. Worse, as Saturday progressed, Abigail's father started getting a flushed face and a sniffly nose. Though he insisted he didn't have time to be sick, he was quarantined to the bedroom with a room heater to ward off chills, and Mrs. Alverson announced that the family was staying home from church. Mark protested briefly and Abigail thought unhappily of the Palm Sunday procession she would miss. But their mother had a look in her eye that made it clear there was no point in arguing.

So the family stayed home for the weekend of Palm Sunday. Mr. Alverson recovered quickly and Bet began to look a little more bouncy. But Abigail found herself slowing down and having trouble finishing her school work. She hoped that it was just boredom from being stuck inside all weekend, but when she woke up Tuesday morning, her throat felt raw and a ragged pain made her wince when she swallowed. Mrs. Alverson took one look and fished through the medicine cabinet for the thermometer.

At first, it wasn't so bad. Abigail didn't like the roughness in her throat, but her mother kept her supplied with fruit popsicles that took the edge off the pain and turned her tongue red or blue. It was different once her temperature began to rise. She couldn't pay attention to books or games and just ended up on the couch watching old videos with a blanket wrapped tightly around her.

It was a very strange couple of days. Abigail had a harder time getting rid of the fever than her sister did, and she found herself sleeping on and off without really knowing what time it was. Her father and Mark read to her and played games, and even Bet would come and cuddle up quietly, but Abigail still felt weak and uncomfortable.

It didn't help to think that it was Holy Week and there were services going on at church that she was missing. Mr. Alverson felt well enough to take Mark off to the Bridegroom Service on Tuesday night, and they described for her how the church had been darkened and one chanter sang a haunting song that was only sung at that time of the year: *Behold, the Bridegroom cometh at midnight, and blessed is the servant whom He shall find awake …*

The next night was Holy Wednesday, and Mr. Alverson stayed home with Abigail while the others went to the Holy Unction service.

"What happens at the Holy Unction service?" she asked him from the recesses of her blanket after everyone had gone and the house was still again.

Mr. Alverson put down his cell phone. "This is when you're anointed with holy oil. You've seen it before."

Abigail tried to think back to last year but gave up. "I don't remember," she sniffed.

"Well," Mr. Alverson said, moving to the couch, "there are special prayers said over a container of oil to consecrate it — to make it into holy oil. The service talks about what was happening in the days before Jesus was crucified, but it also focuses a lot on sickness and healing. Do you remember what happens next?" Abigail looked at him uncertainly, so he answered for her. "People come forward one by one and they are anointed with the holy oil. The priest dips a cotton swab into the oil and dabs it here and here and here." He gently traced the sign of the cross on Abigail's forehead and her mouth and her throat. "And on your hands. Do you remember now?"

Abigail looked vague. "On the backs and palms of your hands. I remember. And the oil can help make you well? I should have gone to the service and then maybe I'd get better."

Her father kissed her forehead and looked at her critically. "Judging from how much soup you were able to finish off tonight, I think maybe you are getting better. But as it so happens, your mom will be bringing a cotton swab soaked in holy oil home with her. After she gets here, we'll anoint you as well." Her father adjusted the blanket for her and tucked loose hair behind her ears.

She got quiet for a minute. "I just feel like I'm missing out on a lot of stuff. There's so much that happens this week."

Mr. Alverson looked at her sympathetically. "You'll have a lot of other years to see it. But you don't have to miss so much. Remember some of the videos I made last year with my cell phone? Here, I'll find them for you. It's not everything, of course, but there are some pretty special moments in there. Holy Wednesday, Holy Thursday ... here it is. Look, you can play some of these and you'll feel like you were there."

Abigail cradled the phone carefully. It was a rare privilege to get to handle her father's cell phone, and she didn't want to do anything wrong. He showed her how to start and stop the videos, and she held the screen close to her face, taking in candles and prayers and songs on the small screen as best she could. When she started to feel sleepy again, she just tucked the phone by her ear so she could hear her favorite hymn from the services.

It ended up later that it was a very good thing that she did.

ABIGAIL DIDN'T THINK she had been asleep long, but she woke up when the door opened. Bet had gone to sleep in church and was carried up to her room, but Mark stayed with Abigail and told her things about the service. He pulled a baggie out of his pocket with an important air and showed her the cotton swab with a tip darkened by the amber oil. Pointing to the shiny place where the oil had touched his forehead, he said, "Can you smell it? It smells like roses."

Abigail couldn't smell it with her stuffy head, even when her parents came back and pulled the cotton swab out for her. Her father read the prayer for the sick from a book while her mother lifted her bangs out of the way and lightly daubed on the holy oil on her forehead, mouth, throat and hands, making the sign of the cross as she went. When she was finished, Abigail surveyed her hands curiously, tilting them in the light to see the streaky marks of the oil.

"I don't feel any different," she reported.

"That's okay, Abigail," said her mother, replacing the swab in its baggie and gathering Abigail up in a hug. "There are miraculous healings sometimes with holy oil, but getting better in the normal way is still a kind of miracle, right?"

Abigail had been hoping for something dramatic, but she had to admit that the prayer and the oil did feel kind of special.

As it turned out, there was a real improvement shortly afterward. In the middle of the night, she suddenly got very hot and threw off all the extra blankets to keep from getting sweaty. It made her think of sick people she had seen in old movies, but her mother smiled brightly when she looked in on her in the morning. "Oh, the fever broke. How do you feel now?"

Abigail realized she felt better than she had in two days. "I don't feel all hot now. And I'm not as achy."

"Are you hungry?"

Abigail looked at her in surprise, but didn't have to think about this question for long. "Yes!" she said forcefully. "I want orange juice and toast."

"Lucky for us then that we happen to have orange juice and toast. But first things first. If you're well enough to get breakfast, you're well enough to help me put this bedding into the laundry."

Abigail bounded up but then felt dizzy and fell back onto the bed.

"Careful, sweetie," cautioned her mother. "Feeling a little better isn't quite the same thing as being all better. Just take it easy today and let yourself get mended up."

ABIGAIL'S MOTHER was usually right in matters of health and well-being, and this time was no exception. Although she was tired of being sick and ready to get back to all her normal activities, the fact was that Abigail still wasn't quite herself. The soreness in her throat was gone and her temperature came back down to normal by mid-afternoon. But her stuffy head still kept her from being able to breathe easily. and she wasn't ready yet to go out and play with Bet and Mark.

The inactivity bothered her most of all. She wasn't as sick as she had been and she was starting to get restless being in the house. Usually, she enjoyed a chance to just keep to herself and doodle or play games, but her room and the living room couch were starting to feel like all she had seen for the past week.

"Is there a service tonight?" she asked her mother fussily after she had finished a word puzzle.

"It's Holy Thursday," replied Mrs. Alverson. "The service of the 12 Gospel Readings is tonight. But I don't think you should go, Abigail. It's a very long service, and I don't quite think you're up to it yet."

Abigail didn't relish the thought of being at home for another night while others were out seeing the church all lit with candles and perfumed by incense. She briefly considered trying to wear her mother down, but Mrs. Alverson seemed to read her mind. "Not tonight, Abigail. We can go to the afternoon service on Holy Friday — it's shorter. And then there are still services on Friday night and

Saturday morning, and the Pascha service late Saturday night. You won't miss out." Her mother stroked her hair gently. "Besides, we've got a little surprise for you."

Abigail glanced up inquisitively, but her mother held up her hand. "You won't get me to tell. It's a surprise. But we're going to have some company, so let's tidy up a bit."

With that incentive, Abigail would have gladly have picked up the clutter without being asked twice. Very shortly, the living room and her bedroom were cleared of signs of sick days and everything was in decent order when the doorbell rang. That sound, of course, brought Bet bouncing into the kitchen, but Mrs. Alverson insisted that Abigail should be the one to open the door. In happy anticipation, she pulled it open wide to reveal Mrs. Jenkins and Mrs. Peasle smiling at her in the bright morning light. And in front of them, a sight that made her smile for the first time in days — Xenia and Photini and Maggie.

Chapter nineteen

"What else has happened?"

Abigail was lying on her bed with Xenia and Maggie while Photini sat on the desk chair. They had finished off one box of popsicles and all of their lips were different colors. Best of all, they had been telling Abigail all the little things they could think of to catch her up with the news.

Photini had led off. She had seen the pages for her reading on Holy Saturday, and to her great relief, they were using a different translation so that she wouldn't have to try to say the dreaded word "sackbut". That was just as well, because even having to say it one time in Abigail's room made them all start giggling again. But they stopped when they realized that it hurt Abigail's throat to laugh, and Maggie tried to think of something else to talk about.

"Ummm." Maggie took the popsicle stick out of her mouth. "Did we tell you that Mrs. Moore is going to have another baby? We did? And we told you that they almost forgot to get eggs to dye red for

Pascha. Hmm. What else?"

Xenia said something, but it was muffled by the popsicle and she had to take it out of her mouth and repeat it. "I said, the bookstore thing."

Photini discarded her popsicle wrapper tidily. "Abigail knows all about that, Xenia. Father Andrew told everybody on Saturday."

Abigail glanced around. "But we weren't there on Saturday. What's the bookstore thing?"

"Oh!" cried Photini with a shiver of excitement. "You don't know? No one told you?"

"Told me what?" asked Abigail, feeling a little stupid.

Xenia was about to answer, but Photini hushed her with a sharp yip and turned to Abigail. "You'll never guess," Photini burbled in delight. That left Abigail uncertain whether she was supposed to try to guess or not, but Photini couldn't stand the suspense any longer and burst out the news. "Somebody robbed the bookstore!"

Abigail's jaw dropped open and Photini nodded vigorously.

"They did what?!" Abigail exclaimed. "They robbed the bookstore?" She turned to Maggie for confirmation, not because she really thought that Photini would make up anything like that, but just out of sheer disbelief.

Maggie-May inclined her head sadly. "That's right."

Abigail still couldn't believe it. "You mean somebody broke into the church and — "

Maggie and Photini both said "no" to that, but Photini got there first. "No," she repeated. "Nobody broke in. It was someone from *church* that did it." She shook her head as if it was the first time she had heard the news. "Isn't that terrible?"

"Do they know who did it?"

"No," answered Maggie gravely. "Father made an announcement on Saturday and again on Sunday. He said that someone took all the bookstore's money sometime last week. No one's sure exactly when they did it because no one had checked on the bookstore for a while. But they sold some jewelry last month so there was a lot of money in the store. It was over 300 dollars."

"Three hundred and eleven dollars and eight-five cents," corrected Xenia, still sucking thoughtfully on the popsicle.

Abigail frowned at her. "How can you be so sure of the amount?" Everyone knew that the sisters who ran the bookstore were notoriously disorganized with the money.

"That's the good part," chimed Photini. "Whoever it was didn't get away with it. Subdeacon Philip found the money all in a pile in the kitchen, so the thief must have wanted to hide it but had to run away."

Xenia made a disapproving face. "That is such a dumb place to try to hide money. If I had stolen $311.85, I would have gone someplace quiet."

Photini was scandalized. "Xenia!"

Xenia regarded her mildly. "Well … I'm just saying … "

"I still don't understand," said Abigail. "If they have the money back, why make an announcement? Maybe the money wasn't even stolen — maybe it was just an honest mistake."

"Father gave the announcement because he wants the person who did it to come forward," explained Maggie. "He said if anyone knows about it, they should come directly to him — no one else. And they know it wasn't an accident because whoever did it broke the lock to get at the money. It's a heavy lock — you'd have to use a hammer or something. The bookstore sisters are kind of mad about that, too. They're going to have to have the whole thing replaced, and it's expensive."

It was just alarming to think that anyone in church possibly could have done such a thing. There was something about it all that just seemed ... Abigail sat forward again and tossed her popsicle stick into the trash.

"There's something really strange about this," she muttered. Her eyes felt tired from the glare of her desk lamp and she rubbed them distractedly.

"We should probably go," said Photini sympathetically. "Your mom said it was okay for us to come, but she told us not to wear you out."

"What? No, I'm fine," said Abigail, but Xenia was rising as well.

"I got a ride with them," she said, hooking her thumb toward Photini. "My mom couldn't bring me, and we wanted everyone to be here."

Abigail smiled. "Everyone?"

"Everyone in the Club," said Xenia flatly, and Abigail felt Maggie give a start. She turned to her in surprise, but Maggie waved in a flustered way and said nothing.

"Well," Abigail said in mild confusion. "Thank you. I mean, really. I had been kind of bored, and I'm glad everyone could be here. Or almost everyone." She suddenly realized who was missing. "Where's Vanessa, by the way?"

Maggie answered quickly that Vanessa hadn't been able to get free, but not before Abigail saw alarm flash across Photini's pale face.

"Oh," Abigail said uncertainly. "Well, anyway, I'm really glad you guys could come."

"We were glad to," Photini said with a nervous quickness. And then she seemed to stop and relax. "We really were, Abigail. It was so sad you ended up home sick this week. You've helped all of us with our problems and —"

"What was your problem, anyway?" asked Xenia with her usual bluntness.

Abigail tried to pretend that she didn't know what they meant, but she was touched to find that the others had noticed that she had been passed by. After everything that had happened in the past week, Abigail no longer felt hurt and disappointed about the whole thing, but she did feel a little silly. With a wry grin, she showed them the drawing she had done of St. Abigail and tried to describe the real icon to them.

"You should have seen it," she said with feeling. "It was so beautiful. I thought if I could just have a real icon done from that one, it would help me with all the things I wanted to get right in church. Maybe I'd pay attention more and not get into trouble so much with my mom. I thought maybe I'd feel like I had someone to talk to … or something. So that was my problem. I wanted help to get that icon."

"How could we help with that?" Xenia inquired.

Abigail shrugged. "I don't know. Father Andrew told me it costs hundreds of dollars to have an icon made and I thought maybe we could think of a way to raise money. Father Andrew was actually going to help me get it, but … " She looked up wistfully. "I kind of think he forgot."

"Well …" Xenia handed back her drawing. "It sounds like a really cool icon. Maybe we could build something to make money. Maybe we could build a game to play on cell phones. I've played a lot of games — I wonder if it's hard to make one … " Xenia had been heading out the door as she spoke, and by the time she got to the stairs, they couldn't hear her anymore.

"Xenia," muttered Photini, her exasperation tinged with affection. And then, "Xenia! Wait. You've got my sweater. Hold up!" and she followed her out.

The door shut behind her, leaving Maggie and Abigail chuckling.

A slightly awkward pause followed, and then Maggie rose from the bed.

"Well, I should probably get going as well," she said. But she didn't leave.

Abigail didn't like the tension between them. She couldn't think of a good way to bring up what was on her mind, so she just said it: "I apologized to Vanessa."

"What?" said Maggie in astonishment. "You did? When?"

"After confession on Wednesday."

"But … why?"

"Because I had been such a jerk to her — trying to cut her down and being rude. I didn't mean it, really. She just made me so mad. But Father Boris helped me see some stuff when I went to confession and … well, I just wanted you to know. I could tell that I was really bothering you."

"No, you weren't. Well … " Maggie shook her head. "I mean, yes. It did bother me at the time. You're right, I thought you were kind of out of line. But, it turned out you weren't totally wrong." She flumped herself down on the desk chair and pulled it forward. "Oh Abigail. Vanessa is the one who should apologize, not you. I was mad at you.

But that was before …"

She hesitated and then exhaled and plunged into a story. "When we heard that you were out sick, all of us wanted to come and see you, because you had done so much for us. And I invited Vanessa because she is a member of the Club, even if she pretends like she's not."

Abigail nodded. "Yes, she is."

"But Abigail, she was awful to us. She turned her nose up and told us she had better things to do. And when Photini and I asked her again later, she threw a total hissy fit about it. She yelled at us, and she pushed Photini so hard, she almost knocked her down. It was crazy!"

Abigail was speechless. She would've been terribly hurt that Vanessa disliked her that much, but to get so angry about it just seemed bizarre.

"Why would she do that?" Abigail asked.

Maggie rolled her eyes. "Who knows? Nothing she said made any sense. There's always something that's so weird about Vanessa, don't you think?"

Abigail had thought that more than once, but she wanted to know how it struck Maggie. "How do you mean?" she asked.

"Well," Maggie frowned. "She can be really cool sometimes and not snooty. It's easy to like her when she's being funny, and she really is kind of smart about some things. But then there are other times … well!" She blew out her cheeks and leaned in close to Abigail. "It's not nice to say," Maggie-May whispered. "But sometimes Vanessa is a real pain in the rear end."

"I know," Abigail whispered back. And they both giggled merrily.

Maggie got up again and this time it seemed like she really would leave. "I just can't figure Vanessa out. It's like with that thing that I messaged you about."

Abigail glanced at her computer. "What thing?"

"A couple weeks ago. Oh, that's right, you never answered me. Well, do you remember back when we were in the Club meeting where you guys helped me with Baby Jacob? And I got so mad and … well, you remember. But here's the thing: When I grabbed Jacob and left, just as I was closing the door, I saw Vanessa just staring at me. With this … look."

"What kind of look?" Abigail pressed.

"I don't know. It's hard to explain. Everyone else was just surprised, but Vanessa was looking at me in this totally intense way. It's difficult to put into words."

Abigail frowned. "That's weird. The Sunday after that, I saw her looking at you and Baby Jacob. Just staring, really."

"What could that mean?"

Abigail tried for a minute to understand, but shook her head. "I have no idea."

Maggie stopped with her hand on the doorknob for a minute and considered. "Me neither," she said. "But I can't stop thinking about it. That's what I mean about Vanessa. For someone who said she didn't have any problems, she sure has given a lot to us.

"But then," Maggie continued in a lighter tone. "I guess that's what we do, right? In the Every Tuesday Girls Club? We solve problems."

Maggie smiled and Abigail smiled back.

"See you tomorrow," she said.

"Bye 'til then," Abigail returned.

After the door was closed, Abigail blew her nose and lay back in bed with the drawing of St. Abigail in front of her.

We solve problems.

"But how do you solve problems for someone that says they don't have any?" she wondered out loud. St. Abigail didn't have an answer to that, and neither did Abigail.

ABIGAIL WAS STILL THINKING about the situation when she got to church the next day. What if she bumped into Vanessa and she was rude to her? And what was Vanessa so mad about anyway? Hadn't she apologized and everything? But there wasn't really anything Abigail could do about it, and anyway, she was just glad to be able to leave the house and see her first Holy Week service.

It was the afternoon service called The Taking Down from the Cross, and as her mother had told her, it wasn't nearly as long as most of the evening services that week. Abigail looked around the church and felt like she hadn't seen it in weeks. It was light and quiet. A few candles flickered in the candle boxes — prayers offered up to God. In the center of the church was a large wooden cross about as tall as her dad with an icon on the cross that was a figure of Jesus Christ crucified. It was cut out in the shape of His body and fit onto nails on the cross. Abigail came near it and venerated it with everyone else before the service, but she found that she couldn't look at it for very long.

During the service, Subdeacon Philip read the words of the prophet Isaiah, words written hundreds of years before Jesus was born. "Surely, he has borne our griefs and carried our sorrows; yet we esteemed him stricken, smitten by God, and afflicted. But he was wounded for our transgressions, he was bruised for our iniquities … with his stripes we were healed." Abigail remembered that the first time she had heard that, she hadn't understood, but her mother explained that the "stripes" the prophet was talking about were the nail wounds and the scars from being flogged.

She glanced at the icon again, and looked away. It was so hard to think about. Could someone else's wounds heal you? She knew that Jesus Christ was perfect. He was God's only Son, and He never committed any sins. So could the things that He did perfectly — even His perfect death on the Cross — fix what was broken in everyone else?

After the Gospel readings, Fr. Boris removed the figure of Christ from the wooden cross and took it away. A cloth was draped over the cross that symbolized the cloth wrappings that Jesus was buried in. The empty cross would remain where it was, Abigail knew, until Saturday night. And late on Saturday night, nearly at midnight, they would begin the Pascha service, and the service would echo and re-echo with joy. This year especially, Abigail could hardly wait. She felt like she had learned a lot this year during Lent and Holy Week, but there had been some parts of it that had been difficult, and she was looking forward to the brighter days of Pascha.

As the service finished up, people shuffled about and formed a line to venerate the cross before leaving. Xenia saw her and gave a solemn wave without smiling. Abigail waved back and then caught a sudden movement out of the corner of her eye. In the crowd behind Xenia, she saw that Vanessa was standing with her family. But she had scrunched down behind her older brother James, and as Abigail watched, she actually moved her little brother Noah in front of her so that she was almost hidden from sight. Did she really not even want Abigail to be able to see her? Abigail still couldn't figure out what she possibly could've done to make Vanessa so mad at her.

She didn't want to think about it right then. The church service had felt really special to her, and she didn't want to spoil it with silly stuff. She venerated the cross by kissing it lightly and then walked into the narthex.

The Friday afternoon service wasn't as crowded as the evening services, and Abigail was happy to find less people milling around. With any luck, maybe she would be able to stay just long enough to say hello to Maggie and the others without her mother getting pulled away to meet with people or do an errand.

But when she saw her mother, Abigail realized that that's exactly what had happened. Mrs. Alverson was walking up with a gentle old lady who always seemed to have things for people to do around the church. She had a shopping bag with some of the altarboys' vestments sticking out of it, and her mother handed it to Abigail as the old lady thanked Mrs. Alverson kindly and moved off to find other people.

"We can go in a minute," said Mrs. Alverson, switching her purse to the other arm and looking through it for keys. "But can you take that to the car for me? I have to talk to Mrs. Murphy for a minute."

Abigail's heart sank. She knew there was no such thing as talking to loud Mrs. Murphy for one minute. But whining probably wouldn't help, so she took the shopping bag and sifted through the clothing. "What are these?" she asked glumly.

"Just some things that need repair. Some of the stitches came out of one stole and — "

Abigail felt something smooth and slick and lifted it free of the clothing. "And what is — ?" And she stopped in mid-sentence.

"What's … " Mrs. Alverson looked over. "Oh, that. Well … " She looked embarrassed. "That's the bank pouch from the bookstore. It's made out of leather, but Miss Dermond wanted me to see if I could possibly fix the zipper. See how it's torn?"

Abigail turned it carefully in her hand and traced the ripped zipper. "The … bank pouch? This is what the bookstore money was in? But … I thought that they broke a lock. I thought a padlock was on a box or a drawer or something."

Her mother nodded sadly. "So your friends told you what happened? Yes, whoever did this broke the lock, but it was the lock on this pouch. See?" She pointed to a heavy metal lock at the top corner of the leather pouch that would keep the zipper closed if it was locked. But the lock had been smashed until it gave way and then the zipper had been wrenched open. Abigail stared at it.

"This is what they put the bookstore money in?" she whispered.

"Uh huh," said her mother busily. "Oh, I see Donna. Here are the keys. Just wait for me in the car — I won't be long." Placing the keys on top of the leather pouch, Mrs. Alverson hailed Mrs. Murphy quickly and the two disappeared in the direction of the social hall.

Abigail looked at the bank pouch in wonder. She lifted the car keys off it delicately and held it up by one corner.

"I've seen this before," said Abigail, to no one in particular. A square-ish green leather bag with a white emblem of an eagle on it and a ripped zipper at the top. This is what Vanessa had been carrying on Wednesday night, when she had been acting so nervous.

This is what Abigail had mistaken for Vanessa's purse.

Chapter twenty

"But you'll definitely come?"

"Photini, I said I'll *try* to come."

Maggie had been dawdling behind the rest of her family with Jacob when Photini had come up to her. She knew immediately that Photini was going to ask her to stay and listen to her rehearse her solo, and she wasn't sure that she could.

"But you said — "

"I said I'd stay if I can. But Violet has to get to work and my mom does, too."

Holding Maggie's book bag for her, Photini walked ahead and held the door open. "Maybe you can get a ride with us," she said, tossing her hair nervously. "Or with Abigail's mom? I think they're staying for a bit."

Maggie followed Photini out into the narthex and spied Abigail standing by herself. "Well, that would work, I guess. Abigail, is your mom going to stay for a bit?"

Abigail turned to her as if she hadn't understood the question.

"Oh wait!" Photini smacked her forehead. "Xenia's mom is staying, because the choir has to rehearse. Let me go get Xenia and see what she says."

Maggie chuckled as Photini sprinted back into church. "She really wants some moral support for the solo she has to do tomorrow. Vanessa helped her last time, but …"

"I've seen this before," said Abigail.

"Seen what?" Maggie stopped fiddling with her book bag and her eyes fell to the green pouch in Abigail's hand. "What's that?"

"It's the thing that the bookstore money was in."

Maggie saw her stricken look and frowned. "Oh. The money pouch the bank gave them." She lifted it out of Abigail's open hand and examined it curiously. "Oh, look. The lock is smashed and …" She sighed and handed it back. "It's like I said. The bookstore ladies say it'll be expensive to replace. I hope your mom can at least fix the zipper."

"Maggie," Abigail said with added urgency. "I've seen it before."

Maggie nodded patiently. "Well, so have I. Nathan and I helped out once with the bookstore, and — "

"No, not like that," Abigail hissed. "I saw it like this. I saw it when it was broken. She was carrying it in a notebook."

Maggie's hazel eyes locked on hers with sudden intelligence. "Who was?"

"Vanessa."

"Oh good news!" came a sharp voice from the church door. Photini emerged dragging Xenia along by her sleeve. "Mrs. Murphy is staying, so everyone can hear me rehearse and — "

Maggie held her hand up. "Photini, hold on. Abigail, what did you say?"

Her eyes flicking to Photini and Xenia, Abigail hesitated. "Um … "

Abigail wasn't sure she wanted to finish this conversation in front of the other two girls, but Maggie persisted. "Did you say that you saw Vanessa with this? With the bookstore pouch?"

Photini eyed the pouch with its broken lock and took in the significance of the statement immediately. "When?" she asked.

Abigail sighed. There didn't seem like much point in evading the question. "Last Wednesday."

"Where?" inquired Xenia.

"Well, kind of … here. I was standing just about where you are. And Vanessa came from the short hallway," Abigail said as she waved the pouch over her shoulder.

Xenia swiveled around to peer into the dark hallway behind her. "From the short hallway?" she repeated incredulously.

"She was — " Abigail looked down at the money pouch, fingering the edges of the torn zipper. It suddenly looked like such a pitiful little thing. "She was carrying it in a notebook, and it fell out onto the floor. I mean, some money had fallen out of it — "

"Some *money* had fallen out of it?" repeated Photini in shocked tones.

"Yes, just … just some quarters, I think." Abigail shut her eyes and tried to remember. "And a dollar or something. I wanted to give it back to her, but I startled her. And this dropped out on the floor." Abigail looked at it again. "So I picked it up for her. I thought it was her purse."

Xenia lifted it up to the light while Photini drew in a long breath.

"Oh. My. Gosh," said Photini with feeling.

Maggie gave her a quick glance. "Abigail, are you sure? I mean, maybe this was before the money got taken. Could it have been another day?"

Abigail shook her head. "No, it was Wednesday. It was just after I gave my confession. Besides," she said sadly, turning the pouch over for the others to see, "I saw that the zipper was broken. I told her I thought that's why the money was falling out."

Photini stared at her, open-mouthed. "What did she do next?"

Abigail thought briefly about her apology and Vanessa's strange reply. Come to think of it, a lot of Vanessa's behavior had been strange. Had Vanessa grabbed the money pouch from the bookstore, smashed the lock and ripped open the bag? It was hard to believe she would do something like that. Abigail grimaced, wishing she could have a chance to think this over without the others around. But it was too late for that now. "She just … left. She went out through the other hall door."

Photini bobbed her head energetically. "The door that leads off to the social hall and the kitchen! Because that's where they found the money. Vanessa must've had to leave it because she heard people coming."

"Photini — " Maggie admonished.

"What? Isn't it obvious? Vanessa robbed the bookstore!"

Abigail felt a little strange. The days of cold and fever were still making her a little woozy, and all of this had come to light so suddenly. "But it's just so … "

"Incredible," Xenia finished, handing the money pouch back to Abigail.

"That's right."

Xenia glanced down the short hallway in wonder. "She must've *wanted* to get caught."

Abigail rounded on her irritably. *Oh, Xenia, not now,* she thought. Abigail wanted to think things through, and she didn't feel like she could handle one of Xenia's oddball comments right then.

"Well, I don't know," Maggie mused aloud. "I just can't believe it."

"Can't believe what?" Photini shot back. "You can't believe Vanessa robbed the bookstore? I can. Didn't you hear Abigail say she was carrying this? And she was hiding it in a notebook? And money was falling out of it? And I'll bet she was acting all nervous and stuff."

Maggie raised her eyebrows in a question, and Abigail nodded. "Well," Maggie continued, "I still can't believe it. Abigail, what do you think?"

Abigail had been hoping no one would ask her that. She looked from one girl to the next. "I don't know what to think. I mean, it's very weird. I guess I can't think what else she could've been doing with this, but … I don't know." She paused and noticed that Xenia was still looking down the short hallway. "So Xenia, what do you think?"

Xenia swung back to Abigail as if she had just noticed her. "What do I think about what?"

Photini smacked her forehead. "About what? About the *bookstore*! Do you think Vanessa robbed the bookstore?"

"Oh that. Well, I think … " Xenia's furrowed look cleared and she pointed over Abigail's shoulder. "I think you should ask her."

Maggie, Abigail and Photini swung around together, just in time to catch Vanessa's shocked look as she turned from her mother and saw all four girls standing together. One swift glance took in the mangled bookstore pouch cradled in Abigail's hand and Xenia's finger still pointed in her direction.

It was the most terrible thing Abigail thought she had ever seen. Vanessa wasn't close by, but the horror on her face was as plain as if she had been right in front of them. For a long, awful moment, none of them could move. Then Xenia let her hand fall limply to her side, and Vanessa seemed to wake up. She turned to her mother and Noah and told them she'd be along in a minute. She drew herself up as tall as she could and walked casually to where the four girls were gathered.

IT WAS STRANGE to notice all of the sudden how quiet it was in the narthex.

A dozen or more people had been milling around after the service, but by ones and twos, they had all walked toward the cold parking lot or the social hall, and after Noah and Mrs. Taybeck walked out, Abigail realized that they were alone. Vanessa crossed to the others in a few steps and looked pointedly at the torn bank pouch. When she raised her gaze, there was a strange light in her eyes.

"So … " she said, with a fixed smile. "I imagine you have some questions for me?"

No one knew what to say. After looking from Maggie to Photini to see who would go first, Xenia broke the silence and said, "Well, I have a question, if no one else does. Why were you coming from the short hallway?"

Maggie turned to Xenia so rapidly that she didn't see how the question made Vanessa jump. "Xenia," Maggie said in exasperation, "that doesn't really matter, does it? I think what she means to say … I mean, I think what we all want to know is just … um …"

"Why you robbed the bookstore!" Photini blurted. "That's what we want to know. How could you do that?"

"Photini!" Maggie threw her a hard look, but Vanessa only jerked a thumb at Abigail.

"Is that what *she* told you?" she said through clenched teeth.

"Abigail didn't say anything like that," Maggie objected. "She just told us what happened."

Vanessa whipped around to face Abigail. "You mean, she snitched. You probably couldn't wait, could you, Queen Abigail?"

"No, Vanessa," Abigail cried out. "I didn't even see this thing again until right now."

"And these guys just happened to turn up, I suppose. And right away, all of you just assumed you knew what happened. You didn't even ask me to explain."

Maggie looked at her steadily. "So what did happen?"

Vanessa returned her gaze, but her boldness seemed to be faltering. "You're asking me who took the money from the bookstore? Is that what you want to know?" None of the girls bothered to answer, and for a few seconds there was no sound but Vanessa's ragged breathing. For all her loud words, it wasn't hard to see that Vanessa was actually very upset.

"What if I did?" Vanessa asked quietly. She continued in a cocky voice, "I mean, maybe I did and maybe I didn't. But so what? What are you going to do about it?"

Photini drew herself up. "Abigail's going to tell Father Andrew, that's what."

"He's still out of town," Xenia said sensibly.

"Well," said Photini through pursed lips. "Father Boris then. She'll tell him just what she saw."

Vanessa assessed Abigail with cool, dark eyes. "Are you sure he'll believe you?"

Abigail's mouth popped open. She hadn't even thought of that. With his talk last week about her being jealous of Vanessa, would he just think that she was making things up? She turned helplessly to Maggie. "I ... I don't know," she stammered. "He might not."

Maggie, however, wasn't about to be intimidated. "But he'd believe all of us. He'd believe us if we backed Abigail up. I don't think she's lying, but I think you are. Why don't you just admit it?"

"Admit I'm lying?" Vanessa tried a jeering laugh, but it came out hoarse. "You don't know what you're talking about."

"Maybe not, but Father Boris will. C'mon, you guys, let's go find him."

"No!" shouted Vanessa. She grabbed Maggie to stop her, but Maggie shook herself free. "The money was all returned," Vanessa pleaded. "What difference does it make?"

Photini gave a sniff of contempt. "Because it's wrong, that's what. Besides, how do we know you won't do it again? You didn't get away with it this time, but what's to stop you next time?"

Abigail didn't like the sound of that. In fact, the whole thing was starting to make her uncomfortable. With four of them against one, it just felt like they were ganging up on Vanessa. She wished again that things had happened differently. It should have been her problem, and now the whole Club seemed like it was involved. Her eyes met Maggie's and her friend seemed to read her mind.

Maggie slowly shook her head. "Vanessa, we really do have to tell Father Boris. You know we do." And with that, she gently steered the group towards the social hall.

"Wait!" Vanessa cried. It was painful to see how slowly Vanessa opened her tightly-shut eyes, but when she did, she raised her head and regained the proud look they had seen so often. "I'll tell," she said.

Maggie looked doubtful. "When?"

"Tomorrow. Father Andrew will be back then. He's hearing the last of the confessions after the Saturday morning service. I'll do it then. I'll tell Father Andrew that I'm the one that stole the money from the bookstore." She seemed to be trying out the sentence to see how it sounded, which struck Abigail as one of the many odd things that had happened in the last ten minutes. Vanessa turned to them one by one. "Will that work?"

Photini made a dissatisfied clucking noise. Xenia had her usual unreadable expression, and Maggie looked more doubtful than ever. Obviously, they weren't convinced that Vanessa would do the right thing. Abigail felt the coolness of the leather pouch in her hand and looked at it briefly.

"Yes," Abigail said, making up her mind. "Let her tell Father Andrew." Photini opened her mouth to argue, but Abigail cut her off. "I really think we should. And until she does, none of us should tell." She looked directly at Photini. "We shouldn't tell our parents or anyone. Let Vanessa tell Father Andrew," she repeated.

This would have been the time for Photini to challenge her or Maggie to politely disagree. After all, who was Abigail to decide what they should do? As Vanessa had reminded her so many times, there was really no reason she should be the leader of the Club.

But the others held their peace, and by that, they signaled that they would go along. Vanessa straightened up and inhaled slowly. "That's what I'll do then," she said. "I'll do it tomorrow after the service."

And as an afterthought, she gave Abigail the closest thing to a smile she could manage. "Thanks, Queen Abigail."

Abigail shot her a look, thinking that Vanessa meant to insult her. But Vanessa's eyes were bright with unshed tears, and Abigail realized that it was taking all the courage she had to keep from crying. Abigail didn't often feel close to people outside of her family and a few friends. She certainly had never felt close to Vanessa — quite the opposite in fact, as Fr. Boris had seen so clearly. But a strong wave of sympathy came over her, looking at Vanessa showing so much bravery, but so much pain. *Vanessa, your sister,* said her small voice.

"Vanessa …" Abigail said helplessly. Her heart ached to say something that would help, because she suddenly had the feeling that Vanessa needed help a lot more than she had ever wanted them to know. But Abigail couldn't think of anything to say, and a second later the side door opened and the quiet of the narthex was gone. Several Peasles and another chatting couple came in, and from the front door, Mrs. Taybeck appeared and coolly asked Vanessa how much longer she thought she'd be.

"I'm coming right now," Vanessa called out brightly. To the four girls, she said in a lowered voice, "I'll do it tomorrow." And turning quickly on her heel, she left.

Two of her sisters caught Maggie up at almost the same time, so that she only had time to call out quickly "I'll phone you!" to Abigail before disappearing into a pack of Peasles on the move. Photini gave a sudden gasp when Mrs. Murphy reminded her that it was time for her to rehearse with the choir, and in an instant, Xenia was the only one left.

Abigail didn't see much point in trying to discuss what had just happened with Xenia. On the other hand, her heart was too full to stay silent.

"I feel really sorry for Vanessa. I don't understand why she did it, and of course Photini is right — it was a bad thing to do. But Vanessa's parents are really going to be mad."

"Don't feel bad." Xenia's puckered expression gave no indication what she was thinking, and for a second, Abigail thought she wouldn't say anything else. But she did. "After all, it's as if she *wanted* to get caught."

Abigail almost dropped the money pouch. "Xenia, *why* — ?"

But she was cut off mid-sentence. Mrs. Alverson entered abruptly and grabbed the bag of vestments. "Come on," she said furtively. "If I hurry, I can get out before anyone else comes up with something for me to do. Let's go." She bundled her two daughters along in front of her like a mother hen and pushed open the door so that they tumbled out together into the vivid light of the spring afternoon.

Chapter twenty-one

CHOIR:
The wise thief, on this very day
Thou didst make worthy of Par
Enlighten me as well by the Tre
And save me.
Enlighten me as well, and save

HOLY SATURDAY dawned cold and clear, but the sun promised great things. On her way in to church that morning, Abigail noted that some of the older trees had lost branches in the last storm. But there were more signs of new life poised to blossom and thrive. The sun shone fitfully but brightly, and the sweetness of early May was in the air.

Her mother commented that it was nice to get good weather for the procession they would have that night. Abigail had to admit that it was hard enough to walk in the inky darkness of midnight without the wind blowing out your candle and the rain lashing your face. But she was too distracted to feel very interested in the weather. She and Maggie had talked over the whole painful episode on the phone after they got home from church on Friday. But they couldn't seem to understand it.

Maggie put it best. "The thing is," she had sighed, "it just doesn't make sense. Vanessa may act tough sometimes, but she never seemed dishonest. I can't believe she's the kind of person that would do something like this."

"But she said she did."

"Well, but ..." Maggie paused. "Did *she* say she did it, or did *we* say it?"

Abigail tried to recollect the exact words, and couldn't. The breeze from her window fluttered a few papers on her desk, including her picture of St. Abigail, and she lifted it out of the way. "But either way, why would Vanessa let us think that she stole the money if she didn't? And why would she confess to Father Andrew?"

Neither of them could answer that question. Hanging up the phone, Abigail addressed her next remark to St. Abigail. "I only wanted to help. But how can you do that with someone who doesn't want any help?" Abigail wished she was looking at the real icon and not her drawing. Maybe those wide, green eyes would give her some idea. But the question just seemed to hang unanswered in the air. Abigail sighed and shut her window.

THE CHOIR PERFORMED WELL at the Saturday morning liturgy. The long services of Holy Week were almost over, and the promise of Pascha gave a much-needed boost of energy. The readers chanted their parts clearly and without mishaps. Best of all, the reading of the Three Holy Youths — the lengthy one that Photini called her solo — was done flawlessly. Photini began a little timidly, but in time her confidence increased and her fine, clear voice began to soar. It lightened everyone's spirits to hear her, and on the other side of the church, Abigail could see that Mrs. Jenkins and her relatives were beaming and recording it on their cell phones. *Well, there's one happy ending anyway,* thought Abigail with pleasure.

Father Andrew's homily was short and direct. He looked tired, but his face glowed with the contentment of the blessed time of Holy Week.

"We've come to the end," he said. "Lent is over. This is the last day of Holy Week. Tonight we will meet here again when the sun is gone and the stars are out. At midnight, we will go in a candlelit procession as the myrrh-bearing women went to the tomb of Christ. We will hear the reading at the door of the church. We will hear, as those women did, 'He is risen; He is not here.'

"And now, in a few minutes, we'll hear words to a hymn that we only sing once a year at this service: 'Let all mortal flesh keep silence …' Today, all is still quiet, and we can ponder. What do we remember now of the services of Lent? What songs or prayers or words come back to you from all of Lent and Holy Week? Usually, there is one or two that stand out — which one is it for you this year?" Father Andrew paused briefly and adjusted his glasses.

"We know what will happen tonight, but what happens now, in the present? What will happen at the end of the service?" Abigail couldn't help jumping a little at the question. On the other side of the church, where Vanessa stood with Noah, she grimaced and pulled him a little closer to her. Father Andrew paused again, gazing around the church at the assembled people.

"That part is up to you. May we use these last hours before the blessed Pascha service in ways that bring glory to the name of the Father and of the Son and of the Holy Spirit. Amen."

All the people murmured "Amen," and Abigail exhaled. That had been a bit of a shock. It seemed that things in church sometimes mirrored what was going on in her life to an astonishing degree.

The liturgy settled into its usual pace and Abigail let her mind wander a little bit, thinking over Fr. Andrew's question. What did she remember of the services? There had been so many. It seemed like forever now since that procession in the first week of Lent where she had sung a song she made up about a fly.

And then there was the second week in Lent when she had learned more about prayer. And the one about the Cross, and the week she heard about St. Mary of Egypt. They all seemed quite distinct in her mind, and they had all had some impact on what happened in the Every Tuesday Girls Club. That was funny, now that she came to think about it. But as the service wore on, she was aware that there was something that was coming back to her again and again, like Fr. Andrew said there would be.

It was a song, one of the hymns. Had it been earlier in Lent? No, more recently — just in the last day or so. Abigail tried to sort it out. It had been something special — something that stood out, and that she had replayed a couple times ... oh, of course. One of the videos she watched on her father's cell phone when she was home sick. It was from Holy Thursday, she remembered that. But what were the words? She hadn't been able to make them out very well. *Something something ... on that very day ...*

It probably didn't matter, but it was strange how the whole thing kept nagging at her. *Life ... light ... lighten.* A rustling and squeaking disturbed Abigail's concentration and she noticed that the service had ended. Pulling her sweater back on, she was surprised to see her mother sit down again with a fretful look on her face.

"Abby, I've got a huge favor to ask. I know it's been a long morning and you want to get right home. But Miss Pasternak said that there was a problem with the flowers and ... well, I may have to stay for about fifteen or twenty more minutes. I'll take Bet, but can you just hang out here for that long?"

"Oh," Abigail said. "Sure. That's okay." In fact, it worked out well. Abigail wasn't ready to go home. Not quite yet. This mystery of the song from Holy Thursday was really bothering her.

Mrs. Alverson hugged her in great relief. "Oh Abigail, you're an angel! I promise I'll be back as soon as I can. I have the best daughter!"

Abigail turned away in shy embarrassment at the unexpected praise, but her eye caught sight of something of interest. "Mom, are those the service books from the other nights? Can I look at them?"

Mrs. Alverson hesitated with one arm in her coat and threw a look over her shoulder. "Oh, sure. I guess. Don't get them mixed up — probably Mrs. Murphy is going to store them for next year. Well, I'm off." And she caught Bet by the hand and swept out the side door.

Abigail started flipping through the different booklets, some thick and some thin, all with different colored covers, until she found the booklet for Thursday night and settled back into a chair. She had no idea how she would find what she was looking for, but she knew that it happened late in the service. She turned pages until a short verse jumped out at her:

The wise thief, on this very day,
Thou didst make worthy of Paradise, O Lord.
Enlighten me as well by the Tree of the Cross
And save me.
Enlighten me as well, and save me!

That was it. Abigail could hear it now. The high part of the song rose up, and the lower parts went lower — the whole thing had a sad, haunting sound to it. *The wise thief.* The song came after the reading from the Gospel about the thief who was crucified next to Jesus. The thief knew that Jesus was innocent and even seemed to know that Jesus was the Son of God. Even though he was dying himself, the thief asked for Christ's blessing and received it. That was why he was called wise, and that was what the song meant about him being enlightened.

But why did the song stand out? *Enlighten me as well.* Abigail looked down at the floor and up at the light coming in through the dome windows. Across the room, people were tidying up after the service and positioning chairs for the last of the confessions.

The confessions. And Vanessa.

The wise thief.

Abigail rose from her chair. Tossing the booklet onto one of the plastic bins, she hurried across church to intercept Maggie.

"Have you seen Xenia?" she asked when she was near enough to be heard.

Maggie turned in surprise. "Uh … She's around here somewhere, I think. Why?"

"I need to talk to her. I think it's important."

Maggie agreed to help look, even though she had little Jacob with her that afternoon. With her brother's hand firmly in hers, Maggie went towards the social hall and left Abigail to search outside the church.

AS IT TURNED OUT, finding Xenia wasn't difficult. In fact, Abigail almost walked into her as soon as she rounded a corner of the church yard. But Xenia and her brothers were having a lively argument about a favorite television program, and it proved difficult to pry her away long enough for a private discussion.

As soon as Abigail had steered her into the narthex where they wouldn't be overheard, she drew a breath and plunged into what was bothering her.

"Xenia, you kept saying that she wanted to get caught." Xenia didn't show that she understood, so Abigail explained. "Vanessa, I mean."

"I know," said Xenia.

"Why did you keep saying that?"

Xenia scratched her nose. "It's obvious, isn't it? I mean, the short hallway?"

Abigail almost grabbed the lapels of Xenia's coat, but stopped herself. "But what does that mean? What difference does it make that she came from that direction?"

Xenia gave Abigail a pitying look. "Think of what you would do if you just stole something. You would want to go someplace private and get the money out of the pouch, right? And you'd be careful not to do anything suspicious. That's what you would do. Do you see now?"

"No," answered Abigail, feeling foolish.

Xenia sighed and pointed down the hall. "What is down the short hallway?"

Abigail turned to look. "There's nothing down there. Just the boys' bathroom."

"Exactly," said Xenia. "Vanessa could have gone almost anywhere else — the narthex is full of places no one would notice you. And there's always the girls bathroom. Why would you go to one place where any girl would automatically get noticed?"

The clouds of confusion parted. "The *boys'* bathroom," said Abigail.

"That's what I mean. Why take the money there?"

Abigail frowned. "But then, come to think of it … she wasn't taking the money there. She had the money when I saw her. She was bringing it out *from* the boys' bathroom."

It was Xenia's turn to be confused. Searching Abigail's face briefly, she asked, "Why would she do that?"

Abigail raised her glance and, just as Xenia had done the day before, she pointed past her. "Maybe we should ask her."

Xenia turned slowly and deliberately, registering only slight surprise at seeing Vanessa standing behind her before turning back to Abigail in silence.

"You don't need to worry," Vanessa glowered. "I'm going to tell Father Andrew everything, just like I told you I would."

Abigail studied her angry expression without flinching. "But you didn't take the money."

Vanessa's hard look changed to amazement.

"You didn't take the money pouch from the bookstore," Abigail repeated. "You just took it away from the boys' room. I think you were going to return it, but … I don't know, maybe you changed your mind."

"Changed my mind *nothing*!" Vanessa shot back. "You got in the way. I could've done it, but you — " And then with a shock, Vanessa realized how much she had revealed and she stopped with a stunned gasp.

A little form tumbled into Abigail from behind, and a moment later, Maggie appeared.

"Jacob, be careful!" Maggie called. Setting him back on his feet, she looked up and took in the assembled girls in some surprise. "What's going on?" she asked.

"Well," answered Xenia, "it turns out that Vanessa didn't steal the money after all."

"Yes, I did," replied Vanessa through clenched teeth.

"No, you didn't," rejoined Abigail, and she told Maggie what she and Xenia had figured out. "You know you didn't rob the bookstore," she concluded, turning back to Vanessa, "but you let us think you did. Why?"

Vanessa looked sullen and said nothing.

"Because someone else stole the money pouch, and she saw them take it," guessed Xenia, watching Vanessa carefully.

"What?" exclaimed Maggie. "Who?"

Xenia shrugged. "I dunno. Someone who went into the boys' room. So ... a boy?"

Maggie swiveled to Vanessa, whose defiant look seemed to be fading. "A boy?" Maggie repeated, perplexed. "What boy?"

Vanessa's mouth was working, but she couldn't get out a sound. Abigail glanced at Maggie. She felt like she knew enough to make a guess.

"Her brother. That's it, isn't it, Vanessa?"

Vanessa's face crumpled, but she still couldn't make a sound. Her silence was frightening.

"You meant to put the money pouch back in the bookstore," Abigail continued, "but that didn't work. So you left the money where it would get found. And when we confronted you yesterday, you said you stole the money just so your brother James wouldn't get blamed for it."

"No," said Vanessa, breaking her silence. "That's not — " But the words caught in her throat, and she couldn't go on.

Maggie found that her eyes had strayed down to Baby Jacob of their own accord. He lifted his face and smiled, and she gave him a thin smile. "Not James," she said gently. "Your *younger* brother." She lifted her eyes and looked at Vanessa levelly. "That look you gave me when I took Jacob from the room weeks ago. You knew exactly how I felt. You would do anything to protect your little brother, wouldn't you?" Vanessa looked at her helplessly. "Noah stole the money pouch from the bookstore," Maggie said.

Vanessa's tears began to flow freely. "He didn't think anyone saw, but I did," she gulped out. "He has been doing some bad things, and I try to keep anyone from finding out, but I never thought ... He just

didn't know. He's … he's always trying to impress James. He just …" and she bowed her head and cried.

"But Vanessa!" Maggie stooped so Vanessa could hear her. "There must be something else you could do. Maybe if we just told —"

"No," Vanessa sobbed out the syllable.

Abigail and Maggie exchanged despairing looks. "But, you can't —" Abigail sputtered. "Vanessa, you can't tell Father Andrew that —"

"I can." Vanessa swiped her hand across her face. "And you all have to be quiet about it. You kept the other Club secrets. You have to keep this one, too. I'm going to tell Father Andrew that I stole the money, and that's all there is to it."

Maggie tried to gather Vanessa in a hug, but Vanessa shook her off. "You don't understand," she snapped. "James is my step-brother. He's always getting into trouble and my parents argue about it all the time. My dad says that he's a bad influence on Noah and … he's probably right." Her features contracted in misery. "If my parents find out what happened, they'll send James back to his dad. We won't be a family anymore. But if I say that I did it…" For a second, Vanessa looked as if she might cry again, but she shook her head, sprinkling teardrops from her face. "If I say I did it, they'll only punish me. And I can take it. I can deal with it. I have to … I *have* to."

The sight of her at that moment took Abigail's breath away. *The wise thief.* Courage seemed to light her up from within. *The wise thief Thou didst make worthy of paradise…*

Maggie reached out for Vanessa, but she took a quick step backwards.

"I have to," she repeated defiantly and stepped through the doors to the nave, leaving the three girls alone behind her.

Chapter twenty-two

"WHAT DO we do now?" asked Xenia. It was the first thing she had said in minutes.

Maggie threw her hands open wide. "I don't know. What do we do now, Abigail?"

Abigail was surprised to find that she had very clear ideas what they needed to do. "Xenia, you have to make some excuse to your family so you can stay in church a while longer. Maggie, go find Photini. You can bring Jacob if you want, but we have to get everyone together. You guys have to talk Vanessa out of confessing to Father Andrew."

"But Abigail, she's gone into church. She's in the nave right now," said Maggie, waving toward the oak doors.

"Then you'll have to go in after her. You've got to find a way to talk her out of it."

Maggie stared at her. "And what are you going to do?"

Abigail had hoped no one would ask her that question. "I have no idea," she said, stepping over Jacob to the door. "I guess I'm going to try to stall for time."

Bumping backwards into the door, Abigail spun around and disappeared into the somber stillness of the church nave.

STEPPING INTO THE NAVE, seeing Fr. Andrew standing before the icons, it was hard for Abigail to believe that everything she had just heard outside was real. But there was Vanessa in the front row, sitting up straight with her head high. Abigail made her way to the front as quickly as she could, mumbling apologies as she brushed past.

"Vanessa," she whispered.

Vanessa looked away from her.

"*Vanessa!*" Several heads turned disapprovingly.

"Shh!" hissed Vanessa. "Go away!"

"No."

"You're not supposed to be in here."

"No, *you're* not supposed to be in here."

Several parishioners shushed her, so Abigail had to sit down next to Vanessa to keep talking with her.

"I don't think you should do this."

Vanessa shifted away from her. "I have to," she said, without meeting her eyes. "I told you why."

Abigail leaned forward urgently. "But it can't be right. You didn't do it. Vanessa, it just can't be right."

There was a rather pronounced throat-clearing directly in front of them that ended the conversation. Fr. Andrew was finished hearing Mrs. Landrew's confession and he looked at the girls pointedly before going into the prayer of absolution.

Flumping back in the seat, Abigail hastily considered the situation. A glance to the back of the church told her that Maggie hadn't found Photini yet, and it would surely take all three girls to talk Vanessa out of her determination. But what could she do? Was there some kind of distraction she could make so that the others would have more time? In desperation, her gaze swiveled to the icon screen — the iconostasis — at the front of the church. There was an icon of Christ, of the Virgin Mary, of Archangel Michael and Gabriel. All these heavenly helpers and still she was at such a loss.

Be yourself.

Abigail started. It was one of those messages she seemed to get sometimes, she was sure of it. But what did it mean? Be herself?

But who am I? thought Abigail miserably. The girl who makes up songs? The one who can't pay attention, who thinks everything is like a story? What good is that now?

Be what you are.

Abigail saw movement out of the corner of her eye. She saw that Mrs. Landrew was headed back to her seat and Vanessa was getting ready to rise.

"Next," said Fr. Andrew.

"That's me!" burst Abigail.

FATHER ANDREW WAS SURPRISED by Abigail's level of enthusiasm. Confessing didn't usually make people jump out of their chairs. But another glance to the back of the church told Abigail that Maggie had found Photini. The three girls were huddled together with little Jacob tottering between them, and Abigail realized she would have to give them enough time to sneak forward and talk to Vanessa.

"I thought you had already confessed," said Fr. Andrew mildly, looking at her over the top of his glasses.

"Well, I did, but …" Abigail left off there and hoped he would fill in the rest. She didn't know what she was going to say and could only hope that some inspiration would come to her.

Be what you are, the voice had said.

Well, thought Abigail, *I'm a storyteller. So let's hope something comes to me.*

Fr. Andrew was still regarding her a little too skeptically for her comfort, but he indicated the book on the stand and drew near to hear her recite the prayer.

"What's on your mind?" he asked when she had finished the prayer.

"A lot of things," she answered brightly.

"What have you come to confess?" he said, with a slight smile.

"Oh … okay. So … well, Father Boris probably told you that I had confessed about some things that — "

"Father Boris and I don't share what anyone says in confession."

"You don't?"

"No. A priest never tells anyone what is said in confession. It's confidential."

"Ohhh. I didn't know that. How … how interesting." Her mind

grabbed hold of the information, which did present certain possibilities.

"Yes. So, Abigail, what is it that you have come to confess?"

"Oh, yes. Well, the other day, I was playing a card game with Bet …" And Abigail proceeded to tell the same incident she had confessed to Fr. Boris, how she cheated at the game and made Bet cry. Abigail tried to include all the extra details she could, but had the feeling that she was starting to get mixed up. At least once, she said it was Mark she cheated rather than Bet, and that they were playing checkers instead of cards. Father Andrew studied her carefully as he gave her some words of advice.

"Is there anything else?" he said, speaking very slowly and deliberately.

"Yes!" Abigail squeaked. "I've been rude and disrespectful to my parents. When I told Father Boris about it, he said that — "

"Father Boris?"

Abigail almost clapped her hand over her mouth, but Fr. Andrew just asked her in the same even tone, "Abigail, are these things you have already confessed?"

She blushed guiltily, which Fr. Andrew took for a yes. "You have already been absolved of these sins. You don't need to confess them again."

"Oh … well …" Abigail stammered, and lapsed into silence.

"So if there's nothing else — " He sounded weary.

"Yes. There is." She could tell she would have to make the next one more interesting, or else she'd lose his attention. "I killed someone."

"You *killed* someone?!"

"Two people. But … not really." There was no point in overdoing it.

"I mean, it was a computer game. And they were, you know, vampires and stuff."

He raised an eyebrow critically. "I'm surprised your parents let you play games like that."

This wasn't going well. "They don't. It was … a dream!"

Father Andrew exhaled slowly. "Abigail —"

"I dreamt I was playing a really bad video game, and there were lots of zombies and vampires. And really bad people."

"Abigail, none of this sounds like an actual sin."

Abigail could see how that would be a problem, but she continued valiantly. "But they were really bad people. And I shot them with a laser gun, which doesn't sound very Christian."

"Are you just making this up?"

"No, it …" Abigail tried to make herself believe it, but she failed. A dream about zombies? Where did *that* come from?

Father Andrew stood up and stretched his back. "Confession is a sacrament, Abigail, and shouldn't be taken lightly. You know that. And I still have other people in line. So if there's nothing else — "

"Um … but …"

She was running out of ideas. Her eyes on the icon ahead, she thought desperately, *What do I do?*

Be as I am.

Her eyes locked onto the eyes of Christ in the icon. Christ in His suffering. Christ in His humility. *Do as I do. Be as I am.*

Time seemed to slow down, almost stop, for that instant. But she could see now that Fr. Andrew was raising his stole, preparing to read the prayers of absolution.

"The thing is …" she whispered. She suddenly knew what she had to do, but the words wouldn't come. *Be as I am.*

She grabbed Fr. Andrew's sleeve and bent close so that she could hardly be heard.

"The thing is … I took the money from the bookstore."

She felt a jolt go through Fr. Andrew. "You what?!"

The weariness was gone from his voice and he sounded completely alert. Abigail couldn't

look at him — she kept her eyes on the icon of Christ, afraid that if she looked away, she wouldn't be able to keep talking.

"I did it. I took the money. No one knew it was me. No one saw."

There was a long pause. She hadn't let go of Fr. Andrew's sleeve and she could hear his shallow breathing. "You robbed the bookstore?" he asked in wonder.

"No, someone else did that."

"Who?" Father Andrew's voice seemed to come from miles away.

"My brother. He took the money pouch. He broke it. I saw him, but he didn't know I saw. I took the money back after he hid it."

"Mark? Mark robbed the bookstore?" Father Andrew was shaking his head.

Abigail didn't want to stop to think about what she was saying. No one would ever believe that Mark had done such a thing. In a minute, Fr. Andrew would accuse her of making this up as well, and then he would be very angry with her.

She crunched up more of his sleeve in her fist and made herself look straight into his round, brown eyes.

"I only did it to protect my brother. I would have taken all the blame myself and said that I did it. But only to protect him — only to save my family. But I can't let anyone know. I have been really afraid, but I have been trying not to let anyone see. That's what I wanted to tell you."

THERE WAS A PAUSE that might have been one minute long or ten. Fr. Andrew and Abigail stared at each other.

"I see," said Fr. Andrew at last, lifting his sleeve free from her grasp.

He cleared his throat and without another word, he lifted his stole and murmured the prayers of absolution. Abigail kissed the cross and his hand and turned to the rest of the nave, hearing her footsteps echo heavily on the wooden floor.

The sights and sounds were familiar, but none of it seemed real somehow. Two things were obvious, though. Maggie, Xenia and Photini were still huddled together in the back of the church, so they hadn't even gotten a chance to say a word to Vanessa.

And Vanessa rose out of her seat immediately, not wanting anyone else to get in front of her. Her proud stance told the whole story — she was more determined than ever to confess to something she hadn't done.

All of Abigail's stalling had been for nothing. She hadn't changed a thing.

THERE WAS NO ONE in the narthex, so Abigail crossed over to the social hall. In time, her mother found her and with Bet in hand, they piled into the car.

"I can't tell you how much I appreciate you being such a sweetheart," Mrs. Alverson said, as soon as they had pulled onto the street.

Abigail felt embarrassed, but her mother wouldn't let her deny it. "I mean it. You have been as good as gold lately, and I don't want you to think your dad and I haven't noticed. All this Lent, you have gotten better and better about behaving yourself in church."

Behaving herself. She was probably in more trouble right now than she had been in her whole life, but her mom didn't know it yet. But when Fr. Andrew told her mom ... how could she explain it? What would she say?

Mrs. Alverson was still chatting happily, praising Abigail's good behavior. "I know that we were having a rough patch there earlier in the year, but look at how far you've come."

She smiled over at her daughter, but Abigail couldn't think of anything to say. Mrs. Alverson surveyed Abigail's wooden expression uncertainly, and her smile faded.

"So ... what were you doing in church the whole time? Just talking with friends?"

"No." Abigail could have come up with some kind of story, but she didn't feel like telling any more lies. "I went in for confession."

Her mother blinked in astonishment. "Again? But you just went a week or so ago." She beamed a smile at Abigail and sighed happily. "That's what I mean — you're just turning into an angel. I can't tell you how happy that makes me. Dad and I are both so proud of you."

ABIGAIL MANAGED to hide her feelings on the drive home. She changed the subject and played games with Bet and found things to say. She helped unload the car and hung up her sweater by the door. She went upstairs, hearing her mother questioning the others on what they wanted in the Easter basket, and turned the handle into her room. There at last she could let the tears fall. She didn't try to stop them.

She wasn't sure if she was crying more because Vanessa's story had made her feel so sad or because she knew her mother was going to be so disappointed in her soon. Somehow, she had made her mother really happy with her, so that she wasn't worried or irritable, and that was about to get swept away. Her mother and father had been proud of her and soon they would either think she was either a liar or a thief, which was much worse than just being inattentive or ir-responsible. And did any of it even matter, as far as helping Vanessa? Everything felt so messed up.

But in spite of the deep sadness that made her cry, she didn't feel the confusion that came when she had done bad things — her mind felt as clear as the spring air that wafted into her window.

She laid her head on her arms and immediately drifted off to sleep.

Chapter twenty-three

"Meatballs!"

Coming slowly out of her heavy sleep, Abigail was aware that she was hearing a voice that was getting closer. Impatient steps came heavily down the hallway and with a sharp knock, Mark poked his head around the door.

"Abigail," he repeated impatiently. "Meatballs!"

She blinked groggily. "Meatballs?"

"Yes. Mom says to come downstairs and help."

"Oh, okay," she said, rising obediently. Her mind still felt a little fuzzy and she looked around with bleary eyes. "I was looking for something, though. Have you seen the drawing I did of St. Abigail? It's always right here, and I couldn't find it."

"How should I know? Come on."

She followed him down the stairs and into the warm kitchen bustling with activity. Mrs. Alverson had a recipe for

meatballs in sauce that was a particular favorite for pot-
lucks. For the Pascha feast, they were going to make up
hundreds and figured out that getting the family involved would cut
the time it took to prepare them. Abigail formed the mixed meat
into little balls and handed them to Mark to dip into a combination of eggs and milk. Bet coated them in herbed breadcrumbs and
passed them on a spoon to her father who would cook them on a
griddle. The kitchen was full of the delicious smell of the browning
meatballs and the savory sauce that went with them.

"Hey, there's my girl," called out Mr. Alverson. "Glad you could
make it, sleepyhead."

Abigail's yawn turned into a smile as he winked and tossed her an
apron.

"I had to call her three times," reported Mark disapprovingly.
"And even then she was still soggy and started going on about a
drawing she lost."

Her dad tested some of the meatballs and flicked them over to
brown them evenly. "Well, I'm glad that Abigail got some extra
sleep. We all should. We won't be home from the service tonight until about three in the morning. Good job, Abigail."

Abigail was tempted to stick out her tongue at her brother, but she
thought better of it. She hadn't forgotten that she told Fr. Andrew a
few hours ago that Mark had robbed the bookstore. Surely Fr. Andrew wouldn't believe it. But what if he did?

"You're … you're doing a really good job. With the eggs, I mean.
You're not getting any shells into the bowl," she told Mark kindly.

Mark regarded her narrowly. "What is that supposed to mean?"

"Nothing. I wanted to say something nice, that's all."

Her dad flipped a few meatballs and playfully threw a potholder at Mark. "It's called a compliment, Mark. You should try one sometime."

Mark's only reply was a grumbling remark about sisters, and Abigail decided to change the subject. "Where's Mom?"

"Uhhh ..." Mr. Alverson took one of the meatballs that Bet was about to eat and tossed it into the trash. "She might be finishing the Easter basket. Or maybe she's still on the phone. Or ... nope, she's right here. Hello, sweetie!" He merrily waved a hand encased in an oven mitt.

Mrs. Alverson waved back and surveyed the work in progress. "Smaller meatballs, Abigail, or we won't have enough for everyone. And Bet, honey, I need you to not to put the breadcrumbs on so heavy, or they won't cook right. And as for you," she continued, giving Mr. Alverson's apron strings a tug, "Any way you can cook those faster? Looks like we'll have to leave a little early tonight."

"Early!" groaned Mark. He had a hard time keeping his eyes open for the whole service and didn't want the night to start any earlier than it had to. "Why early?"

"I don't know," Mrs. Alverson replied. "Father Andrew said he needed to talk to us for a bit."

"Really?" said Mr. Alverson in surprise. "What about?"

"He didn't say."

"He wants to talk to all of us?"

"No," answered Mrs. Alverson, and there was a slight pause. "You, me and Abigail."

Abigail almost dropped the spoon.

"Uhh ohhh," sang out Mark in obvious delight. "Abigail's in trouble."

HOURS LATER, the three of them were sitting in the large conference room at church, and a heavy silence made conversation impossible. Father Andrew had directed the Alversons to go up to the room, promising to be along shortly. But when they entered, they found that they weren't the only ones called to come in early. Maggie was there with her parents, Vanessa with hers and Xenia with hers. The adults held a hushed conference of their own, but since none of them knew anything, they had lapsed into mystified stillness. The four girls exchanged furtive looks, because they had some ideas about what might be going on, but they didn't dare ask each other any questions.

I wish Father would just come and get this over with, Abigail thought. But for the life of her, she couldn't figure out what the others were doing there. Her, Vanessa, Maggie, Xenia … that was almost all the Every Tuesday Girls Club, and they were only waiting for —

The door opened as if on cue, and Mrs. Jenkins threw the same astonished look around the room as the others had done. Her hand went up nervously to adjust her head covering, until she remembered she didn't have it on yet. She clutched instead at Photini, who seemed to be on the verge of exploding from sheer terror, but to everyone's relief a light footfall announced Fr. Andrew's approach. A second later, the side door swung open and he entered, apologizing as he came.

"So sorry," he muttered, adding stray comments about the last-minute details that had been keeping him busy. His eyes swept the gathering to make sure that everyone was there, and then he grabbed a chair.

"Well, I have to prepare for tonight's service, so shall we begin?"
The group murmured agreement. He smiled, and with the merest glance at Abigail, he cleared his throat.

"I have asked you all to come early tonight because something quite unusual happened today. It touches on some matters that affect our church community and are quite sensitive." Several of the parents exchanged concerned looks.

"As all of you know," he continued, "we had a theft in the church. A few weeks ago, someone stole the money pouch from the bookstore."

This is it, thought Abigail.

"The money and the ripped pouch were found in the kitchen, but we didn't know who the thief was. Until today." Abigail saw her mother's fingers twitch on her purse.

"Today, after the morning service, something very strange occurred: These five girls each confessed they robbed the bookstore."

Five! Abigail's eyes flew open. All around her, a little storm of astonished noises was breaking out. Abigail spun to Maggie, who was looking at her in amazement.

A small fist banged onto the table and Vanessa scooted her chair back. "But it was me!" she cried. Mrs. Taybeck barked out her name, but Vanessa ignored her. "It was me! I did it!"

"No, I did," yelled Abigail, pushing her chair away.

Maggie and Xenia's chairs shot back as they rose in unison, and two more voices joined the chorus. Last of all, Photini stood on shaky knees, and the room was filled with the sound of five girls all admitting their guilt as loudly as they could.

The parents were completely dumbstruck. Mrs. Jenkins seemed in danger of fainting, and loud Mrs. Murphy, for one of the first times in her life, was completely speechless.

"Girls, please," implored Fr. Andrew, directing them to return to their seats. "Now then, you parents see the problem. Five girls confessed. Who actually robbed the bookstore? And the answer is … " Fr. Andrew, seemed to enjoy the dramatic pause. "The answer is … none of them."

You could have heard a pin drop, although Abigail was pretty sure she saw one or two parents breathe a sigh of relief. Fr. Andrew turned to each of the girls, and Abigail last. "None of you robbed the bookstore. You were all willing to take the blame in order to spare someone else pain. I believe now that I know what happened and who the real thief was, but it wasn't any of you. I will be in touch with that family, because some counseling will be needed. But I wanted you all to know that I am very touched by what you did. It takes a lot of courage to sacrifice for another person and risk condemnation for yourself."

His face, which had become pensive, split into a wide smile as he turned to the parents. "This is what I wanted you to know about your daughters. I am going to ask all of you to say no more of this, once you leave this room. It is a private matter and I will handle it.

But you should all be proud of your girls today. They have made me very happy."

There was still a lot that the parents didn't understand, but Mrs. Murphy felt she had been quiet for long enough. She broke the silence with a hearty cry of "WELL then!" and gathered Xenia into one of her great big hugs. A ripple of laughter and delighted embraces broke out on all sides. Locked in her parents' loving arms, Abigail was pleased to note that the Taybecks had drawn Vanessa into a hug that didn't look like it would ever end.

And it might not have, if Fr. Andrew hadn't arisen from the table and exclaimed that it was time to go. A flurry of movement followed and, still laughing, the throng burst out of the room and down the stairs.

As they drew near the church, Abigail had just a moment to find Maggie. "You guys each told Father Andrew that you stole the money?"

"It's all we could think of. It was Xenia's idea," Maggie said. "But we didn't know you were going to do it too. How did you come up with it?"

"I don't know," admitted Abigail. "It just popped into my head."

"You guys — " said a voice behind them. They turned to find Vanessa looking at them with shining eyes. "You … you did that for me? You told Father that —" Her voice choked with emotion.

"We lied to our priest," said Xenia solemnly.

"Just like you were going to," added Maggie.

"It was a really bad thing to do," whispered Photini, her face lit up with guilty delight.

"Yes, it was," agreed Abigail. "It's a good thing it made him so happy."

They had just a few moments to grasp each other tightly in a thoroughly awkward and giggling hug before they heard the clear words that announced that the Pascha service was beginning.

"Blessed art Thou, O God of our Fathers, now and ever and unto ages of ages ..."

Chapter twenty-four

There might have been better Paschas, but Abigail couldn't remember any. It's true that the weather didn't cooperate as well as it might have — it wasn't rainy or cold, but the wind turned gusty, and during the procession, faint exclamations of dismay announced when candles went out or blew hot wax onto cold skin. These were some of the things that were remarked on afterwards when everyone enjoyed the buoyant good humor of breaking the fast together in the social hall. But Abigail didn't notice any of that.

She had a unique sense during the service of being really awake, really aware. She felt as if her eyesight was clearer and her hearing more sensitive than usual. Her heart was so light that all of the Pascha service felt as pure and clear as a walk on a brilliant spring morning.

She loved that the service started with the church darkened. Subdued chanting told of good things to come, of a tomb that was empty and angels that were amazed. When that portion of the service came to an end, the lights in church were turned off and Fr. Andrew came forward with a single candle lit. He sang a song that the choir picked up and sang over and over.

"Come, take light from the Light not overtaken by night. Come, glorify Christ, Who is risen from the dead."

Fr. Andrew lit the candles of those around him, and then they turned and did the same until every candle was lit. Little children might be held by parents so they could share the candlelight, or tended by older children if they wanted a candle of their own. And when all the candles were lit and faces glowed in the flickering light, the song would change;

"Thy resurrection, O Christ our Savior, the angels in heaven sing. Enable us on earth to glorify Thee in purity of heart."

Fr. Andrew and Fr. Boris led the procession, followed by subdeacons and altarboys with banners and a cross, and the choir, and then all the people. Around the church they wound, singing the song and keeping candles lit as best they could. And then, when they came back to the front door, there were prayers and songs.

Fr. Andrew read the Gospel account of the blessed morning that the women came and found the stone rolled away from the tomb. He then exchanged words with someone on the other side of the closed door. It looked almost as if he would break down the door as he struck it a deafening knock and called, "Make way, for the King of Glory enters!"

And finally, the church doors were thrown open from inside. Everyone streamed back into the church where every light had been turned on. The church bells and their clamorous ringing sounded the beginning of the jubilant Pascha service that was an explosion of light and song. As they all poured back into the church, the people blew out candles and hugged each other, greeting one another as

Christians had done for centuries: "Christ is risen!" "Indeed, He is risen!"

Abigail saw all this and thought her heart would burst from happiness. It had all been there before and she had loved it before, but she never felt it as keenly as she did that year. On that Pascha, it was as if her eyes and ears and mind were like the doors of the church that just couldn't stay shut.

OTHER PEOPLE didn't have Abigail's acute senses and might not have thought the Pascha service that year was anything special, if it weren't for two things.

Firstly, no one could remember when the moon and stars had shone so bright. The blustery wind had chased all the clouds out of the night sky and the full moon lit the way for everyone better than a flashlight. The glittering stars more than made up for any candles that refused to stay lit.

For another thing, there was a certain sight that warmed a lot of hearts that night. Abigail was walking in procession and singing when she noticed another candle come near to hers. Turning, she saw that Vanessa had drawn even with her and was walking by her side. Her face was aglow with gratitude that didn't need any words. Instead, the two girls held hands and walked together. Maggie was behind them, and Xenia and Photini made their way forward as well — they all felt like being together that night. Maggie reached out for Photini on one side and Xenia on the other, and the threesome marched along hand in hand.

For the girls to walk in such sweet and simple harmony was more touching than they knew. It had been a hard year at St. Michael the Archangel church. There had been a lot of arguments and problems that had to get solved that year, and some people worried that they would never stop fussing and carrying grudges. But if the daughters of the Murphys, Peasles and Jenkinses could go along together, then maybe they could as well. If Abigail Alverson and Vanessa Taybeck could walk hand in hand, then really anything was possible.

Abigail didn't know it then, but that was when the Every Tuesday Girls Club began in earnest. That was when those five girls truly began to help the church.

"SO DO YOU understand everything now?"

Abigail was glad that Fr. Andrew had found her during the potluck and asked her for a moment in his office. She loved the service, but the potluck that came after it was a little overwhelming. It was great fun to talk and laugh and feast in the middle of the night, but it had gotten a little noisy and it was a relief to step into Fr. Andrew's office where the babble of voices was lessened.

Did she understand everything? "I'm not sure. The last week or so, everything happened kind of fast."

Fr. Andrew nodded sympathetically. "I thought it might have. I know that you wanted to help other people — that's how you thought you could be like your patron saint. But remember what I told you: People's lives are not easy these days. If you get involved, you could find that it's a lot more difficult than you thought."

Abigail was quiet for a minute. "You know who it was that really stole the money, right?"

Fr. Andrew's expression clouded briefly. "Yes, I know that it was Noah."

That made Abigail curious, but she thought of another question that was more pressing. "Is Vanessa's family going to be okay?"

The priest drew a breath and let it out slowly. "I don't know. They still have hard work ahead of them. There are some very deep wounds here, and those are the hardest to mend sometimes. But it will have to be done privately, Abigail. I don't want the Club to stay involved in this. All the same, I'm very, very glad that you girls came to the rescue when you did. If you hadn't, Vanessa would have gotten the blame and punishment for something she didn't do."

The words of praise for the Club were music to her ears, but she looked away shyly. "I bet you would've figured out that Vanessa was lying."

Fr. Andrew tutted doubtfully. "I'm not so sure. I realize she was trying to help her family, but I don't believe that good things are ever built on a lie. And sometimes it's very hard to know when a person isn't telling the truth. How did you girls figure it out?"

"Mmm." Abigail considered the question. "Xenia knew something was wrong with Vanessa's story right away — Xenia is pretty smart like that. Maggie and I didn't think that it was something that Vanessa would do. But it was that song from Thursday night that really convinced me."

"What song?"

"The Wise Thief." Abigail told him about the way the song had stayed with her, and how the words struck her. "Because it was right there. The thief was like someone that wasn't really bad. It was like actually he was good."

Father Andrew nodded. "It's called a paradox. The Bible has a lot of them. Powerful people who are actually weak. Foolish people that are actually wise. Saint Paul says that God uses our weakness to show His strength. But there was another quality of that thief that might have been why you remembered him. He had the kind of discernment I talked to you about a few weeks ago. God gave him insight to see that the condemned man on the cross next to him was not only innocent, but was the promised Messiah. I think you and Maggie knew in your hearts that Vanessa hadn't committed this crime, but to find the proof, you needed that same kind of discernment."

Abigail wasn't quite sure she understood that, but maybe if she had more time to think about it, she might. "I … I guess so. Suddenly, I just knew that Vanessa hadn't done it. But we couldn't change her mind about confessing, even when she told us the truth. That's why I came up for confession before her. I was just hoping the others would talk her out of it if I gave them time."

"Ah," said Fr. Andrew, adopting a sage-like expression. "So that's why you told me tall tales about killing vampires in a dream. Not the kind of thing I usually hear in confession. But what gave you the idea of saying that you were the thief?"

Abigail looked at her fingernails and then at her shoes. "Well, the other girls came up with it when they talked together, but I didn't find out about that until tonight. It's kind of hard to explain."

Abigail proceeded to tell the priest, as best as she could, about what had happened and what she had heard — first, to be herself, and then to be like Christ.

Father Andrew watched her with keen interest. "Do you think you heard voices?" he asked.

Abigail considered that and rejected it. "Not voices. Maybe just a voice — one voice. Mom calls it my still, small voice."

"She gets that name for it from the Bible, from something that happened to the prophet Elijah."

"But that's not quite right either. It's like when things just come to you and you don't exactly know where they come from. Or when you suddenly know what the truth is, even if you couldn't possibly know … or something."

Father Andrew nodded very slightly with his beard tucked against his chest. "I think I understand what you mean."

"Was it … did God talk to me? Or Jesus?"

He looked at her over his glasses. "Well, we need to be very careful about saying things like that. But I think we can say that you got some help at just the right time. These are great blessings when they happen, because they don't happen often. But I can think of a very good reason why you experienced it right then. Can you?"

Abigail considered, but couldn't come up with anything that sounded right. "Because I asked?"

"I'm sure that helped," Fr. Andrew admitted. "But when you were willing to stand in the place of a guilty person, just to help them, you were acting a little like Jesus Christ acted for us. When you acted out of self-sacrifice and risked punishment when you were innocent, you were also able to receive a special blessing — help when you needed it." Abigail tried not to look confused, but Fr. Andrew seemed to read her mind, and he restated it in simpler words.

"You happened to be in a place in your heart this year where you could see a little of the Light that dawned on Easter morning. In that way, you were like the Wise Thief yourself."

She couldn't think of anything to say. "I guess we all did okay," she mumbled at last.

"You all did beautifully, and I wish I could reward you all. I don't have presents for everyone, but I do have something that you might like." He reached across and placed a rectangular board in her hand.

"Oh. Thank you," said Abigail, not knowing what to say.

"Turn it over."

"Oh. *Oh.*" She jumped up. "Oh! It's my — my — "

"It's your Saint Abigail icon," finished Fr. Andrew, smiling broadly.

"You got it! You got it!" She flew over to him and hugged him around the neck with the icon still in her hand.

"Careful now," the priest laughed. "The last coat of varnish isn't totally dry yet. I only finished it this afternoon."

Abigail stopped dancing. "*You* finished it. You painted this?"

"Uh … yes." Fr. Andrew looked embarrassed.

"But you said that you used to know an iconography student or something."

"I know," he admitted sheepishly. "That wasn't quite true, Abigail. I apologize. The iconography student was me. I used to paint icons, but I had to stop because the work was causing pain in my hands. I just didn't know if I could do it again after all this time, and I didn't want to disappoint you."

Abigail tilted the icon up and looked at it with new appreciation, letting the light play over the lines of St. Abigail's garments and hair. "It's perfect," she whispered. "Can I have it?"

"Of course. You earned it. But you will need to leave it here overnight to let the varnish dry."

Abigail placed it carefully on the desk and looked up at him with a brilliant smile. "Thank you, thank you, Father. Thank you for everything."

He returned her smile. "Believe me, Abigail, I should be thanking you. But in any case, you are most welcome. I better get back to the feast, but you can have another minute or two. Just turn out the lights when you go."

Abigail's eyes followed him thoughtfully as he crossed the room. "Father?"

"Mm?"

"How did you figure out it was Noah? I tried to let you know Vanessa was protecting her brother, but how did you know James didn't do it?"

"Oh, that." Fr. Andrew's smile became a little mysterious. "Priests need to have a few secrets, I expect. Let's just say that I also have a still, small voice." They exchanged a meaningful glance before he added. "I'll leave you alone with Saint Abigail for the moment. You probably have a lot to say to her."

She looked at him wide-eyed. "I wouldn't know where to begin."

Fr. Andrew turned with one hand on the door. "Probably you just begin where it all started — with a little song."

And with a click, the door closed behind him.

SO, ABIGAIL MADE UP A SONG because that's one of the things that she did best. She knew that it wasn't the best song anyone had ever done in church, and probably there were better songs for this saint as well. But it pleased her, and she sang it a time or two for St. Abigail, dancing in solemn circles with the icon held in front of her.

Saint Abigail, we did it!
(I'm still not quite sure how.)
You helped me solve some problems,
And things are better now.

Saint Abigail, we did it —
My friends all did their part.
The Every Tuesday Girls Club
Is off to a good start.

Saint Abigail, He did it —
He made hidden things clear.
God help me to see Pascha's light,
All throughout the year.

Abigail's
Christmas Cookies

"Do you have everything you need?"

Abigail looked in the grocery bag next to her on the car seat. "I've got a spatula, a potholder, our cookie sheet, our drying racks."

Her mother thought briefly. "A big bowl?"

"Maggie said she had all that we needed."

Mrs. Alverson nodded, looking in the side mirrors to make sure no branches had blown into the driveway. There hadn't been any snow in Missouri that December, but it had been cold and windy. "And of course you've got the fancy cookie mold?"

"Yes." Abigail held up a large cookie mold. It was made of reddish terra cotta clay and had features to make a cookie that looked like St. Nicholas – not the usual Santa Claus, but the real saint and bishop, with a bishop's stole and the pointed hat called a miter. Abigail's fingers lovingly traced the delicate features, including the immense beard. The mold had been a gift from her favorite aunt, and she had never had a chance to use it. Until now.

Sitting next to her in the car, her mother scanned her face. "Are you nervous?"

Abigail carefully put the mold back into the bag. "A little bit."

Mrs. Alverson gave her an encouraging smile. "Don't worry. The parish council is full of very nice people. You already know Photini's mother, Maggie's dad. They'll be there, along with Xenia's father." Mrs. Alverson knew that hearing that parents of her friends would be there would help Abigail feel less alone. Abigail had started a girls' club in her church called the Every Tuesday Girls Club, and the other members – Maggie, Photini, Xenia and Vanessa – had grown into good friends over the past year.

"There's also Miss Hemmings, who runs the Burger Bagger in town," Mrs. Alverson continued. "Mr. Broadmere – you know him from choir. And of course, Fr. Andrew will be there." Abigail nodded, trying to keep the butterflies in her stomach under control. She thought how nice it would be to look out and see Fr. Andrew's friendly face, his patient eyes and wise, owl-like expression. "And he said he'll help me if people ask me too many questions or anything?"

"Absolutely," Mrs. Alverson replied. "I don't think you'll have any problems. But all the same, it's a good idea to feed them gingerbread cookies and egg nog. The parish council doesn't usually have to meet this close to Christmas – they might as well get a treat. And it'll put them in a good mood."

Abigail grinned proudly. "That was my idea."

Her mother leaned over and tapped her forehead. "You're a smart one. Like your father."

She started the car.

At Maggie Peasle's house, preparations were already underway. Xenia and Photini had arrived together and were helping Maggie get the kitchen ready for baking. With their large family, the Peasles had the biggest kitchen and everyone agreed it was the only place all five girls could work together without bumping into each other. Abigail would have liked if it had just been them, but her mother was called in to work at the drug store and had to leave five-year-old Bet with the group. And Maggie had to watch two of her brothers, Nathaniel and Jacob, and her little sister Isabelle while her mother was on the phone for business. Abigail regarded the boisterous youngsters nervously, but Maggie assured her that they could get the little ones relaxed once things calmed down a little.

Vanessa arrived last of all – giving directions and issuing orders as usual. And with that, the Every Tuesday Girls Club was all accounted for.

Mrs. Alverson kissed her daughter on the head and left through the kitchen door while Mrs. Peasle, with a notebook and a steaming coffee drink, stepped over toddlers, took a right turn and disappeared through the living room.

For a few minutes, the kitchen was all talk and no action. Utensils and ingredients and bowls had to be found and set up, and there were other details to get straight.

"Xenia, did you bring a white shirt?"

Xenia was still looking at the baggies she and Photini had brought, and it took a moment for her to realize that Vanessa had asked her something.

"What?"

"Did you bring a white shirt?"

"And did you bring the cardamom?" Photini added.

Vanessa was annoyed. "Never mind about that right now –"

"Yes," responded Xenia, without looking up.

"Oh good," Photini said.

Vanessa turned from one to the other. "Wait, yes on the cardigan – "

"Cardamom," Photini corrected.

"Whatever. Yes to that or yes to the white shirt?"

"I couldn't find a white shirt."

"Xenia!"

"I still don't see why it matters."

Vanessa pushed her hair out of her face. "We talked about this. We all have to dress in blue and white. They're good colors for winter, and it makes us look like a team or something. Things like that impress people. So if we *all* have to be there –" she glanced over at Abigail, who was peeling a banana for Bet.

"We *all* have to be there," Abigail answered promptly.

Vanessa nodded once. "Then we have to dress in blue and white."

"It's fine," Maggie soothed, lifting Jacob's hand away from the softened butter on the counter. "I've got one she can use. She can change after we finish so it won't get messy. Will that work?"

Vanessa was surprised to admit that the problem was solved. "Yes."

Abigail glanced around her. "And we have everything else we need, right?"

After a few quick checks, everyone agreed that they did.

"Then we're ready to start. Photini, can you say a prayer?"

"Um." Photini looked around until she found a cross and an icon of St. Euphrosynus the Cook with his steady gaze and one hand holding a branch loaded with apples. "In the name of the Father and of the Son and of the Holy Spirit. Dear Lord, please lead your servants in this undertaking. Guide our hands in your service. Help us to make … um .." She frowned. 'Make good cookies' didn't sound very prayerful. "Help us to prepare satisfying food for everyone."

Everyone thought she was done, but she wasn't. "And help your servant Abigail to know what to say to the parish council. Amen."

Abigail crossed herself glumly and said, "Amen." She sort of wished Photini hadn't said that – it seemed to wake up the butterflies in her stomach. But she stood up straight and put her shoulders back and tried to sound confident.

"Okay, let's get started. Maggie and I are going to be out in the dining room with the little kids. That'll keep them out of your way. In here, you guys are making the dough – "

"Including the spices," Photini added proudly.

"Oh right. What have you got?" Abigail actually knew the answer – they all knew the answer – but she knew that Photini was especially proud of the contribution she and Xenia were making to the baking project.

Photini lifted up baggies of strange-looking greenish, black and brown things. "We bought nutmeg, cinnamon sticks and cloves at the store. But the ones we grew ourselves are this vanilla bean, the cardamom pods and of course, the ginger." She held up a bizarre object that looked like a lumpy brown stick figure.

Vanessa eyed it doubtfully. "Photini, are we sure we want all these to go into the cookies? Aren't we worried these gingerbread men will taste really strong?"

"They're all home-grown!" Photini insisted. "Do you know how hard that is to do? Xenia's dad does it as a hobby, and when he saw we were interested, he helped us with some plants of our own. Some of these took months before they were ready. You said yourself we need to impress people."

"Well yes, but – "

"And if you're worried the cookies will taste too strong, why don't you leave out what *you* wanted to add?"

Vanessa held up the two oranges she brought. "That's different. Just scraping a little of the outside of an orange peel into the dough is something my grandmother does, and she's a really good cook."

"You guys?" Abigail tried to interrupt.

"Vanilla bean will taste better than orange peels," said Xenia crossly.

"Guys?" Abigail repeated.

"It's not the *peels*," argued Vanessa. "It's called the *zest*. And it's called that – "

"Guys!"

"—because it's *zesty!*"

"GUYS!" Abigail shouted. "It's fine. Let's stick to the plan we had. Everything goes in. Photini and Xenia, you make the dough. Vanessa, you roll it out and bring it to us in the dining room, and then bake the cookies. Maggie and I keep the little kids busy and we'll decorate the cookies. And we'll all get them ready to take to church and clean the kitchen. We don't have a lot of time and if we stick to our plan, it's the best way to make sure we don't make any mistakes."

Vanessa looked a little grumpy, but after a pause, she shrugged. "You're right," she said. "We really don't want any mistakes."

There was no arguing with that, and everyone got to work. Without any mistakes.

For the first 10 minutes or so.

Things started off well in the kitchen. After Abigail and Maggie left with the little people, the other three girls looked over the recipe briefly and figured out that Xenia could be combining the butter, sugars and eggs while Vanessa was mixing flour, baking soda and salt together in another bowl. That would give Photini time to cut up the vanilla bean and ginger. It seemed like everyone would be done at the same time, but when Vanessa finished her part, she saw that Photini was still scrunched over the cutting board, slowly cutting up the pungent-smelling ginger.

"Those pieces are too big," said Vanessa critically.

Photini didn't look up. "No, they're not. They're perfect."

"But you know you don't want big chunks of ginger like that."

"Yes, I know. They have to get a lot smaller. In fact, they need to be tiny."

"Well?" asked Vanessa impatiently. "Do you want help with that?"

"No." And with a last precise cut, she added, "Because I'm done. Here, Xenia." With that, she brushed the pieces into a bowl with the other spices, handed it to Xenia and looked at Vanessa triumphantly.

Vanessa was miffed. She had learned a lot from the group since Abigail had started the Every Tuesday Girls Club during Lent – they had all learned from each other. It had taken her some time to realize that just because she was the oldest didn't mean she was always right. And she had never forgotten that she owed the Club a lot, because they had all helped when she had some really serious problems with her family. Things were better now – not perfect, but better – and she had never forgotten how kind the girls had been to her. All the same, it was hard to stand there in the kitchen and have Photini looking so smug when it was perfectly obvious that she was in the wrong.

Vanessa plumped both fists onto her hips. "What did you do that for? You just said – Xenia, do you have to make that much noise?"

"Yes," said Xenia, and the grating racket went on.

"Fine. Go ahead!" Vanessa snorted. And she said louder, so Photini could hear her, "You just SAID that the SPICES NEED TO BE TINY."

"BUT THERE'S NO TIME!" Photini hollered. Then Xenia's noise stopped as soon as it had started, and she repeated in a normal tone "There's no time. And we want everything turned into powder – dust, almost. That's why I brought a spice grinder."

Vanessa sighed melodramatically. She hated when she had to ask questions. "What's a spice grinder?"

Photini reached into a grocery bag and pulled out a rounded metal contraption with a glass lid. "See? It's like a little bitty blender. Once

I give it to Xenia, she'll be – "

"Done!" Xenia finished and proudly showed them the bowl of mixed butter and sugar with a dusting of multi-colored powder on the top.

Vanessa and Photini both looked at the bowl and then at the appliance in Photini's hand.

"How did you grind up the spices?" asked Photini, perplexed.

"Duh," answered Xenia, giving the ingredients a couple good stirs. "With the spice grinder."

"But … this is the spice grinder."

Xenia stopped stirring and glanced at it. "Oh. Well, so I used theirs, then." And she waved the spoon over her shoulder to indicate a little white appliance on the counter.

And it did sort of look like what Photini was holding. It was small and cylindrical and had a little container that was coated with the remnants of the spice dust.

But there was another faint smell that Vanessa could just make out.

"Maggie?" she said, raising her voice.

"Yeah?" came a voice from the next room, after a pause.

"Does your mom have a spice grinder?"

"A what?"

"You know. A little gizmo for turning spices into powder."

"No, we don't have anything like that."

The three girls digested that information in silence. Then Vanessa called out again.

"Maggie?"

"Yes?"

"What's this funny white appliance next to the coffeemaker?"

"The what? Oh, you mean the coffee bean grinder? My mom uses it to grind up espresso beans. It turns them into this really fine dust. I think she just used it a minute ago. Why? Is the dust making you sneeze?"

Photini made a strangled cry in her throat, but Vanessa just called out, "Um … no."

"Okay. Anything else?"

"No," said Vanessa lightly, grabbing Photini as she reached out for Xenia. "Thank you."

"Okay," Maggie answered politely.

"Xenia!" Photini cried, but Vanessa immediately hushed her. "*Xenia*," she continued in a hissing whisper. "What did you *do*? You put coffee grounds into the cookies!"

Xenia had that look she got when she wanted to go away and hide. But she raised her chin and said, "Not coffee grounds. It was like she said. It was a fine powder."

"But didn't you think to clean it out first?"

"No. I thought you put it there because you wanted it in there."

"Couldn't you smell that it was coffee? Espresso is like this really, *really* strong coffee."

Xenia shrugged in a helpless way. Things like this always made her want to leave and play a computer game.

Photini threw up her hands. "Ruined! It's totally, totally ruined."

Vanessa had been standing with one hand covering her mouth in horror, but she made herself calm down. "Hold on, Photini. Let's not panic. Xenia, was there a lot of the espresso dust left in there?"

"No."

"Well then … I don't know, Photini. Maybe this won't be so bad. I think sometimes people add that in to recipes on purpose."

"But not *this* recipe." Photini continued glaring at Xenia and refused to be consoled. "It'll have all this caffeine in it. They'll be like these over-caffeinated cookies and the parish council will get all buzzed from them."

"No, they won't."

"And they'll have *germs!*"

"What germs?" Xenia asked.

"Coffee bean germs! Like from dirt and stuff."

Vanessa shook her head. "Photini, I don't think coffee beans have dirt on them – if they did, no one would drink coffee."

"But that's because people use a paper thing to trap the dirt. But we didn't and now our cookies will have caffeine and dirt and –"

"We could put some of this in," offered Xenia helpfully, holding out a bottle from the counter.

Photini looked closer at the label and pointed at it in shock. "That's rum!"

"It's alcohol, so it would kill any germs that are there."

"Put that down right now! That's just for the grown-ups to add to their eggnog if they want."

Vanessa was trying not to laugh, but she put on her best serious face to try to get control of things. "Thanks, Xenia, but she's right – that needs to stay where it was. Look, Photini, it's done now. We can't start over because we don't have enough stuff. And there really isn't a lot of espresso powder in there. Let's just finish making the dough and see how it tastes."

Photini wasn't convinced. "We have to tell Maggie and Abigail about this."

"No! Abigail has enough to worry about right now. She's got to get up and talk about the Club in front of the whole parish council. The last thing we need to do is stress her out. It'll be fine. Come on, trust me."

Photini crossed her arms. "It's going to be all caffeinated."

"No, it won't. You'll see. We'll finish up the dough with the flour and stuff plus the orange zest I've got, and it'll be fine. But Xenia, you have to promise us that you won't put anything else in the cookies – like *a-ny-thing*. Right?"

"Right," agreed Xenia. She was happy to agree if it kept Photini from scowling at her any more.

"So … we're good, right?"

Photini turned from one to another and gave a resigned sniff. "Not yet. If everyone else is putting something in, then I will too." She reached behind her to a vial she had seen on Mrs. Peasle's shelf and squirted a little clear liquid into the bowl.

"What's that?" asked Vanessa in alarm.

"Holy water," declared Photini. "If this is going to work, we'll need all the help we can get."

vanilla bean

"I wonder what's keeping them," Maggie mused, turning towards the kitchen.

Abigail stopped drawing and glanced over her shoulder. "Well, there was actually a lot to do, when you figure the fancy spices and all that. It's just as well, really. I didn't want to try to do this with *some people* crawling all over the place." She indicated their younger siblings with a significant look.

Maggie smiled. "I know what you mean. *Some people* were pretty worked up for a while." Jacob, Nathaniel, Isabelle and Bet had all started out by being very excited that they were together, and needed to talk and run and generally act up until they had gotten it out of their system. But to Maggie and Abigail's great relief, the afternoon sun glinting in the window had finally put them into a more subdued mood, and they were guided gently to quieter activities with a minimum of fuss. When the brightly colored clay came out, they all settled at their little table and kept up low-level chatter while they pummeled, poked and prodded it.

Maggie was glad to see it, because she didn't want Abigail to have little fingers getting in the way while she was trying to use the mold on the dough. Her eyes wandered over to it on the table, and she picked it up, tilting it into the light to see it better. "This looks brand new. Have you ever used it before?"

"No, but I've wanted to. I wanted to save it for a special occasion, and this seemed like a good one."

Maggie nodded thoughtfully, and watched Abigail's marker move across the page for a time. "Do you know what you're going to say? To the parish council?"

Abigail put down her marker. "Not exactly. I mean, I know some basic stuff. My dad told me that in business, you usually start out by introducing yourself. But everybody knows us, and besides, I think Fr. Andrew will do that part. I just have to tell them about the Every Tuesday Girls Club. I don't really think it'll take that long – at least I hope not. I just want to make sure they understand how helpful we could be."

Maggie looked at the drawing. Abigail had drawn the image of St. Nicholas from the cookie mold, and as usual, she had done what Maggie thought was a really good job. "And are you sure we want to ask them to give us stuff to do? I mean, they're grown-ups."

"I know," Abigail agreed solemnly. She had been thinking about this for weeks, maybe even months. When she first started the Every Tuesday Club, she had really wanted to do something important for people, and for St. Michael the Archangel Orthodox Church. She hadn't known how it would go, but through the weeks of Lent and then Pascha and over the course of the year, all the girls had come to see that their time together meant a lot to them. They had all benefitted from it and been able to take on some problems that they were having – things they never would have been able to do by themselves.

"The Club has helped us so much," she sighed to Maggie. "But I can't help it, there just keeps being something that tells me that we could do more, that the Club wasn't supposed to be just for us."

"Your still, small voice," Maggie said simply.

Abigail grinned shyly. "I probably talk about that too much, huh? I think everyone has something like that – just a time when it almost feels to you like God is talking to you. Fr. Andrew says I need to remember to use good judgment and not get carried away. But ... well, yes. I do think I keep hearing that we need to do more, even if it's for grown-ups. Fr. Andrew thought it would be a good start to just tell the parish council, and see what the Club can do with whatever they give us."

"That's right, Fr. Andrew did say it was okay," Maggie said, almost to herself. She still felt very unsure if they were doing the right thing. She was afraid that the parish council would think the whole thing was silly and Abigail would end up embarrassed and disappointed. "Still, I mean … don't you think —?"

But at that point, her thoughts were interrupted when Vanessa appeared with a large floury cutting board. "Here we go!" Vanessa sang out brightly.

"Hooray!" said Bet and Isabelle, over at the little table. They had no idea what was going on, but it seemed like things had suddenly turned festive and both loved a celebration.

"Put it down anywhere," Maggie told her. "We've got an old plastic tablecloth down so the table won't get dirty."

"This looks great!" Abigail chimed. "Does it taste good?"

"Of course!" said Vanessa quickly. "Taste it for yourself."

They both pinched off a little bit from the edge and popped it into their mouths. "Mmm," said Abigail, as she savored it. "I love gingerbread dough. And the flavors keep going on – it's amazing what a difference it makes that all that stuff was home-grown."

"It's really good," said Maggie, but she was finding the cookies a little unusual. She liked nice, basic things, and this tasted sort of complicated and odd. Plus, there was one flavor she couldn't quite place. "What's in it again?"

"Oh … the usual stuff – butter, eggs, sugar, flour – plus the spices they grew, and my orange zest, and … you know, just stuff," Vanessa finished nervously. *At least Xenia didn't put any rum into it,* she thought.

"Well, I love them," said Abigail enthusiastically, popping another lump of dough into her mouth. "They have such a snappy flavor, they just make me happy. Don't you think, Maggie?"

"Absolutely," said Maggie, a little distracted. That one flavor was still bothering her. It was almost like … No, it couldn't be. She looked up and smiled at Vanessa. "These are just the kind of cookies that grown-ups really like."

"Thanks! Well, there's more coming, so … " Vanessa had a brief impulse to make the sign of the cross over the cookie dough, but instead she just turned back to the kitchen. "So … bye!" she called back.

Abigail and Maggie exchanged slightly mystified looks, but then they both got to work doing their part.

They had agreed that Abigail would handle the dough and the mold while Maggie kept the little people occupied so they didn't get in the way or snatch any cookie dough. But luckily for them, Jacob didn't like gingerbread very much, and the others were still interested in their clay. The boys had gotten some plastic forks and seemed to enjoy making crisscross patterns, and Bet was showing Isabelle how to roll perfect long strings of clay to turn into miniature pots. So Maggie watched Abigail work and provided utensils as she turned the mold upside down, pressed on it and then began cutting away the dough from the edges.

Abigail had gotten quiet as she worked. "Maggie," she asked, "you do think I'm doing the right thing, don't you?" Maggie looked over the dough and cutting board in confusion, so Abigail added, "With the parish council and the Club?"

"Well, of course," said Maggie, wishing that she meant it. "I mean, it's like you said. If we just keep doing things for ourselves, how are we ever going to help the church? And we all wanted to do that."

Abigail turned the mold over and pressed the dough into it. "But you're right. They are grown-ups. I want to ask them to give us things to do, but I don't really know what I mean by that. I don't want to mess it up."

"But that's why you've got a flier," replied Maggie, glad that there was something that she could give a good answer to.

"Oh, that's right. The flier," Abigail mumbled, taking a spoon to pry the cookies out of the mold.

Abigail hadn't been totally happy that Xenia made up a flier. It was just a sheet of paper that had the Club's name at the top and a drawing Xenia found of a smiling group of children standing in a circle holding hands. There had been a little disagreement in the Club, because Abigail was used to drawing things herself and it bothered her that the children didn't look anything like them. Plus, she didn't know why they should all be holding hands when the whole point was that Clubmembers go to work solving problems. In the end, they had come to a compromise where Abigail got to add some symbols like a magnifying glass ("because we figure stuff out," she said), a paintbrush and rake. Abigail still wasn't sure about suggesting that they would do all kinds of chores, and it didn't help that Xenia had put things like "Odd jobs! Errands! No job too small!!" in tilted type scattered on the page.

"The flier is bound to help, really. I mean, we kind of wish she hadn't run it off on bright orange paper. It's a little hard to read and it might give someone a headache. Still, it … " She stopped, because Abigail had put down the spoon and was looking at her in obvious distress. "What's wrong?"

"It's not working."

"What's not working?"

"The mold. I can't get the cookie dough out. It's stuck, and I can't get it out unless I scrape it out with a knife."

"That's weird. We put butter in there so it should come right out. Well, let's just get all the dough out and clean the mold. We'll butter it up more and try again."

But the next cookie came out the same, and the one after that. More butter, more dough and all manner of mold tapping was tried, but in the end, they always had to pry the cookies out in bits and pieces, and in a short time, Abigail was looking gloomily at a pile of imperfect shreds and strips of spicy dough.

"What are we going to do? The mold doesn't work."

"Or else maybe the dough isn't right – too goopy or too dense to work right in the mold. I mean, we don't have to make St. Nicholas cookies, but if we still wanted to, maybe we have to tell Vanessa and Photini and Xenia to fix the recipe so that –"

"No." Abigail shook her head stubbornly. "I really don't want to bother them. They worked so hard to grow those spices and put everything together just right. I don't want them to think they messed up, and I don't want to feel like we couldn't get our part done perfectly, too. Let me think for a minute."

She nibbled on another piece of dough. Maggie reached for one and thought better of it and put it back. Her sister and Bet had started to sing one part of their favorite song over and over and she put a finger to her lips.

"Not right now, girls. We're trying to think."

"About cookies?" said Isabelle in round-eyed wonder.

"Yes. Something's gone wrong and we need a bright idea."

Bet looked up in solemn curiosity. "Are they Bright Idea Cookies?"

Maggie looked over at Abigail, who shrugged. Her little sister Bet said unusual things like that often, and she loved giving names to things. "Yes," Maggie responded, with a little smile. "They're Bright Idea Cookies, and we need to be quiet if we want them to work."

"Okay," nodded Bet sagely, and put her finger on Isabelle's lips.

The clock chimed while the girls contemplated. Abigail picked up the mold and her finger traced the details. Then she glanced over at the drawings she had done. *It's not really that hard to draw,* she thought. *If I used the mold just to give me the shape, I could put the lines in myself with the edge of a knife, and we could add on some other things with icing after they were baked. But what about the different patterns they've got? It's so interesting where they made it look like fabric or like hair.*

And Maggie contemplated the younger children at their play. She saw the lumps of clay all crisscrossed by the boys and the thin rolls of clay the girls had made. And she thought, *If we let them do that with rolled-out dough and then cut it into the right shapes, it would look as good as those parts in the mold – better, in fact. But does that help us?*

Abigail lifted her chin off her fist in surprise. "I think the Bright Idea Cookies have given me a bright idea."

"Me too," said Maggie. "You guys, put the clay away. I've got a job for you."

"Hooray!" said Bet and Isabelle together.

cinnamon sticks

A few hours later, the Every Tuesday Girls Club pulled up to the darkened church in the Peasle van. With Mr. Peasle's help, they transferred everything out of the back and into the social hall kitchen. "These cookies look fabulous," Mr. Peasle commented.

"They really do," agreed Vanessa, putting the container of them down on the counter. "I still don't know how you got them all to look so different. It's much more interesting that way."

"Oh," said Abigail haltingly. "We, um, we decided we didn't really need the mold after all. I just drew some of it, and Maggie got the little kids to make other bits of dough look like patterns."

"Well, it's very fancy," nodded Mr. Peasle. "Are you all set?"

"Almost," Maggie responded. "We're going to make up special plates so everyone has their own."

Mr. Peasle whistled in admiration. "Sounds amazing. Well, whenever you're ready, come over to the big conference room. We'll let you guys go first so you don't have to sit through a boring meeting. And let me just take this – " he grabbed the bottle of rum with a wink " – so you don't put some of that in there, too."

Photini glanced over at Xenia with her lips in a thin line, but Xenia pretended not to notice.

"Okay, let's go!" said Vanessa with satisfaction, and they quickly set up an assembly line to finish the final tasks. She set out the pretty blue and white paper plates and the girls added two of the large gingerbread St. Nicholas cookies to each one, followed by some chocolate gold coins. Then each was wrapped in decorative cellophane and tied up with a ribbon that had a candy cane in it. Last of all, each of the mugs got a long cinnamon stick in it to add a festive touch.

One by one, they finished their part of the work and stood back.

"Are we done?" asked Vanessa. "All the plates finished?"

"Yes."

"And we've got the mugs and the spoons and the tray?"

"Yes."

"Someone has the fliers?"

"Yes."

"And Xenia is in a white shirt?" Vanessa grinned, with a sidelong look.

Xenia frowned. She had almost forgotten to change when she was through, and Vanessa had been going on about it in the car. "Yes," Xenia answered glumly.

"Time to move 'em out!"

They made their careful way down the hallway, loaded down with goodies. Mr. Peasle had left some lights on for them, but it was still a long way to go in a cold, shadowy hallway, and they were glad to see the beacon-like light of the conference room door left open for them.

With a quick look back at the other girls and the sight of their encouraging smiles to steady her nerves, Abigail rapped lightly on the door and walked in. They were met with welcoming waves and pleasant greetings. While the girls set up the refreshments on a side table, Fr. Andrew rose and give a few opening remarks.

"We're glad to have some of our young ladies with us tonight. I think you all know Abigail, Vanessa, Xenia, Maggie-May and Photini. They have something very exciting that they've been doing together this year, and Abigail is here to tell you more about it. Miss Alverson?" As scattered applause broke out, he turned to let Abigail come forward.

She realized that he had made things easy for her to get started. She didn't have to introduce anybody now — all she had to do was jump in. Taking a quick breath, she raised her chin up and said, "Good evening. I'd like to talk about our group, the Every Tuesday Girls Club."

Abigail was right that it didn't really take all that long to give her speech. It was all over in a few minutes, and there was more polite applause as she wound up and the refreshments began to be passed out by the others.

She wasn't really sure how it had happened. She just began talking about how the Club began back in Lent. She was glad to notice that once she got started, the story did just seem to come out more easily – especially the part about the hand-painted icon that she had earned with the Club's help. All the same, the fliers had helped – as she had feared, it was hard to explain what the Club actually wanted from the parish council. Being able to point to the items in the flier helped her through that awkward moment. The truth was, she still wasn't certain what assignments she expected them to give the Club – that was what they were supposed to figure out, and she didn't know if she could tell them.

Mr. Broadmere looked over the flier with a squint, because it really was a very bright orange and he was having a hard time reading it. "So you want us to give you jobs to do?"

"Yes," said Abigail.

The church treasurer also looked at the flier, tilting her head so she could read all the words that were on an angle. "So gardening, then? And cleaning?"

"Well –"

"And babysitting!" said a lady that Abigail didn't know.

"But not only that," piped Abigail hastily. She didn't want to turn down any offers, but she really didn't want them to turn into a baby-sitting service. "We'll do those things, but we also can help you fig-ure things out. Like if you've lost a pet, we can try to find it. Or if you don't know what to say for a special occasion, we can make sugges-tions." She couldn't tell whether they liked that part or not. Some of them had rather blank expressions. "Or just … you know, problems you have."

"You want to know our problems?" said a man in the back. Abigail had a feeling that he wasn't taking her seriously, but she answered him anyway.

"Anyone's problems. Like, what's a problem the parish council has?"

That made the room go silent. As all the parish council members knew, the church was having trouble making ends meet. For a year and a half, their finances had been looking rather grim, and there were some repairs to the buildings that were going to cost a bit of money. They probably would have said something nice and then waited for the girls to leave, but Fr. Andrew broke the silence first.

"I encourage the council not to underestimate what these girls can do. I didn't ask them here just to be kind. I have been impressed with what they are capable of, and I ask you to consider that they might be able to help you more than you think. I believe all of you at this point have seen the icon that Abigail received of her patron saint?" There were nods from a number of them. It was a really beautiful icon. "Well, believe me, that iconographer is quite happy that the Club commissioned it from him." That elicited smiles and some chuckles. "I believe our church has benefited financially and spiritually from the extra iconography sales we have had this year. And I know there are some families in church that are a bit better off because of the girls' other efforts."

There was a longer pause at that, and some of the parish council members looked thoughtfully at the five girls. Others looked at each other. Eventually, Miss Hemmings, in the back, decided a change of subject might be welcome.

"Well girls, if you don't mind me saying, these cookies are absolutely delicious!" As Miss Hemmings thought, that brought a relieved exhale from everyone and general expressions of agreement. "What are they – gingerbread men? Or gingerbread saint cookies? Or ...?"

"They're Bright Idea Cookies," said Abigail, with a half-smile. That brought perplexed looks, so she explained, "That's what my sister Bet called them."

"Well, they're really, really good." ("See, I told you," whispered

Maggie to Abigail.) "I would put these in my restaurant in a heart-beat, or … well … " Miss Hemmings looked at the cookie wistfully. "Maybe not my restaurant. They don't sell homemade treats like this – only packaged things. But –"

"I love the special touches you added," exclaimed Mr. Broadmere with gusto. "Having them all tricked out and you guys in matching colors … that's clever stuff. I feel like I'm eating in a fancy restaurant." Vanessa couldn't resist throwing a smug look at the others at that point.

"And did you see all the details and the little patterns? How did you get that much work done in the time you had?" asked Mr. Peasle.

"I still want to know what's in them. Did I hear you guys actually grew your own vanilla? And *cardamom*?" said Miss Hemmings in amazement.

And two different conversations broke out, with Abigail a little be-wildered in the middle. On one side, Maggie told Miss Hemmings and her dad about the mold not working so that they had to use a combination of Abigail's drawing skill and the industry of their younger siblings to make the cookies turn out. On the other side, the topic of the spices had turned rather excitable when it was discovered that they had been grown from Mr. Murphy's plants. Apparently, no one knew that a person could do that in a place that got as cold as Missouri, and with some pleasure, Mr. Murphy discussed the finer points of his hobby. He made sure to give credit to his daughter Xenia and to Photini for their part in it and pointed out that they were really the ones who nurtured, harvested and prepared the spices for these particular cookies. Xenia didn't know what to say and looked like she wanted to just leave the room. But Photini remembered to put things in the right perspective. "We grew the spices just for fun, but it made it a lot more important to us when we knew we could use them for something for the church."

Fr. Andrew, standing behind her, heard that and was touched. However, he could tell that the meeting was getting a bit too chatty and conversational, so he got the council's attention by tapping with a pencil on his mug. "I know we all want to thank the girls for those delicious refreshments, and also thank Abigail for giving such a good presentation on the girls club. I think they've given us a lot to consider, and I'm very grateful to them for the time, energy and love that went into this."

"Amen," commented several of the parish council members, and there was applause that was a little more enthusiastic than it had been before.

Abigail almost felt like she should curtsey, but she controlled herself and just acknowledged the round of applause with a shy smile while they all sidled out of the room and closed the door. It was really a bit of a relief to find themselves in the subdued light of the hallway again, and once the girls knew they were far enough away not to be overheard, they indulged in a celebratory group hug with a couple barely-suppressed squeals.

"Well," said Vanessa, throwing a fond arm around Abigail as they began the march back to other parts of the social hall. "How do you think it went?"

"I don't know," answered Abigail honestly. She was glad it was over, but she felt like she had missed something somehow. "Okay, I guess. Only, why did they end up talking so much about the cookies?"

Back in the conference room, a few members of the parish council were relieved also. They were naturally fond of the young girls, and they had tremendous respect for Fr. Andrew. But hearing little Abigail offer to help made them a bit uncomfortable, because they really didn't see what she and her friends could possibly do. And having Fr. Andrew back her up just made them wonder if he was really taking the church's problems seriously.

Still, there was no denying the cookies were a hit. There were still some bits and pieces left, and so it was agreed that they would all take a short break to finish them off along with the egg nog.

"Mmm," said Miss Hemmings for the fourth time. "I've got to see if I can find this recipe online. What did she call them? Brilliant cookies?"

"Bright Idea Cookies!" the treasurer recalled.

"Oh. Well, we could certainly use some of those," Mr. Broadmere chuckled.

For a minute or more, there was a pensive silence broken only by the clinking of utensils and the sound of contented chewing, as the parish council members retreated briefly into their own private thoughts.

Mr. Murphy was thinking with pleasure about his daughter Xenia and the interest that she and Photini had shown in growing spices. It had been so satisfying to see the vanilla and other things put to a good purpose. He had tumbled onto this challenging kind of gardening as a hobby and had been amazed how few people knew that it was possible to grow spices that were really quite expensive – saffron and cardamom, for example – without living on a tropical island. All it took was some special equipment for indoor gardening and a little experience. It had become a bit of a passion for him, and for years he had toyed with the idea of quitting his job as a pharmacist and setting up a really decent spice-growing operation, instead of the few heat lamps and shelves he had put together in his spare bedroom. But he knew it really wasn't practical. What you would need was a proper greenhouse, and those were expensive to build and equip. Even with that, it would work a lot better if you had a buyer all lined up – a person or business that had agreed to buy what you were producing. It would be such satisfying work, he thought sadly.

But it needed a greenhouse and someone to sell to, and where could you get those things?

Miss Hemmings was thinking about the artistic flair that Abigail had shown. The decision to make some treats was smart, but using such delicious home-grown ingredients and making each cookie unique seemed even smarter. It was the kind of thing she wished she could do at her job at the Burger Bagger, but it really wasn't that kind of a restaurant. Miss Hemmings had liked the work when she first got it – it was a nice, steady job and the customers never expected much – but lately she had been getting restless. She had been experimenting at home with better and better recipes, and she knew she could make some really wonderful food if someone would give her a chance. And she didn't just want to cook the pre-packaged, pre-cooked meals that ordinary restaurants used. She wanted to use only the freshest ingredients – she wanted to have one of those enticing little places with a garden out front where the chef would go gather herbs and spices for whatever was on the menu that day. The food would taste … well, it would taste like these cookies tasted, because there was just something about fresh ingredients that tasted better than frozen, dried ones. It would be so lovely, but … impossible. Miss Hemmings sighed, popping the last bite of the cookie into her mouth. It was too cold most of the year in Missouri to harvest anything from a garden. So not only was she talking about a brand new restaurant, but one that had its own *greenhouse*.

It would cost a fortune. How could you ever afford it?

Mr. Broadmere couldn't get over Vanessa's smart sense of style. Imagine figuring out what an impression it would make to dress everyone alike and put together fancy plates with matching colors and other goodies. It was the kind of thing that people really liked, and it made his mind wander back to his father's old house. After his father passed away a couple years ago, Mr. Broadmere had inherited it, and he loved the grand old place. They just didn't build houses like that anymore, with lots of carved wood and old-fashioned brickwork. It was a real beauty, but it had turned out to be such a bother. The neighborhood around it had really changed – the old homes had been bought up and turned into tiny, artsy shops where people went to buy overpriced trinkets. He couldn't move into the house himself, and he knew he should just sell it. But he just couldn't stand to think of it turning into another boring little boutique – it should be someplace warm and lively, where people felt comfortable. Besides, it was just too big. It would have made a good restaurant, but he hadn't been able to find anyone to buy it for that, and he knew why. His father had a passion for growing tropical plants, and he had insisted on putting a giant greenhouse on one side of the house.

Who would ever want to deal with a bothersome eyesore like that at their fancy restaurant?

Mr. Peasle frowned in thought as he sipped his egg nog. Interesting about Maggie putting the little ones to work to help make the cookies a success. Of course, being one of six children, she knew what he knew: That even at that age, they love having a real job to do. It was on his mind a lot these days, not so much with the young children but with the ones in high school. Not only did he have two teenagers of his own, but he worked with the church's young people, and he knew that one of the big problems for them these days was finding a job. In his day, there had always been some work to get – just some starter job to get you into the work world – but these days, there were less and less things like that around. It could even be volunteer work, he mused, as long as it gave you some skills and showed that you could handle some responsibility. Mr. Peasle's background was in running restaurants, and he naturally thought of things like that first, because he knew that a decent restaurant always needed to have people to work the tables, help in the kitchen and run the cash register. He tried to secure those positions for the church kids when he could, but what he really had in mind was something where they could all work at the same place. A lot of them had grown up together, and it would be wonderful if they could keep that sense of fellowship. And it would be even better if it was a nice place where they weren't likely to get into trouble.

But where could you find a place that would hire them all?

Fr. Andrew couldn't get Photini's remark out of his head. "It made it much more important for us when we knew that we could use it for the church." What a wonderful attitude. Imagine if more of his parishioners thought like that. But then, he reflected sadly, maybe they did.

He knew that quite a few people were having a difficult time with their money, and it was a lot to ask them to give more to the church when they were just trying to make ends meet. The parish council really did try to come up with ideas to raise money. He had heard so many, but most of them took too much time or energy for too little money. What they really needed was something where everybody won – something that would put people to work and also funnel some money to the church. And it should really be an ongoing enterprise, not just a one-time event. What was the term he was looking for? A *cottage industry*. Maybe some business that the church people could run together. Especially if it was something that they really liked doing and that, as Photini had said, would be important to them because it was really for the church. But … no, that was crazy. He shook his head. The St. Michael parishioners all had very different backgrounds. Surely, there was nothing that they would all want to go in on together.

And even if they did, where could they ever find such a place?

Crazy.

And yet …

Fr. Andrew shook his head and chuckled. "Bright Idea Cookies," he said, breaking the silence and drawing some questioning looks.

"Well, I don't know if they're working or not, but they have made me think of something really kooky."

"You too?" said Mr. Broadmere. "I was just going to say –"

"Me too," laughed Miss Hemmings.

And then they all started to talk.

"Do you think it's okay for us to be in here?" Photini said, peeping her head around the reading room door.

Maggie switched on the light and turned to her. "I know it is. Father Andrew told me we could come in here to wait. The parish council has to finish up, and it's too cold in the other meeting rooms. Besides, this is the most comfortable room in the hall."

"I'll say," said Vanessa. She settled down into one of the wingback chairs with satisfaction. "This is much better than hanging out in the little conference room. Here." She passed around some sodas she had picked up in the kitchen, and before Photini could object, she said, "Father said it was okay as long as we were careful and used the coasters." And as an afterthought, she added, "A coaster is a thing to put your drink on, Xenia."

"I knew that," said Xenia. But she hadn't really, and she made a mental note of it.

"So, Xenia, your dad comes to these meetings," said Vanessa after her first sip of soda. "How long do they usually take?"

"Mm, it varies. Not too long, if they don't have much to say. But …" Xenia tipped her head sideways so she could hear more of the low hum of voices from the conference room. "It sounds like things have picked up. I guess we'll be here a while."

"Well, I don't mind," said Photini, kicking off her shoes so she could put her feet onto the couch. She never got to do that at home.

"Me neither," said Maggie. "It's so quiet here. It's never *ever* this quiet in my house."

"Mine either," agreed Vanessa with a wry smile. Her eyes drifted over to darkened windows that looked out on the parking lot and the woods beyond it. It was almost possible to hear the sighing wind outside that made the tree branches lightly dance, but she gave up after a minute. It was too hard — the conversation from the conference room had gotten too loud. She tried to make out what they were saying, but they were too far away. Plus, it sounded like people had started talking over each other.

"You've been quiet, Queen Abigail," she said with a smile.

Abigail had been looking out the windows as well, because she was hoping that it would snow. "Still thinking about how that went just now. Do you think I did all right? It just doesn't seem like it turned out well."

"What do you mean? You did fantastic!" said Photini staunchly. "I never could've done something like that."

"And they ate all the cookies," said Xenia.

"Well, yes but … I still feel like they kind of missed the point. I have the feeling we can really help with stuff, but I'm not sure they got that."

Maggie had been thinking the same thing. Everyone had been nice, but they had said the kind of thing that grown-ups say when they just think you're being cute. "Well, maybe you just have to pray about it."

Abigail said softly, "I did."

"Okay, then. And if you hear from your still, small voice, you can let us know what it says. In the meantime, I admit I like just being in the Club no matter what we're doing. I'm really glad we got to do something together for Christmas."

"Me too," said Photini, and Xenia nodded.

"We need a toast," said Vanessa, raising her soda can. "Here's to us, and to the Every Tuesday Girls Club and ... Photini, do we get to give the Christmas greeting, even if it's not Christmas yet?"

"Definitely," Photini said with feeling.

"Then ... Christ is born!"

"*Glorify Him!*" the girls all said together, leaning forward happily to bang the cans together.

Abigail had to laugh, and a burst of laughter from the room down the hall happened to echo it. But she was still daydreaming a little. Because it really seemed to her that she had heard something from her still, small voice. Downcast when she left the parish council meeting, the question just seemed to come out of her: "What happens now?"

And the voice said: *Wait and see.*

Abigail looked away from the window, so she missed seeing the first fluffy snowflakes that started falling. She couldn't help thinking what wonderful words those were to contemplate, as Advent came to an end and the feast of Jesus' birth came near.

Wait and see.

More in the Every Tuesday Club series
by Grace Brooks

Vanessa the Wonder-worker
A Year of Every Tuesday
Xenia the Warm-hearted

What is the
Every Tuesday Club
going to do next?

For news and updates, check out
www.QueenAbigail.com

Find us on Facebook at
facebook.com/QueenAbigailtheWise/

Made in the USA
Columbia, SC
28 October 2023

24683543R10167